Darkscapes

Steven E. Wedel

PublishAmerica

Baltimore

First printing

ISBN: 1-59129-323-5
PUBLISHED BY PUBLISHAMERICA BOOK PUBLISHERS
www.publishamerica.com
Baltimore

Printed in the United States of America

Darkscapes is dedicated to Kim,
my junior high school sweetheart for more than 21 years.

Table of Contents

Reunion	13
The Interrupted Journey	17
A Drink from the Springs	20
The House Beside Soldred Quarry	28
Bridges	35
Chip	39
Like Dying	43
Unholy Womb	48
Dining at Sea	57
Governing	64
Aces Over Eights	70
Dawn's New Coat	74
The Night Cloak	76
New Blood	79
SKN-3	85
The Pollination	92
The New Disciples	97
Going Places	105
Barney the Boa	107
Summer Offspring	112
Soul Trap	124
Grandpa Frost	131
Digging Up the Past	139
Souls in Motion	141
Last Trick	149
Phaethon Reborn	151
Ghosts	156
Nocturnal Caress	161
Particles	165
Success	173
A Change of Clothes	176
The Halloween Feast	180
Elijah	188
Warren Pepper's Victory Choir	201

Foreward

You're holding a collection of short fiction that means a great deal to me. The stories contained in this book were all written between 1985, when I first began to think about becoming a professional writer, and 2001, the year I made my first professional sale of fiction.

Many of the stories in this collection have been published before in either small press magazines with limited circulations or online in electronic 'zines. Others were written during that time but were never published for one reason or another. Some existed only as fading ink on yellowed notepaper before I finally fleshed them out specifically for inclusion here.

As a writer, I always like to hear the little stories authors tell about the creation of their tales. So, if you'll bear with me for just a little longer, I'll introduce you to each of the stories you're about to read.

The first one, "Reunion," is one of my most popular stories. It won the Best Fiction contest for *Short, Scary Tales* electronic magazine, where it was first published in 2000. The story was inspired by a conversation between J.R.R. Tolkein and C.S. Lewis over whether there would be any difference in resurrecting a body that was cremated and one that had decayed to dust when Gabriel blows his horn.

"The Interrupted Journey" was published in *Phantom Fantasy* magazine in 1997. It's a ghost story about young lovers separated by tragedy.

I earned my first money from fiction with the sale of "A Drink from the Springs" to *Terminal Fright* in 1994. This one's about some cowboys driving cattle up the Chisholm Trail and what they find in a watering hole that later became Government Springs park in Enid, Oklahoma.

H.P. Lovecraft was an early influence for me and that shows up in "The House Beside Soldred Quarry," which was first published online at *Dream Forge* in 1996. It's a story about a tentacled creature living in the depths of the quarry.

"Bridges" was originally written as a college assignment and, despite receiving an honorable mention in the Short-Short Fiction category of the

2001 Oklahoma Writers Federation, Inc. contest, I seldom submitted it for publication and it was never accepted. The story is about a man facing a bridge that will change his life if he chooses to cross it, and remembering another bridge he refused to cross.

Reading Clive Barker's "The Body Politic" opened my eyes to the possibilities of truly bizarre horror fiction. That story showed me that I could write about anything, no matter how weird, as long as I made it plausible to the reader. That resulted in my story "Chip," which is about a gynecologist who orally gives birth to a son and his reaction to the child. The story was published online at *Short, Scary Tales* in 2000.

I was never able to find a home for "Like Dying." This story about a man who slips away from his wife to be with a prostitute either wasn't violent enough, not erotic enough or the magazine I chose was full.

The first piece of fiction I ever had published was "Unholy Womb," my first Halloween story. It appeared in *The Midnight Zoo* in 1992. It's about a boy and what he finds growing inside the pumpkins he plans to carve into jack-o-lanterns.

A shanghai victim and one of his captors find themselves in a life raft on the ocean in "Dining at Sea." They get company when they discover a piece of their ship's cargo floating with them. This was the first story of mine to be included in an anthology. It appeared in *COLD STORAGE*, a collection of stories about the undead, published by Short, Scary Tales Publications and Booklocker in 2001.

"Governing" was written before the scandals of Bill Clinton's administration, but I have to admit his problems seeped into revisions of this story before it was published online at *DeathGrip* in 2000.

Two college buddies gamble until one is out of money and has to bet his immortal soul in "Aces Over Eights." This ghost story also was published by *DeathGrip* in 2000.

"Dawn's New Coat" is a very graphic unpublished erotic horror story about a young woman who can't accept her boyfriend's excuse for leaving her.

"The Night Cloak" is one of those stories that was just a draft before being revised for this collection. It's about a boy who meets the man in the moon.

When I wrote "New Blood" and had it published in *Mausoleum* magazine in 1996, the idea of AIDS and vampirism wasn't the cliche it is today.

"SKN-3" was originally written to be a comic book, but I never got around to adapting it properly. The story is about a doctor getting revenge on the man who caused him to lose his medical license.

In "The Pollination," an expedition lands on an unfamiliar planet covered in flowers and brings one of the strange plants back to Earth. The results are not good. This is another old story revised for this collection.

"The New Disciples" is another homage to Lovecraft. The setting of an old insane asylum was a real place some friends and I used to explore south of my hometown. The story asks if gods exist simply because we believe in them. It was first published online at *Lurid Fiction* in 2000.

"Going Places" really isn't much of a story—it's more a vignette about a man who decides his life isn't going anywhere and decides to do something about it. I never submitted it anywhere, so it's published here for the first time.

There's a reason "Barney the Boa" is in a cage where he can see only his own reflection. A fired zoo employee finds out what that reason is when he sets all the snakes free. This one was published online at *Short, Scary Tales* in 2000.

I left the world of newspaper reporting to become a corporate writer late in 2000, a year of record drought in Oklahoma. I missed my old job, so I wrote "Summer Offspring" as a series of newspaper reports about what happens when condoms are flushed down the toilet and eaten by rats. This one first appeared online at *The Kovacs Files* in 2001.

"Soul Trap" is another of my very early stories being published here for the first time. It's about a man who was pulled back from death and finds himself trapped in his own body.

I turned off all the heat and wrote "Grandpa Frost" wearing a pair of shorts and a T-shirt one winter day to get an arctic feel for this story about a heat vampire. It was published online at *Frightnet* in 1998.

"Digging Up the Past" is another college writing assignment, this time about a man who goes to the old family farm to find where his life went wrong. It was published by *EOTU* in 2001.

A ghost asks a ghetto fortuneteller to help him exorcise the spirit that evicted him from his body in "Souls in Motion." The story was published in 2000 by *DeathGrip*.

"Last Trick" is one of my least favorite stories. It's about a young girl who has suffered all the abuse she can stand. It was published online at the *COLD STORAGE* support Web site in 2000.

"Phaethon Reborn" is about a boy who can shape fire as if it were clay.

This story existed as a one-sentence outline for about 15 years before I finally wrote it for this collection.

"Ghosts" is about a man who meets himself as he might have been had he made different choices in his life. It was published by *Phantom Fantasy* in 1998.

In 1987, I signed a contract to have "Nocturnal Caress" published by a small horror magazine, but, to the best of my knowledge, it was never published. It would have been my first fiction publication...and my first sale. To make things worse, I'd sent the editor my only copy. The version here is a complete rewrite and, I think, much better than the original.

Anybody who writes horror fiction and doesn't name Stephen King as an influence is a liar. "Particles" probably shows his influence more than anything else in my work. It's about a tiny lakeside town in Oklahoma and how the people come together when the lake dies. It was just an old draft for about 12 years before I edited it and it was published by *Infernal* in 2001.

Many friends have told me "Success" is my most moving story. Despite that, I never found a home for this one about a farm boy and the girl who leaves him at the train depot to be a star. This one was inspired by REO Speedwagon's song, "Son of a Poor Man."

For a while, I was obsessed with various types of hauntings. "A Change of Clothes" is about the psychic battery phenomenon as it applies to clothes left at a dry cleaners while a very charismatic traveling evangelist is in town. The story was first published by *DeathGrip* in 2000.

"The Halloween Feast" has been published three times prior to this collection and I have received more letters on it than any other story. In this one, a man is invited to an unusual Halloween party attended by the ghosts of his dead wife and son, and he's given the opportunity to stay with them. "The Halloween Feast" was first published in *The Ultimate Unknown* in 1996.

"Elijah" is the oldest story in this collection. It was first written in the mid-1980s and went through too many revisions to count before being published in the final issue of *DeathGrip* in late 2000. It's about a demonic parrot that comes into the life of a young woman who has a phobia about birds.

The Horror Writers Association bylaws dictate that a professional-level sale must earn at least three cents per word for the author. With that in mind, "Warren Pepper's Victory Choir" was my first pro-level sale, appearing in the online men's magazine *1000 Delights* in December 2001.

There's the lineup. Now for the "thank-yous" that won't interest anyone who isn't named. First, thanks to Wilda Walker, the Enid High School creative writing teacher who started me on this path—rest in peace, friend. Also, to Johnny Quarles, Sara Orwig and Carolyn Wheat for their support and advice. Thanks to Shanley Wells, Sandy Dickey, Bruce Mitchell and anyone else who has proofread for me over the past fifteen or so years. And finally, thanks to my parents, my wife and my kids for putting up with me as I spent time alone, casting these demons out of my mind and onto paper.

Steven E. Wedel
Ponca City, Oklahoma
February 28, 2002

Reunion

"I'm so glad you could all come today," said Beverly Bauman. "I hope no one had trouble finding the place. I know Windy Acres, Oklahoma, isn't the easiest place to find. Praise God our cars have air conditioners now. Driving out here during August could be unbearable without air conditioning. God is good."

Beverly smiled with a mouth that had never known lipstick. The mouth was part of a round, weathered face that showed more years than it owned and had never been introduced to the cosmetic artifices that would have made it look its real age. Beverly ran a hand up her forehead and over her hair, which was pulled back into a severe, deadly tight knot at the back of her head. She wore a long-sleeved, white blouse with red and blue pinstripes, and a dark blue wool skirt that fell in pleats to mid-calf. White tennis shoes were bound snugly on her large feet.

"Our house, John's and mine, is so small. We couldn't have all squeezed in there. I'm so glad our Glorious Resurrection Church let us use the sanctuary. It seems fitting we meet here. Bobby's funeral was here. This was the last place his loved ones saw what was left of him. Until now."

Beverly smiled. The fourteen people seated in the first two center pews of the small church shifted in their seats. Some smiled politely. Others munched on homemade cookies or quietly sipped dark red punch from clear plastic cups.

"I want to tell you a story," Beverly said. "I want to tell you about our son Bobby. I think you should know something about him, considering he has become such an important part of you all."

Beverly paused. Every eye was fixed on her. She could read the expression in most faces. Only a few seemed interested in what she had to say. Some were already glazing over, as she had heard people often did in churches with uninteresting sermons. A few pairs even looked angry that she was talking about Bobby and God. Beverly looked away when she met a familiar pair of blue eyes looking back at her.

John moved silently to the doors of the sanctuary. He closed them and quietly fixed the lock. He turned to face his wife and nodded. His dark, rough hands were trembling, Beverly noted. John seemed to see her looking at them. He shoved his hands into the pockets of his navy pants.

"The Lord blessed me and John with just the one child, Bobby," Beverly said. "Oh, it was a long time ago he was given to us. I was young. Too young, really. When Bobby was delivered, the doctor said I could never have another child. But that was okay with me and John. We had one beautiful, healthy son. Praise God. We certainly did."

The people shifted a little more, chewed slowly, sipped delicately. They had no idea what they were taking into their bodies. Bodies that, in some cases, should already be as dead as Bobby's.

"In many ways, Bobby was a wonderful child," Beverly continued. "He was smart. He did well in school. He made the principal's honor roll three times in grade school and was on the honor society two semesters in junior high and one in high school. And he was good around the house. He took out the trash and milked the cows and helped with the planting and the harvest.

"It was only in church that our son was a disappointment," Beverly said. She shook her head and toyed with a button on the long striped sleeve of her blouse, taking her eyes away from her audience for a moment.

"He had no passion for the work of the Lord. It was that, finally, that caused us so much trouble. Bobby started to rebel when he became a teenager. Oh, I know that's common enough." She smiled. Only a couple of people smiled back at her. One man was already unconscious, his chin resting on his chest.

"Bobby didn't like the way we practice our faith here at the Glorious Resurrection Church," Beverly said. "He said we were too strict. He said he wanted a television. He wanted to watch that MTV channel and listen to rock and roll music and dance heathen dances. We forbade that, as is God's will.

"When Bobby turned eighteen, there was little we could do to control him. That was just one year ago today. He left home and went to that big city. Oh, I know Oklahoma City isn't such a big city, but to poor country people like us, it might as well be New York or Chicago. He went there, and only God knows all the things he did. One thing he did, though, was take up drinking. May those accursed souls of the legal moonshiners rot in Hell forever.

"Bobby had a car wreck on Interstate 40 one night, just about four months after he left home," Beverly continued. Now she took a tissue from a pocket of her skirt and dabbed at eyes that had become moist. "He was drunk, or high, or wasted, or whatever they call it. He wasn't himself. The devil had taken control of him through the drink. He was possessed by an evil spirit just as sure as if Satan himself was inside Bobby's skin.

"Me and his father never knew that Bobby had marked his driver's license to allow the state to parcel out his organs like jewels from a mine," Beverly said. She straightened herself up and wadded the tissue in her strong, farm-wife hands. More than half her audience was unconscious now. The rest were nodding or staring groggily forward.

"They took him to one of those big Oklahoma City hospitals and cut him apart and sent pieces of him all over America. Even some of his skin was taken to replace skin of people who had burned themselves," Beverly said in a hard voice.

A woman slumped forward and toppled out of the pew where she had fallen asleep. Beverly stepped away from the podium and walked carefully down the three steps from the stage and around the wide oak bench that served as an altar before the pulpit. On Sundays and Wednesdays, people crowded around the oak altar to pray.

"You have all cheated your fates, some of you have cheated death, cheated God's design for you, because of the ignorance of my son," Beverly said. "But I am his mother, and I have to forgive him. I have to make it right. I'm his mother, after all."

"Amen." John's voice was soft and cracked as it floated from the back of the sanctuary. Beverly glanced toward him and saw the look of euphoria in his eyes. The Holy Ghost had been slow, but had come over her husband at last.

Beverly smiled and approached a middle-aged man asleep in the first pew. She took him by the chin and tilted his face up so she could look into it. "You drunkard," she accused. "You made a stone of your own liver because of the devil booze, and then they took it out and put in the young liver of my Bobby so that you could live a little longer.

"The Rapture is coming, people," Beverly shouted at the unconscious crowd, releasing the face of the liver transplant patient. "Our Lord will return and raise the bodies of the dead from their graves. But the body of our Bobby is not complete. What was his must be returned before the coming of our Lord."

"Praise the name of the Lord," said John. He had moved forward and

15

taken a position beside Beverly.

"Yes, praise God," she said.

John's two-pound sledgehammer arced down and struck the holder of his son's liver on the crown of his head. The still, sticky, humid air of the church seemed to hold the sound of the skull cracking for a moment before letting it die with the man.

"Glory be," Beverly said as she wiped a splatter of blood from her cheek.

Suddenly, "Ringing in the Sheaves" burst forth behind her. Beverly did not turn around as the other parishioners of Glorious Resurrection Church poured from the room behind the pulpit, carrying Bobby's unearthed casket among them. She heard the box being set on the oak alter and smelled the decaying meat when the lid was opened.

"Glory be to God," John whispered as he moved to the next person, a young woman who held Bobby's beating heart within her chest. The hammer rose and fell.

"Amen," Beverly said in a quiet voice. She took the knife offered by her pastor, a short, balding man with a happy, wondrous look on his face.

Beverly knew tears were flowing from her own eyes as she sliced open the old man and lifted Bobby's liver out of the body. She handed it to her pastor and he passed it through a chain of human hands until it was placed in the coffin with the body from whence it came.

"Praise his name," Beverly said again as she moved toward her son's heart.

The Interrupted Journey

Vaguely, she heard a door close. She knew she was alone in the mortuary. But not really alone. Best to wait another half-hour before leaving her hiding place in the bathroom, just in case the undertaker returned.

She waited. She picked at the crease in her black slacks. She studied the laces of her shoes. She toyed with a button on her blouse. She wept quietly. With a piece of toilet paper, she wiped off the final smudges of makeup.

It was time. She rose from the toilet where she had been sitting for the last hour, walked to the bathroom door, pulled it open a crack and listened. She heard nothing. She left the small room and hurried through the casket showroom, down a short hallway, then stopped before the closed doors of the chapel.

Her sweating palm gripped one of the knobs of the double doors, but she did not open it yet. She studied the doors—finely carved oak, about seven feet high, each door three feet wide with brass knobs. She remembered hearing that oak was a sacred wood. She twisted the knob and pushed the door open, then squeezed inside and closed the door behind her.

Red carpet. Twelve short, gold-cushioned wooden pews divided into two sets of six with an aisle of the lush red carpet running between them. At the end of the aisle, on a black-draped stand, lay the coffin. Beyond the casket stood a podium, and beyond that a bare, white wall.

She walked up the aisle, her hands clenched at her sides. She studied the coffin, though she had already memorized every detail; black, six brass rings for the bars held by the pallbearers, white satin lining. The upper section of the lid was open. She stopped walking when she could see the contents of the box.

The human remnants of a car accident lay inside.

A plastic license plate on the front of the Oldsmobile had read, "Dennis loves Annette." It had smashed and broken into three pieces when Dennis ran headlong into a tree. An elm tree, not an oak. Oak trees were sacred.

Annette saw it again as if she were still nervously standing behind the curtains of her living room window.

Prom night. Dennis driving up the street in his red Cutlass. A child, another girl, maybe eight years old, darted in front of his car. Dennis's car swerved violently. The sound of the car hitting the tree filled the neighborhood, smothering all other sounds. Dennis died instantly upon impact, said a man from the ambulance. Dennis's throat was crushed, his skull fractured.

No dancing. No envious looks from classmates as Annette clung to the arm of the cutest boy in school. No giving up her virginity in the expensive motel room after the dance.

Dennis went to the morgue. Annette went into hysterics.

But they would not be denied this night. Annette wiped her eyes and looked into the coffin again. She would spend this last night by his side, mourning him as no other did.

Dennis wore a black suit, white shirt, and black tie. He wore makeup. And wax. The wax filled the dent in his skull. The thought of Dennis, the living, masculine Dennis, wearing makeup brought a tiny, sad smile to Annette's face. The smile was soon drowned in salty tears when she remembered the time she had dabbed his face with blush and how it had embarrassed him to have the makeup on for even a moment. A sob burst suddenly from her body. The sound echoed ominously through the chapel.

"Don't cry, Annette."

A voice. His voice.

She stepped closer to the casket. The body lay motionless. The sound had not come from there. It had come from... She looked around the chapel. Nothing. No one. Had it come from inside her head? She had lost Dennis; would she lose her mind, too? More tears ran from her eyes. More sobs. Her body twitched spasmodically as the sorrow flowed from her.

Annette cried in the darkening chapel. The body of her prom date lay impassively in its wooden box.

"Don't cry, Annette. Please."

She looked at the body again. Looked around the room. She found him. Standing in the darkest corner, to the right of the double doors where she had entered. He was wearing a suit, not the one his body was wearing, but the one he had died in. His eyes were sad. She started to go to him.

"No." He held one ghostly hand up to stop her. "Stay there. I can't stand to have you too close. "That..." His thin voice became more distant. "It wouldn't be good. There are rules—"

"Dennis." Annette's voice rose so that the single word was more of a wail.

"You can't keep crying, Annette," he told her. "It makes it hard to go on. Every one of your tears is a weight on my feet. And there are other rules…" he repeated, then looked over his shoulder as if listening to something Annette could not hear. "I have to go on."

"Where?" she asked. But he was already gone, faded to a smoky wisp, and disappeared. She cried. She sobbed. She beat her fists against her thighs. She kicked the pew in the front row. She turned her despairing wrath on the coffin where her loved one lay emotionless, still, cold and dead.

As her fist beat the smooth, uncaring wood, a tear flew from her eye and landed on the face of the corpse. She stopped pounding.

The tear splashed near a closed eye. It ran down the cheek. The warm liquid left a trail through the makeup as it ran toward the ear. She could see the pale skin of death in the rivulet left by the tear.

She stepped closer. She cried harder. Her tears cascaded onto the dead face. They washed the makeup away. Their warmth melted the wax. She could see the purplish-black crater where the skull had been smashed. Still she wept. The nose, his cute nose, sank into the face. The tip drooped to one side.

"No, Annette, no." His voice again, desperate. She looked around, back to the corner where he had been. He was there, coming closer, drifting through the wooden pews, his arms outstretched. He came closer. She waited.

"No tears on the corpse's face." His voice was full of grief. "It's the rule. No tears on the face. I have to bring you with me now. You cried on my face. You can't do that."

A cold, translucent hand touched her shoulder. He was cold. Annette shivered; it was as if she was shrugging herself out of her body. The flesh seemed to fall away from her, from the core that was her being, the only part that mattered, the part that loved Dennis. The hand on her shoulder no longer felt like ice. She reached out to Dennis and saw that her own hand was now as ethereal as his.

Dennis scooped her up in his arms, just as he had promised to do when they got to the hotel room. "I have to take you with me," he repeated. "You cried on my face. No tears on the corpse's face. It's a rule."

Annette stopped crying. Dennis turned and started back the way he had come. Annette lay her head on his shoulder. She had known all along they were meant to be together.

A Drink From the Springs

Ben Redding leaned forward in his saddle and spat over the bank of Black Bear Creek. The dusty spittle was the only moisture covering the sun-cracked bed of the small, winding waterway. He lifted his stained hat and swiped a sleeve across his sweaty brow as a gust of dry, dirty wind swept through the tall prairie grass.

"Reckon Bogey Creek an Skel'ton Creek'll be bone dry, too," Franky, the younger of the two cowhands, said.

"Likely," Ben answered. He looked toward the sun. "'Bout four hours of good light left. You better head on back and tell the boss the creeks are dry. I'm going on ahead to see if the Salt Fork River has any water."

"That's a good forty miles," Franky announced.

"Yep. The herd'll probably still be close to the Cimmaron. You can get there in time for supper."

"The Cimmaron," Franky snorted. "Nothin' but a damn mudhole."

"Tell Will I'll be back late tomorrow. He might want to move the herd a little to the west, try to hit the lake in the salt plains. We'll lose a lot of beef if we have to do that." There was a moment of silence as the two men looked at the dry creek bed one more time. "Better go now," Ben said, then urged his horse down the bank and across the bottom of Black Bear Creek. He heard Franky turn around and start back the way they had come.

"Kid talks too much," Ben told his mare as they climbed the opposite bank. He pushed her into a trot and began covering ground on the parched earth of the Indian Nation, heading north.

He found Skeleton Creek just as the sun was leaving the sky. Except for a very few stagnant, shallow puddles, the creek was dry. Ben made camp for the night, keeping his rifle tucked up close to his body in case the redskins came to investigate him. He knew it wasn't likely; this was Cherokee country, but there had been bands of marauding Comanches reported back at the fort.

At daybreak, he was back in the saddle and moving steadily across the changeless countryside. His throat begged for the last drops stored in his canteen, but he ignored it. His bowels, however, couldn't be put off any longer. At the closest growth of brush, he slid off the mare's back and hurriedly dropped his trousers.

When he emerged from the bushes, he was momentarily stunned to find he was alone. He looked around frantically, and soon saw the backend of his horse jogging away toward the north. Ben shouted at her, cursed her, and finally pleaded, but the mare never glanced back at him.

He started walking, going just fast enough to keep the horse in sight. He didn't dare go faster; it was far too hot to run. His canteen was strapped to his saddle, as was his rifle and most of his food. The mare never wavered, but kept moving at a steady, almost leisurely pace, as if she knew where she was going.

The sun reached its zenith and hovered, staring down at the stumbling, cussing man on the prairie. A stray cloud floated into the blazing blue of the sky, but the angry sun burned it to vapor before its shadow could touch the man.

Ben fell to his knees, staggered back to his feet and pushed himself forward. The mare's ass seemed to shimmer ahead of him as the heat rose in waves from the ground. Then she disappeared into a valley and Ben was forced to look at nothing but the motionless grass that waited for his dusty boots to trample it down on his way to a thirsty death.

After an eternity, he reached the crest of the valley and looked down into it.

Water!

A small lake lay winking up at him, the surface silvery in the bright afternoon sun. Trees, evergreens and maple mostly, stood sentinel around the edges of the water. The prairie sloped gently down toward the shore, and Ben tried to walk, but soon found himself rolling and sliding through the brittle grass toward the blessed water that awaited him. At the floor of the valley, he regained his footing and ran as fast as he could make himself go.

Then he stopped dead, his feet suddenly as heavy as if they had taken root in the soil. Ben saw his mare laying on her side next to the water's edge. His nostrils filled with the coppery smell of fresh blood. A strange woman was standing in the water. Ben's eyes widened in disbelief as the woman bent forward and buried her face in the wound on his horse's throat. A sickening, sucking sound carried across to him and Ben felt his stomach roll over.

The woman looked up and her colorless eyes locked with those of Ben Redding. They studied one another, Ben confused over the long white hair and pale flesh of the beautiful, morbid woman. Her skin and hair were smeared with bright blood; the blood highlighted her severe whiteness all the more. Her shoulders were bare, and Ben wondered about the rest of her, but could not pull his gaze from the colorless depths of her eyes.

"I haven't eaten in weeks," the woman said. Her voice was like water lapping stones on a lakeshore.

"My horse…" Ben said in a faltering voice.

The strange albino woman looked at him for a moment, as if she didn't understand, then smiled and reached into the mare's neck. She tore off a piece of flesh and extended the dripping offering to Ben.

"No," he said, turning away, sure he was going to cover the grass with his breakfast. "That ain't what I meant. I was gonna ride her, not eat her."

"Are you thirsty?" the woman asked. Ben's burning throat forced him to look back at her. He nodded. "Then come and drink." She waved a bloody hand over the surface of the water.

"Why is there water here?" Ben asked as he edged closer. "Creeks are all dry. Rivers are mostly dry."

"This lake is spring-fed," the woman answered in her weird, soft voice. "There are five springs here that bubble up from the dark places in the center of the world."

"How'd you kill her?" Ben asked, seeing no weapon the woman could have used to open the horse's throat.

"It wasn't hard," the woman laughed. "I was hungry."

"Aren't there any fish in there?"

"No. No fish."

"It's not poison, is it?"

She laughed again, but gave no answer.

"Maybe you'll swim with me?" she asked. She raised herself in the water, revealing her ample, snowy breasts. Ben stared in fascination at the round, pale nipples and couldn't help but let his eyes travel down her belly to where the water licked at her navel. He loved a woman with good legs and tried to take advantage of the crystal-clear water to catch a glimpse of what waited below her waist, but curiously, he saw nothing at all.

"Come closer, come into the water," she said in a seductive whisper.

Ben's eyes slid from her beckoning, bloody hand to the corpse of his horse. He broke from his position so suddenly he startled himself. He snatched the canteen from his saddle and ran for a stand of thicker trees, his free hand gripping the butt of the revolver at his hip. He heard the woman's eerie laugh ring out behind him as he entered the shade of maples.

He tried to slow himself. Ben Redding was a man accustomed to the dry plains. He knew how to ration a small portion of water to last for days and days. But the canteen was soon empty and he found himself running his tongue around the inside of the opening to catch the last hint of moisture. Finally, he dropped the container and peered out of the trees.

The woman was gone. Only the leaking body of his horse remained by the shore of the lake.

Ben waited in the trees until nightfall, arguing with himself about his irrational fear. His mind knew that the woman in the lake had been just a little "touched," as the Indians said. But his heart insisted she was something more, and that she was waiting for him, eager to taste him the way she had tasted his horse.

When the sun had fallen from the sky and only the stars and a sliver of moon shone down on him, Ben moved quietly from the cover of the trees and edged toward the water. He dipped his canteen into the cool lake and heard it gurgle as it filled. His eyes roved the woods and grass around the shore, one hand always near his pistol. When the canteen was full, he pulled it from the water and reached down to screw on the cap.

His muscles suddenly loosened. He felt dizzy and swayed on his heels. He knew he was going to fall forward, and it was the thought—the horror of falling into the polluted water—that anchored his brain and allowed him to regain control of his body.

The bottom of the lake was carpeted with bloated bodies. Whites, Indians, a few Negroes. Mostly men, but also women and children lay entombed below the glassy surface.

Eyes round with terror and a strange, choking sound coming from his gaping mouth, Ben turned quickly and ran. His open canteen, still clutched in a taut hand, sloshed liquid over his fingers as he pounded across the floor of the valley.

By dawn, the lake and all its strangeness was far behind. Ben had convinced himself the woman was only a lost crazy, and the bodies only visions brought on by his fear, hunger, and intense thirst. In his hurry to leave, he had lost nearly half the precious water from his canteen.

He was once more the calm, levelheaded cattleman, second in command under Will Bond. He had a duty to perform. The herd of cattle was somewhere behind him on the plains of the Indian Nation, and it was up to him to find the water needed to make Dodge City, Kansas.

Soon the sun made it too hot to move, so Ben lay down in the shade of some brush to rest for a few hours before getting his bearings and trying to figure out how to get back to the herd.

He unslung the canteen from his shoulder and unscrewed the cap, forcing all images of the lake, the woman, and the bloated bodies from his mind. He lifted the container, tipping the opening toward his mouth, eager for the clear, cold water to splash the back of his throat.

"Yeessss…"

Ben froze. His eyes fixed on the small opening of the canteen. He could see the water rolling and sloshing within. His hand was steady; the canteen was not moving, and yet the water inside was active, as if eager to come out.

Slowly, Ben opened his hand and let the canteen fall to the ground. It made a solid *thunk* as it hit, then fell over. Water came rushing out to cover the hard earth of the prairie.

Ben stepped back, his mouth shaping inarticulate words as he watched every drop of water pull itself out of the canteen and onto the ground. Then the puddle shaped itself and stood to face him. He gaped at the two-foot-tall miniature of the albino woman from the lake. She extended her arms to him and smiled.

"Drink me," her tiny voice whispered. She advanced a step. Ben staggered back a step. The woman advanced two steps, then a third, moving faster. She came to within a few inches of Ben's dusty boots and prepared to pounce on him.

"No!" Ben's revolver jumped from the worn leather holster and spat burning lead at the small figure. The pale miniature woman jerked when the first bullet hit her, but the missile simply passed through her body with nothing more than a splash and a small gout of steam. The bullets came so rapidly, however, that the form finally broke apart and fell to the ground where it spread out in a glittering puddle.

Ben continued to stand, watching, his empty six-gun still pointed at the ground. When the water began to move and come together again, he broke and ran.

He ran until his legs ached and his sides were sending sharp jabs of pain throughout his body. Ben finally slowed, but only long enough to catch his breath and let the pain ease before resuming his former frantic pace. He felt certain that somewhere behind him the small, white-haired figure of a woman was running through prairie grass taller than herself, trying to catch him.

Ben continued to run until the world swam in his vision. Then he paused and jogged a while. He heard a rustling noise behind him and immediately broke into a run again. Within a few paces, he stumbled and crashed to the ground. His eyes rolled up and he knew nothing for a long while.

When he awoke, it was to the sound of cattle lowing and shuffling somewhere close by. Ben heard a horse snort and stamp less than ten feet from where he lay in the shade of a covered wagon. A shape bent over him, blocking out the noon sun, and Ben shrank away.

"You awake, Ben?" The voice belonging to the shape was one he recognized. A male voice. The cook.

"Zeb?" he croaked.

"That's right." The black-bearded cook grinned, then straightened. "Will! He's awake now." Zeb leaned back down and offered a dipper full of water.

Ben took the dipper in a trembling hand. "From the barrel?" he asked, his eyes flicking to the container fastened to the side of the wagon. Zeb nodded.

"It's gettin' mighty low. Men don't get no more'n a dipperfull a day." Ben drank, the whole while listening for a voice in the water.

"Ben? You okay?" The tall, lean form of Will Bond stood before him. The trail boss hunkered down to a squatting position and studied Ben with his sun-faded blue eyes.

"I guess I've been better." Ben tried to grin.

Will only nodded. "Did you find any water? We need it bad."

Ben couldn't answer at first. Finally he turned his face away and said, "No, I didn't find any water."

"Ben, what is it?" Will always knew when he wasn't being straight with him.

"I found water." Ben looked at his boss. "But…but we can't go there."

"Why not?"

"It…it…" Ben looked into the weathered face and knew he couldn't explain the woman. "It's poison, Will. It killed my horse."

The trail boss looked at him for a long while, then finally nodded. "Okay. I'm gonna have to ride out. I sent Franky looking for water again when we found you yesterday evening. If there's a poisoned pond out there, he won't know it's bad till he drinks it."

"I'm going with you." Ben forced himself to his feet. Both Zeb and Will protested, but Ben insisted. "If I hadn't been asleep, I could have warned him. And I know where it is. I can tell you if it's the right place. You can't drink that water. You can't."

"You can't be going off in the sun again," Zeb argued. Ben ignored him and went to the horses. He picked one out and borrowed a saddle. He was ready to ride when Will was.

"He started back up the trail you left," Will said, spurring his mount out of camp. Ben followed.

The heat was incredible and soon Ben found himself licking his swollen tongue across cracked lips as he swayed in the saddle. Only his determination to keep anyone from finding and drinking from the spring-fed lake kept him going.

They found Franky near dusk. What was left of the young cowhand was lying face down in the sod. He was nothing but a broken skeleton, recognizable only by the torn clothes he wore. Both men bent over the heap, Will lifting a dusty, broken rib bone.

"Morrow's gone right out of the bones," he said in an awed voice. "I've never seen anything strip the flesh off a man like this, and then break the bones to get to the morrow." He dropped the bone back onto the skeleton, where it crumbled and turned to dust. He stood and glanced around, as if looking for the killer but not expecting to see anything. "Ain't that your canteen?"

Slowly, Ben turned and looked into the grass behind him. His canteen lay uncapped and empty, but not in the same position he had left it. He had a sickening image of the water-woman crawling back into the container and waiting until some poor fool found it and took a cool drink. Ben looked back to the skeleton.

Where is she now?

"Something's moving over there," Will said. He started forward, his pistol in hand. Ben followed, his own gun drawn, though he had doubts about its effectiveness against what they would find.

The two men moved cautiously toward the spot where the tall grass was rapidly parting as something moved away from them. They separated and advanced quickly on the thing, one on each side, until they were level with the shifting grass, then they closed on it.

Ben shrieked like a woman when he saw the long, narrow puddle stretching before him, cutting through the prairie grass like a fish through the ocean. The amount of water had increased greatly from what he had held in his canteen, and Ben could still see streaks of pale red as the puddle shifted and flowed forward with the fluid of Franky's body added to it.

Ben turned and ran, jumping back into the saddle and setting spur to the horse. He heard Will slapping the rump of his own gelding as he tried to catch up in the mad dash away from the mysterious puddle that was moving quickly to the northwest, back to the spring-fed lake where dark things bubble up from the center of the world.

The House Beside Soldred Quarry

Dear God, I can't believe I'm going through with this. Why did this shit have to fall in my lap?

Sean Prescott was crazy, just like the sheriff said, but now I know what made him crazy.

My name is Deputy Sheriff Daniel W. Perriman of Iman County, Pennsylvania. Today is the fifth of December, 1995. I am of sound mind and body as I write this testament, though I'll admit to being so scared I can barely hang onto this pen.

I doubt I can forget what I saw, but I want to write it all down now, just a couple of hours after the fact, because someday someone may need a written account of what happened. If something happens to me, I want folks to know what it was. I didn't let Sean Prescott escape, and I sure wasn't helping him in what he did. No way.

Sean Prescott was a horror writer from Pittsburgh. About a month ago, he moved out here to the town of Laroux, into the house beside Soldred Quarry. Sheriff Burnett drove up there one day after somebody reported they saw a moving van in the driveway. I don't know how Prescott got in touch with the firm that owns the place, but he had legal papers saying he had rented the house for three months. He said the house looked haunted and he thought it would inspire him to write a great horror story. Big Luke Burnett snorted and said the boy was likely to find more spooks than he ever wanted.

Spooks! A simple ghost would have been a blessing compared to…the real thing. Just yesterday, I didn't even believe in ghosts. Or souls. Now that I know what can happen to them—My God I wish I was drunk.

I've lived in Laroux for twenty-three years, and that house has been empty all that time. I understand it was there before the quarry was dug, and that the company that dug the quarry used the house for offices and living quarters for the supervisors. It's a big three-story house—I think the style is Victorian. It has gables and broken windows and the paint has turned gray, so Prescott was right when he said it looked haunted. Something happened to all the records from that quarry company. All the records that had anything to do with the workers who drowned, anyway. There's a bunch of folks in Laroux who'd tell you their daddy's in that water. That company left town shortly after those records were requested by the governor. Well, there was the lynching of a foreman, too. Not many company men were willing to hang around after that.

Right after he moved in, Prescott disappeared. Nobody thought much about it; he was a stranger, and a long-hair to boot and everybody knows writers like to hole up by themselves and they're kind of weird anyway. He wasn't so bad really. Dear God, I wish I could get his last look out of my mind.

Then, just after Prescott disappeared, one by one, about a week apart, other people started missing.

Two days ago, Sean Prescott came staggering into the sheriff's office screaming he was a murderer. His body was bloated and a strange greenish color and he smelled like month-old road-kill. Sheriff Burnett locked him up and had him sign a confession, but the sheriff didn't buy the details of Prescott's story. He drew his own conclusions, ones he believed were more logical. Sheriff Luke Burnett don't get excited over anything but food and dirty movies, so he didn't even bother to look for the bodies. He said everyone knows Soldred Quarry ain't got no bottom to it. I think he was right on that part, anyway.

Prescott told me his story, and I have to admit I didn't believe it either. Not until tonight. God knows what I'd give to say I still don't believe it! If I was Sean Prescott, I would have hung myself with a bed sheet rather than go back there and do what he did.

This is what Sean Prescott told me before he died, in as close to his own words as I can recollect:

* * *

"I had explored the house a couple of times, and it was perfect for what I wanted, all dark and musty-smelling. It was a spooky old place, just like something from a Poe or Hawthorne story. There's a huge basement under the house, and in one dark corner there is a thick wooden door.

"The door was stuck shut with the damp, the planks swollen so badly the iron bands were bulging. I tried everything I could think of to get that door open, but it wouldn't budge.

"I was finally finished exploring and down to work the day after I moved in. As I sat there pecking at the keyboard, I got cold, a deathly kind of cold that went right to the bone. I knew where the cold was coming from without so much as turning my head, let alone going down to check the door in the corner of the basement. I knew that door would be open now if I went down there. I knew all this because it's a horror cliche, and I went down there, just like a good character should. Pretty stupid, huh?

"The basement was like a deep freeze and I could imagine slabs of freshly butchered beef hanging from the ceiling. The door was open, just like I had known it would be, and I went through it. The walls on the other side were stone and covered with a thin crust of ice, as were the steps, at least a hundred of them, hard and slick. It was dark, but I didn't dare go back for a flashlight because I was afraid the door would close and I would miss my chance at seeing what was at the end of that staircase. Still acting like a character. A stereotype character, even. The Macho Male or the Dumber Than Dirt Woman.

"When I made it to the bottom, there was a pale phosphorescent glow coming from the greenish water. There are two skeletons on the floor, and a hole in one wall of the chamber at the bottom of those stairs. The hole is about eight feet high and five wide, and it opens onto the water of the quarry, but the water doesn't come through the hole. It's really strange, like a curtain there behind the hole.

"You know the surface of the quarry is black and thick, more like old engine oil or tar than water. I threw some rocks in it and they didn't even splash, they just plopped once and were gone. The water behind that hole looks different, it's more like normal pond water, except for the color.

"You can tell one of the two skeletons on the floor of that little room is really old, but the other one's only been there maybe fifty years. It still has part of a uniform hanging on the bones, so I guess he must have been one of the quarry workers.

"I was just wearing a thin flannel shirt and jeans and standing there in front of that curtain of water shivering like a whipped puppy. I knew I should go back up the stairs to at least get some warmer clothes and a better light, but I couldn't seem to stop staring at that wall of water. I was amazed that it didn't come pouring into the room.

"Then, just like the Dumber Than Dirt Woman should, I reached out and touched it. I put my hand through the hole and into the cold water, which, regardless of how normal it looked, felt more like thin pudding. Something wrapped itself around my wrist and jerked me forward so that the upper half of my body was drawn into the water. I just knew that breaking the surface was going to make all the water flood the room and I would drown down there. I opened my eyes and saw a thing I never could have dreamed of for my meager fiction.

"The thing was a huge gelatinous mass, hovering there in the water like a blimp over a football game. But it was alive. The thing was covered with eyes and tentacles. It was one of the tentacles that was wrapped around my wrist. It kept me there until I was ready to drown. I couldn't hold my breath any longer, and I started to panic. I opened my mouth, and that's when this thing sort of twisted me and gave a tug. Like pulling a cork from a bottle, is what I thought at the time.

"My soul was jerked out of my body just that easy. I felt so strange. Naked in a way that can't really be described. It was…I really can't describe it. It was awful. You just don't know what it means to feel vulnerable until you realize you're not inside your body anymore.

"My soul was in the water with that monster, but it was my body the thing was interested in. I watched it pull my corpse through the opening and hold it close to its core, or body—the blob where all the tentacles came from. It held me there for a few minutes before it thrust me, my body that is, away and back out of the water.

"My body staggered backward and fell on the rock floor. I couldn't believe it, but as I watched, my body stood up and turned around and started back up the stairs, just like I was still in it. I didn't know what to do, and the panic was coming back, clouding my thoughts and making me forget whatever danger my soul might have been in. I tried to go back through the opening in the wall, but I couldn't pass through that strange portal. The thing was watching me and enjoying my terror. I felt like a wild animal just locked into a zoo cage for the first time.

"My body came back after a couple of hours. It may have been longer, or maybe shorter, it's hard to say because there was no sense of time in the water. It was carrying another body, an old woman, and I could see she had been smashed in the face by some hard object. My body stepped up to the curtain of water and heaved the old woman through like a bale of hay.

"The demon surged forward and gripped the corpse of the woman in all its arms and hugged it close to itself. My body fell to the floor like a marionette whose strings had been suddenly cut. The beast devoured the woman. It was horrible to watch, but I couldn't help myself. The thing emitted a dark, inky substance, like an octopus, that covered the corpse, and the old woman was just kind of absorbed into the mass. The last thing that went was her long white hair. I remember it sticking out of the jelly-like body of the monster, floating in the water like pale seaweed, then it was gone, sucked in like spaghetti.

"Three more times that creature came to the wall of water and somehow made my body get up and fetch food for it. My body was decaying. I'm bloated with gas, discolored, and I can even pull bits of my flesh off the bone. I can feel I'm getting better though, now that my soul is back inside. I bet some doctor could have fun studying me. Of course, they wouldn't believe any of this, so maybe not.

"I'm getting tired. I get tired easy. My muscles are still so weak it's pathetic.

"The last time I watched my body go for food, I decided to try to escape. Of course, I had been trying, but now I thought I knew a way to succeed. I had tried to escape by going to the surface of the quarry, but the higher I went, the harder it became to move in the thick, oppressing fluid. There was no way to push back through the hole where I had entered. The stone walls of the quarry were impassable. Maybe ghosts can't really pass through walls. I sensed I could go deeper in the quarry, but I was afraid of what I would find, so for the most part I stayed around the hole where I could look at my body. I didn't dare challenge the creature or demand he let me go. No more heroics from the Macho Male.

"The monster stayed right around the hole, too. It didn't harass me, my soul form, and I kept my distance from the thing, but I could always feel dozens of its eyes watching me.

"Except for feeding time. When my body brought a fresh corpse, all eyes and all tentacles were intent on the prize, and that's when I planned to make my escape. While the beast was distracted, and, more importantly, while the dead body was being pushed into the water, there would be a break in the liquid and I hoped I could go out while the food was coming in.

"The last victim was a child, just a small boy of about four. I know I wasn't in my body at the time, but I feel responsible. How can the parents deal with the loss of a little child?

"But my plan was a success; I was able to slip through the break in the water as the boy was passed in. My body fell to the floor just like always. The black cloud started forming around the child's corpse on the inside of the curtain. I stood there in the little room for a while, looking down at my body, wondering how to get into it. Meanwhile, the creature figured out I had escaped. The water began to vibrate and I was sure the room would flood now, just so he could catch me again.

"I dove into my body like diving into a warm bed. It was that easy. I jumped up and tried to run up the stairs but had a hard time of it because my dead muscles just wouldn't work like they used to. I had to crawl most of the way, with a lot of rest stops before I got out of the house.

"I came here because I'm a murderer. I've killed four people. Maybe I didn't, but my body did. I'm responsible. If I hadn't gone down there in the first place, none of this would have happened. Those people would be alive. That boy would still be with his mom and dad. Somebody has to pay for that."   •

* * *

Who could believe a word Prescott said, except maybe the part about killing those folks? His descriptions of the bodies fit the descriptions of the people who are missing. He begged me to trust him, and finally, last night, we came to an agreement. I would handcuff him and we'd drive out to the house and have a look.

That was my big mistake. I've heard of people who live on top of old toxic dumps. Their families die too soon and they have some bad birth defects, but as long as they don't know what's causing the shit, they don't feel the need to do anything about the toxic dump. I wish Prescott hadn't told me about the problem in Laroux. I wouldn't feel like I had to do anything about it.

When we got to the house tonight, the door in the basement was closed and stuck, but we were able to open it with tools from the patrol car. The stairs were just like he said they were, and there at the bottom was the small room, just a hollow in the rock, really, but there were the skeletons and the wall of water, just like he had described.

And it was cold! That soul I didn't know I had felt the cold and started to freeze inside me.

Prescott began to mumble about being guilty. I was kind of in shock over the fact that maybe he had been telling the truth about everything, otherwise I might have guessed what was coming. Prescott rushed at the curtain of water and jumped into it, his hands still cuffed behind his back.

That's when I saw the dark shape in the water begin to move and I realized it wasn't just a shadow. I had my flashlight, and I shined it on the water. I could see pale, silvery eyes reflected in the light, and at least two dozen octopus arms wrapped around Prescott. The man was struggling, but not like he was trying to escape, it seemed more like he was trying to get inside that monster before he drowned. Then the cloud of black stuff started coming out of the thing and I couldn't see Prescott anymore.

I knew a man once, Jim Lohmann, who killed his wife. We had him in a cell here, the same cell Prescott was in. For two days Jim sat in there and cried because he had killed his wife. He was dead drunk when he did it, but that didn't matter to Jim. Finally, he got Sheriff Burnett to let him use an electric calculator one day. Jim took the extension cord and put it in his toilet, then stuck his bare feet into the stool and fried himself. I guess guilt does things like that to men who are basically good.

I don't know how many times I fell on those icy steps, but I hauled ass up out of that room as fast as I could go. At the moment, I never had any intention of going back down there, or anywhere near that damn house.

But now... That thing's worse than any toxic spill, worse than a meltdown, in my opinion. It won't leave me mind. It'll make me crazy knowing it's up there and not doing anything about it.

I "borrowed" some dynamite from our supply room and I'm going to try blowing up that house beside the quarry. I don't look forward to going back down those steps to the little room with the water behind the wall, but I have to plant the dynamite there. I have to be sure the wall caves in and floods that room even if it means I don't make it back up the stairs. If nothing else, this testimony will at least let folks know what happened to Sean Prescott. And me, too, if I don't make it back. I don't want the sheriff to think I skipped town with a criminal.

Sheriff Burnett wouldn't be much help in what I have to do. I doubt he'd even go over to the quarry with me. He'd have me relieved of duty for letting a prisoner escape. I might do the same if I hadn't seen what's living down there in the water. There's no one else I can tell. I sure don't want to start nothing like those Loch Ness stories and have people actually diving in the water looking for this thing. No way.

I doubt I can kill the thing in the water, but at least I can block off that entrance and maybe it'll go back down deeper in the quarry. I have to try. For my own sanity, if I live through this, I have to try.

Bridges

The old flatbed farm truck that had followed him for the past few miles rattled past and across the precarious-looking wooden bridge. John Garvin sat in his Chevette and watched the truck disappear around a bend in the northern Oklahoma state highway. The upper portion of a white grain elevator stood prominently against the bright blue sky straight ahead of him. Across from the elevator was a church steeple, complete with a cross at the apex. A dust devil rose from the barren wheat field to John's right and raced toward the highway, then died in the shimmering heat rising from the pavement.

The Chevette idled roughly. John goosed the accelerator and fed the gasping carburetor more gas. *Damn car. Damn little weenie car.*

He didn't deserve a weenie car. He was no weenie. Despite what others thought, he had never been a weenie.

Another summer day came to mind, so hot it seemed the earth should boil. The smell of overripe pears was heavy and almost sickening. In the center of the field was one tree that did not bear fruit. It was a tall, stout elm tree. In the mid-section of the tree was a treehouse built by John's friends, James, Danny, and Eddie. John wasn't sorry they had built the house while he was in Missouri with his parents.

"You coming up?" James leaned out the door of the treehouse and looked down on him. "Danny stole five sex magazines from the store, and Eddie brought a whole six-pack of his dad's beer. Come on."

John put a hand on the first rung of a ladder made of wood scraps nailed to the tree's trunk. He began climbing.

"Watch that one," James called when John grabbed the fifth step. "It's a fake. Only nailed up with one short nail. If you pull on it, it'll come out and you'll fall. It's to keep strangers from climbing up here. Just reach over it."

It was a long stretch, but John made it. At last he stood on the small platform at the top of the ladder. The hard part was still ahead of him. A single two-by-four, five feet long, stretched from where he stood to the door of the treehouse. John could see James and Danny inside, looking at a centerfold. Danny was drinking a beer. Eddie suddenly leaned out the door.

"Don't be a fucking weenie, man. Get in here." Then he was gone.

"We need a rope or something to hold on to," John said.

"Hell no," Danny answered. "The whole purpose of that board is to keep Ronnie out of here. He's too fat to cross it. The board would break. If there was a rope, he'd have something to grab. I wanna see his fat ass splatter on the ground."

"Oh. Yeah." John looked down. He knew that was a mistake. How far away was the ground? Ten feet? Twelve? Fifty? Would the butterflies in his stomach be strong enough to keep him from hitting the ground if he fell? He raised his eyes and the act made him dizzy...

John tried to shake the memory away as he watched a tractor drive across the bridge leading into town; it was an old green John Deere. The driver, who wore a stained straw hat, waved as he drove past.

John could still hear Eddie's voice calling from the treehouse. He wasn't sure if it was an echo from when they were thirteen years old, or if Eddie was standing on the road beside the Chevette. "You're being a weenie. What a puss. Either get in here, or get the fuck away. I'll start throwing pears at you in a minute."

"Those are for Ronnie," Danny reminded.

"Ronnie or any other weenie," Eddie answered.

"I wouldn't have built it like this if I'd known you was scared of heights." James put his magazine down and came to sit by the open door.

"I'm not scared," John lied.

"Whatever. It's not hard. Just walk fast and straight. The two-by-four is good and solid. It'll hold you."

"I'm not a weenie."

"I didn't say you were."

"I did," Eddie called.

John put a foot on the board and carefully tested it. If he crossed it, he would prove he wasn't a weenie. If he tried and failed, he could break his neck on the hard-packed ground beneath him. If he didn't try...

It had been nineteen years ago that he stood on that bridge, John thought. Today, he was no better off than he had been then. If he crossed the bridge into this little town, he would have to go through with his plan. He had decided that. This rickety wooden bridge was the point of no return. If he crossed it, the bitch would die, and he would prove he was not "a thirty-two-year-old hamburger-flipping failure."

"I'm the manager," he mumbled, as if she could hear. "I'm the manager of a store. A store that is part of an international corporation. I have twenty-two people working under me. Maybe I'm not some small-town banker. Maybe I don't own a fucking town in the middle of a god-forsaken wheat field, but I am not a failure. I am not a weenie!" He slammed his hand down on the steering wheel and sounded the Chevy's puny horn.

She would be there, in *his* house—the mansion on Third Street. The banker. Emmitt Thompson's house was bigger than most of the houses in the ritzy additions of the small city where John lived and worked. The city where Leah had always complained about being bored.

"What do you do for entertainment out here? Watch fireflies fuck?" John wondered aloud. Of course not. She was too busy giving the banker everything she couldn't give her husband. "Bitch. Whore. You damn slut." He glanced at the shoebox on the seat beside him. The lid was not closed properly; the smooth wood-grained butt of the Smith and Wesson .38 stared up at him. Not the best gun, but it would be effective. Maybe the banker would be home, too…

"You really are a weenie." From that treehouse in the past, Danny agreed with Eddie. "Have a pear." He tossed one, lightly, and it hit John in the chest. John tried to dodge the next missile and almost lost his balance. He wobbled for what seemed forever, his heart begging to explode between his teeth. At last, he steadied himself.

"Come on, just cross it fast and don't look down," James said.

"I'm not a weenie." John put both feet on the board and spread his arms for balance. He stood for a moment, teetering, reaching for support that wasn't there, and then he jumped back onto the platform.

"Weenie!"

"What a fucking puss."

Pears began flying from the treehouse. Some were rotten and exploded when they hit. Others were hard and left bruises. Tears burned and ruined his vision as John tried to hurry down the ladder. He forgot the trick rung, kicked the board loose, and fell to the hard ground. The pears still came as he rolled to his feet and ran. Behind him, the jeers and laughter slowly faded into the distance.

* * *

Of the three, James was the only one who still spoke to him after that day. Unless taunts and catcalls counted as conversation.

Things might have been different if he had crossed that two-by-four bridge.

Danny and Eddie both had high-paying jobs and devoted wives. James made just a little more than John did himself, but had respect as a school teacher. His wife had died in an auto accident. His life was still good; he wasn't a burger-flipper.

None of them were burger-flippers. None of them had married women with no care for expense and no respect for wedding vows. None of them were on the brink of murder. Murder and suicide.

If he crossed this bridge, John knew he would not enter into a clique of friends. He could never jump back to safety and continue taking what life offered and trying to get by with it. Crossing this bridge was final. He would kill Leah, her lover, and then himself.

Suicide. The final act of a true weenie.

John crammed the Chevette's gear shift into first, gunned the little engine, and spun the car into a U-turn. He started for home.

"There'll be other bridges. Surely one of them will lead to something good."

Chip

"Okay. All done." Dr. Aaron Steele stood up and pushed the stool away from the examination table. "I still think it's going to be two weeks from today. Come back next week, and keep taking those vitamins."

"But they constipate me," the woman complained, though she smiled. "I'm afraid I'm going to push the baby out and she'll fall in the toilet."

"Don't be silly," Dr. Steele said. He put a hand to his own abdomen as a cramp clutched at his insides. "That's not going to happen."

"Are you okay, Dr. Steele?" the patient and nurse asked in unison.

"I'm fine," Dr. Steele said. "I guess my breakfast didn't agree with me. I've been cramping all morning. If you'll excuse me, I'll see you in one week." He smiled and hurried out of the examination room and into the nearest restroom.

He barely got the lid up before his stomach revolted against him and began sending its contents upward. Bits of cinnamon roll and chunks of partially digested orange splashed into the bowl. More was coming. The doctor heaved. His throat became raw with the effort. A heavy lump of something was stuck in his chest, but insistent on escaping through his mouth. He tried to swallow it back and couldn't. It felt too big—too solid—to be bile.

This is not just indigestion. This is not vomit.

Dr. Steele grabbed his neck as the solid, hard lump entered his throat. He couldn't breathe. He couldn't cough. Still his body pushed the thing up. His hands were forced apart as his throat swelled like a balloon. His larynx exploded. Blood coated his tongue and dripped into the water of the toilet bowl. The solid mass would not fit into his mouth. The doctor's jaw trembled as it stretched to accommodate the thing. Someone pounded on the door behind him.

His jaw suddenly tore loose from its sockets. Dr. Steele tried to scream but had no voice other than the bubbling of blood and the white light of pain from his torn vocal chords and sagging jaw.

The thing fell from his mouth and splashed into the toilet. Dr. Steele saw that it was a tiny, misshapen fetus. The glistening, looping umbilical cord snaked out of the water of the bowl up to the doctor's mouth. Dr. Steele toppled sideways and slipped into darkness.

"Don't be silly," he remembered telling his last patient.

* * *

The supermarket tabloids loved it. "Man Gives Birth." "Doctor Vomits His Own Son." "Alien Born Through Doctor's Mouth." There had been more. Too many more. But only one had really interested the subject of the wild tales. "Local Witch Cursed Child-Bearing Doctor When He Killed Her Baby."

The local witch named in the article, Lilly Golden, had been a patient of Dr. Steele. She had insisted on using herbs and ancient remedies during her pregnancy, despite the doctor's warnings. She had only consented to come to see an obstetrician-gynecologist in the first place because her brother had threatened—with cause—to have her committed to an asylum.

There had been complications. Dr. Steele induced labor. The Pitocin used to induce labor reacted adversely with some concoction Lilly Golden had drunk at home—something to soothe the process for the baby.

It had been stillborn. The mother snatched the baby from Dr. Steele and clutched it to her breast. She raved and screamed, saying Dr. Steele had killed her baby.

Lilly Golden was placed in a psychiatric hospital a week later. She was calm then, a colleague had reported to Dr. Steele. But she had promised her fancy killer doctor in the stiff white coat would get what was coming to him.

A month after he gave birth to his own living, abominable child, Dr. Aaron Steele returned to work. Most of his patients had immediately changed doctors when word spread about what had happened. His jaw remained in a brace; he could not speak to his patients—those who remained. His nurses explained what the pregnant women needed to do, then the doctor worked on them in eerie silence.

His first day back, Dr. Steele examined one patient who looked at him warily and announced she would be finding a doctor "closer to home" before she left. Her face told him, "I saw you on all the supermarket tabloids."

Dr. Steele spent the rest of the day in a windowless room on the top floor of the nearby hospital. His son slept in an incubator, wires and tubes fastened to his body like so many tentacles. The internal organs worked, though they were weak. The thing was hideous, with gray flesh, absolutely no hair, and only one eye, slightly to the left of center. There was brain activity—the monster had a very active mind. The thing had the brain activity of an adult under great stress. Always. The mind never rested.

"He's a chip off the old block," a friend had said, perhaps hoping to cheer him up, Dr. Steele remembered. From then, the shape had been called Chip.

I hate you.

Dr. Steele wished he could express himself with words. His larynx was permanently damaged; he would never speak again. He left the room and went home.

Three weeks later, the brace came off his jaw and he was able to eat solid food for the first time. He had no patients left. The tabloids were still running story after story about the male gynecologist who had given birth to his own son. Three hospital staff members had been fired for taking pictures of Chip.

I hate you.

The words still wouldn't come out. The doctor thought them at his child as if they were stones he could cast at a monster.

Dr. Steele could no longer drive, as he kept losing his car and ignoring traffic signals. If any of his patients had remained with him, Dr. Steele couldn't treat them; he had been ordered by the medical board to take a leave of absence. He was diagnosed with some unknown form of dementia similar to Alzheimer's disease. He couldn't think straight anymore. His brain wave activity had slowed.

He stared at Chip. The thing had grown from the seven inches it had been at birth to nearly twelve inches now. The organs still could not function on their own. The brain remained very active. More active than before, according to doctors who were still allowed to practice.

"I hate you," Dr. Steele mouthed. He rose from his chair and started to leave the room. He paused at the door and doubled over as if in pain. Chip's attendant hurried over to him, offering to help. Dr. Steele leaned on the man's shoulder and let him open the door.

Dr. Steele shoved the man into the hallway and slammed the door. He locked it and tossed aside the key ring he had slipped from the attendant's pocket. He returned to Chip's incubator and glared at his child.

I hate you. You stole everything from me, and you're still doing it. I know you're sucking up my brain activity so I'll go crazy. So I'll have to go to the funny farm where Lilly Golden is waiting for me. I know all about it.

Well, baby boy, I'm taking it back. I know you hear me, you hear my thoughts. I know how to get it back.

He took the top off the incubator, removed the wires and tubes from his son's body, lifted the child from the bed and bit into its tiny stomach.

When security arrived to open the door of the private room, they found the doctor sitting on the floor, tiny, broken bones scattered around him as he gnawed at the head of his son.

Like Dying

Sam Davidson awoke with a start, thrown out of a sweaty sleep into the oily blackness of the night that had filled his bedroom. He could hear his heart pounding and the blood rushing in his ears. His sweat-soaked pajamas clung to his body. The need was back—insistent, demanding. He knew he had to obey.

Quietly, Sam pushed the covers back and slipped out of bed. His wife, Natasja, lay motionless on the other side, apparently sleeping soundly, unaware of the torment her husband suffered. Sam tip-toed to the bathroom and dressed in yesterday's clothes. He combed his hair and started to leave, but decided to have one more look at his wife before slipping out to satisfy himself.

He crept back down the hallway and stood in the open doorway. She hadn't moved. Sam noticed the smell was coming back. It was a dark, clinging odor, like something had spoiled in a secret corner of the room. *Maybe a mouse.* He would spray more air freshener when he got home—the new rose-scented aerosol he had bought just for Natasja. He turned away and left the house as quietly as he could.

The night outside was so much different than the darkness within the little house. Outside, it was never totally dark—there were always street lights, and tonight there was a moon, not quite full, but close. And millions of stars. It was a nice night, warm with a soft breeze that seemed to wrap itself around him like the embrace of an eager lover asking him to run away.

The urge that had awakened him pulsed within his body and Sam hurried up the sidewalk toward the downtown area. As he passed the darkened windows of closed stores, he remembered his sister, Sheila, and the window of the department store where she once stood as a model before the drugs stole her beauty. Sheila had told him secrets. Unlike Sam, Sheila had friends. And lovers.

"What's it like?" Sam asked one morning after Sheila's boyfriend of the moment had left the house before their mother awoke.

"When it's really good," Sheila answered, "it's exhausting. A lot of work, but worth every minute of it."

"What's an orgasm like?"

"The best ones are like..." Sheila paused, thinking. "I guess they're like dying."

"Yes," Sam whispered to the night. "The good ones are like dying."

Sam found what he was looking for on a city block lighted with garish neon and smelling of stale beer. Sometimes when he felt the urge, he would go to a club where they had dancing and he would try to find a nice girl to take to a nice hotel. But tonight his need was too strong, and trying to pick up a nice girl would take too long. The prostitute standing in front of the little cinder-block bar would have to do.

Her imitation black leather skirt looked slick and glossy in the reflected lights. She wore black fishnet stockings, red heels, and a tiger-striped tube top that hugged her breasts in a way Sam hoped to imitate. She chewed a wad of gum with such enthusiasm that her bleached-out hair bounced on her naked shoulders. Sam approached her boldly and tried to suppress the eager tremor in his voice.

"How much?" he asked.

She looked him over, rotated her wad of chewing gum, then blew a big pink bubble as her eyes remained fixed on Sam's wedding ring.

"Wifey not giving it up?" she asked after the bubble popped and she had sucked the pink gum back into her mouth. "Maybe you like to play rough?"

"Never mind that," Sam said, wondering if he should move on up the street. No, the need would not wait. "How much?"

"Thirty-five and a room. The motel across the street charges fifteen." The woman nodded at a squatty green building with several doors of different colors.

"All right." Sam turned to walk across the street.

"In advance." The voice made him stop. He dug out his wallet and plucked out a twenty, a ten, and a five. The woman came to stand beside him. Sam couldn't help but notice the lingering look she cast at the remaining contents of his wallet. She stuffed the bills into a pocket of her mini-skirt.

For fifteen dollars more, Sam received a key from a fat man in a dirty undershirt at the motel's desk. "Enjoy yerself." The grizzled man grinned around the unlucky end of a submarine sandwich. Sam ignored him. Only his need spoke to him.

His marriage had been one of necessity resulting from one of the few parties Sam had ever attended. He got drunk and woke up in one of his host's spare beds, a woman he barely knew laying naked beside him. She had turned up pregnant and demanded Sam marry her. Sam had felt it was his responsibility to do so.

The baby miscarried in the fourth month of pregnancy, after Natasja fell off the front porch of their home. She had been drinking. The embryo had been formed and destroyed with the aid of alcohol.

Natasja began to demand sex afterward. She said she wanted to get pregnant again. She said she wanted to replace the baby she had lost. But, even more than the baby, she wanted a good orgasm. Sam couldn't seem to give her either. After each act, she would ridicule Sam on his performance. She often said she must have been really wasted to have gone to bed with him that first time.

Sam's craving for sex, and his hate of being made fun of, drove him to go elsewhere, as he knew Natasja was also doing. It was almost a year after the miscarriage when he finally remembered what his sister had told him about really good orgasms.

"You can call me Daphne," the hooker said as she bent to examine her face in a mirror hanging on the wall. "If you want to call me anything, that is. It doesn't matter to me." She turned to face her customer. Sam froze for a moment with one hand under the thin pillow of the bed. He recovered himself, fluffed the pillow, and stood up.

"Daphne's fine," he said. "That's a pretty name. I'm Sam."

"Glad to meet you, Sam." Daphne pulled the tiger-striped tube top over her head, setting free her firm, pale breasts. Sam trembled like a school boy about to get his first lay. He couldn't help it, even after all these years. He stood smiling, watching with eager eyes.

"You like 'em?" Daphne asked. She brought one hand up and fondled a light brown nipple. The other hand reached around and unzipped the mini-skirt. The imitation leather fell to the floor and she stepped out of it, kicking her shoes off as she did so.

The black stockings came to an abrupt stop on her milky white thighs. She was wearing no underwear, only the black stockings and her equally black pubic hair. The curls of hair reminded Sam of tiny fingers, all beckoning him closer. He stood still as Daphne slowly peeled the fishnet stockings from her white skin. She dropped them onto the ratty carpet and stood before him, naked.

"Aren't you going to undress?" She glided to the bed and stretched out on top of the covers. One hand reached down and massaged her vagina. Sam could hear the crinkling sound of her palm rubbing the hair, the squishy slurp of her fingers slipping in and out. She pulled the lips apart to show him the glistening red meat within.

Sam hurriedly undressed, throwing his clothes around the room as he pulled them off. His stiffened penis pointed the way to the woman on the bed.

He lay beside her and let his hands explore her body, tracing every curve, investigating every orifice. They gripped buttock and breast alike, holding them firmly as he brought his tongue to each.

She let her hands run free on him as well. They snaked up the inside of his legs, pulled his cock. Her long fingernails raked gently across his testicles. Sam felt as if he could happily explode under the sharp tickle of those fingernails.

The couple worked their way under the scratchy blankets. When Sam could take the foreplay no longer, he rolled Daphne onto her back and wriggled on top of her. She guided him in. Their bodies moved together spasmodically at first, but soon she adjusted her rhythm to match his. She moaned and gasped while her hands continued to caress and squeeze.

Balancing himself on one elbow and keeping his hips moving, Sam reached his other hand under the pillow Daphne had seen him fluffing. It was nearly time, and he had to make a decision: Did he feel any emotional love for this woman he was physically loving?

He knew emotional love didn't really matter. He could give her a really good orgasm whether he loved her or not. But he was a sentimental person, and he thought the really good ones should only be given to women he loved.

The hand under the pillow gripped the handle of an opened lock-blade pocket knife. He let his thumb play along the blade. His sister's words echoed in his mind. *I guess the best ones are like dying.*

The time was close. Sam felt his testicles gathering for the explosion. He had to decide.

Do I love this woman named Daphne? Should I give her a good orgasm?

He thrust more erratically as he neared climax. He felt his fingers and palm sweating around the opened knife.

Do I love her?

He couldn't decide.

Daphne threw back her head and let out a half-moan, half-howl.

Sam looked down at her exposed throat with its smooth white flesh and two light brown freckles near her right shoulder. Her pulse—her throbbing life—beat slowly. The key to her happiness. Sam's hand gripped the knife tighter.

His eyes moved to her face. Her eyes were open. There was no emotion in them. There was nothing. She was staring up at the ceiling, waiting for him to finish. She moaned again, and now Sam knew it was only theatrics. He released the knife and ejaculated hurriedly, eager to have the deed finished.

"Not bad," Daphne told him as she got out of the bed. She picked up the pile of her clothing and went into the bathroom, closing the door behind her. Sam heard water running in the other room and a few minutes later Daphne came out, straightening the tube top over her breasts. "Come see me again." She was gone, the motel door closing behind her.

Sam lay in bed for a while. He felt dirty for leaving his wife at home alone. Natasja had calmed down lately. She never complained about his love-making anymore. No nagging, no criticism. She had become the perfect wife.

He got out of the bed and gathered up his own clothes, pulling them on as he found them. He took the knife from its place under the pillow, folded the blade and returned it to his pocket. Sam tossed the key to the room on top of the dresser drawers and left the motel.

The night outside was lightening with the coming of dawn. He looked across the street to the corner where he'd met Daphne. There was nobody standing in front of the little bar now.

Sam filled his lungs with the early morning and started walking, heading home—home to the only woman he had ever loved enough to give a really good orgasm.

Unholy Womb

The horror began on a day Danny believed to be a perfect prelude to autumn. Autumn was his favorite season. The air was charged with electricity; harvest smells filled the breezes and gave the first winter goose pimples. But most of all, the season led to The Day.

Halloween.

It was because of the coming holiday that Danny was walking along the sidewalk of Ash Street in the little town of Windfall, Illinois. A breeze sent leaves scurrying around his feet with a sound like old bones knocking together. Danny was going to get a pumpkin for his Halloween jack-o-lantern. For as long as he could remember, he had been getting pumpkins from Farmer Sutton.

Of all the farmers who grew pumpkins around Windfall, Farmer Sutton was Danny's favorite. They had an agreement through an old friendship between the farmer and Danny's father; Danny got the privilege of going through the entire pumpkin patch before the majority was trucked off to market and the rest picked over by the townspeople who came to Sutton's farm for their jack-o-lanterns.

Danny didn't think he would have any trouble securing two pumpkins from his friend this year.

The sidewalk he was traveling on showed cracks and was crumbling in places as he neared the edge of town. The walk soon petered out completely and Ash Street changed from a paved avenue to a dirt road. Danny kept walking. He had forgotten about the rundown little shack he had to pass on his way out of town…until he looked up and saw the ramshackle building where Voodoo Charlie lived. He hurried to the other side of the road.

The dwelling was gray from lack of paint and only about as large as Danny's father's tool shed. Bowed two-by-fours held a sagging roof over a packed-dirt porch. The shingles remaining on the building were of rotted pine; a rusty stovepipe pointed crookedly at the sky.

As he crept past, a little white dog left his place in front of the door and ran under the fence and across the road to bark at Danny's heels. Danny knew from previous journeys that the dog wouldn't bite him, so his only worry was that the noise the little cur made would bring his owner from the shack. But Voodoo Charlie didn't come out of the house.

Danny made two more turns and then the Suttons' farm came into view, acres of gold, with small splotches of just-ripening pumpkins under the waving corn stalks. A quarter of a mile up the dirt road was the driveway that led to the pale green farmhouse.

Coming from the direction of the drive, and less than half that distance away, was a shuffling scarecrow. Danny's heart increased its pace as he realized he would have to confront Voodoo Charlie after all. For the second time, Danny crossed the road to be as far away as possible from the old man.

As Danny crossed the road, Voodoo Charlie stopped walking. He stood on his side of the dirt lane and watched the boy advance.

The closer Danny came to the waiting figure, the more features he recognized—the stained tan pants, the yellow shirt with black buttons and a limp collar, the dusty brown shoes, and dark, withered skin of the hands and wrists. Voodoo Charlie's short gray hair curled close to his scalp. There were bags under his eyes, and deep lines marked his chocolate-brown face like cracks on a dirty egg. As Danny passed, he could see the few remaining teeth in Voodoo Charlie's mouth, rotted black and yellow. A pink tongue licked the gaping, crooked holes.

"Goin' ta git yer Hallereen punkin?" Voodoo Charlie asked in his cracked voice.

Danny tried to answer, but only managed to croak a positive response. He didn't stop walking.

"Git a biggun," the ancient black man said as Danny passed.

Danny upped his brisk pace until he turned onto the dirt driveway leading to the little farmhouse. Heck, the Sutton's golden retriever, greeted him halfway up the drive. Mrs. Sutton appeared on the porch of the house and a smile spread over her plump, farmwife face.

"Hi, Mrs. Sutton," Danny said, hopping onto the porch beside the woman.

"Hello, Danny," she answered. "Come on in. I just took an apple pie out of the oven a little while ago. I don't think Gene's ate it all yet." She turned to lead him into the house. The dog followed behind Danny, tail wagging as if he, too, wanted a piece of pie. "No, Heck, you can't come in. Go on." Mrs. Sutton shooed the dog off the porch. He began to chase one of the chickens that had wandered to the front of the house. Mrs. Sutton shook her head at the dog's antics. "Spoiled rotten," she whispered to Danny.

Inside the kitchen, they found Farmer Sutton sitting at the table eating a piece of steaming pie. He had obviously just come in from the fields; dust coated his faded bib overalls and red flannel shirt, the sleeves of which were rolled up past his elbows. His blue eyes lit up and his whiskery face split into a grin when he saw Danny.

"Hi there, boy," he boomed. "The old lady there was just telling me today that you'd probably be over soon. For once, she was right." He winked at Danny.

Mrs. Sutton, who had gone to a cupboard to get a plate for Danny's pie, turned at the remark; she too was smiling. "Watch what you say, old man. I just might take a rolling pin to your head."

Danny noticed the huge pumpkin on the countertop near the sink. It was two pumpkins, actually, Siamese twins grown together to form one vegetable. They had grown together at an angle so that when one sat directly upright, the other was tilted. The odd gourd was still green on much of its surface.

"Do you like it?" Farmer Sutton asked.

Danny nodded, his mouth full of pie.

"We thought we'd carve two faces in it, like on *Truth or Consequences*, one happy, one sad. What do you think?"

"That'll look good," Danny replied, thinking it would be a good time to make his request for an extra pumpkin. Mrs. Sutton spoke before he could.

"I guess I'll go out and finish hanging up the laundry now that Gene got rid of that nutty black man."

Danny tried hard to swallow a mouthful of pie, but by the time he got it down, Mrs. Sutton had already gone out the back door. "Voodoo Charlie was here?" he asked the farmer.

"Yes, he was here. Again, I should say." Gene Sutton shook his head. "I don't know what it is about that old man. We haven't bothered him, but he's been hanging around a lot lately. I've lost count of the times I've caught him in the fields. He started coming around just after I fertilized last winter, then he stopped until I started planting. Since then, he's been coming around every few weeks. I'll see him just meandering through the fields.

"It's not just here, either. All the other farmers I've talked to have told me he's been around their farms, too." He paused in his speech, then snorted. "I said we hadn't bothered him, that's true, but not completely. When I was a boy about your age I bothered him plenty—me and every other boy in town. Most of the girls, too. Do the kids still tease him?"

"Some," Danny said. "He doesn't come into town much." He paused, ate another bite of pie, then asked, "How old do you think he is?"

"I don't know. He looked exactly the same when I was a kid, and that was, well, a while back."

"Why does everyone call him Voodoo Charlie?"

"Because he's so weird, I guess. There used to be stories about him stealing dead babies from their graves to use in his evil potions." Farmer Sutton smiled, but immediately the man's laughter died and his face took on a troubled look. The past four or five years had seen a rash of grave robbing in the area, all the victims being infants. The crimes had stopped just shortly before the previous winter.

"I better get back to work," Farmer Sutton said. "When you finish there, you can just help yourself to the pumpkins. I'm sure you'll find one you like." He got up from his chair and turned toward the back door. His hand was turning the knob before Danny found the courage to speak.

"Mr. Sutton?" The farmer turned back to face him. "Would you mind if I took two pumpkins this year? There's this girl, and she asked me to carve one for her." Danny rushed the last words.

The farmer grinned broadly, winked, and said, "Sure, you take as many as you need."

Danny wolfed down the last few bites of apple pie and hurried to the pumpkin fields. It took him nearly two hours to find two pumpkins that would suit the faces he was planning to put on them. He carried them to the house and put them on the back porch. For the first time, he wondered how he would get them all the way home.

Mrs. Sutton provided the answer. "Think you can get them home in this?" She brought a rusty red wagon with squeaky wheels from the barn.

"Yes, thanks," Danny said, relieved to see the squeaking relic. He put the pumpkins in and took up the handle. "Well, thanks for the pumpkins. I better get home." The sun was already nearing the horizon and his shadow was long and dark. The air had taken on a nippy coolness.

"Okay, Danny. Have a nice Halloween."

"I will. You too."

Mrs. Sutton waited until Danny was nearly out of earshot before calling, "I hope your little girlfriend likes her pumpkin, too!"

Blushing from neck to hair, Danny only waved and hurried on up the drive. He could hear the woman laughing as she went inside the house.

Back on the road, he forced the blush off his face and concentrated on hurrying home.

He crossed to the other side of the road long before he reached Voodoo Charlie's shack. He hoped with every ounce of his being that he would not see the old black man. He willed the wheels of the wagon to be silent while he passed.

As soon as the ramshackle dwelling came into view, Danny saw the man in a rocking chair on the front porch. Voodoo Charlie rocked steadily and looked in the direction Danny came from, as if waiting on the boy.

The squeaking wheels brought the dog from his place at the old man's feet. He slipped under the fence and ran up the road, barking. The dog began his usual pouncing and nipping at Danny's heels. Danny saw the smile on Voodoo Charlie's face as he grew closer.

As Danny was passing the house, the rocking chair ceased its motion. "Gotcha two ub'em, huh?" Voodoo Charlie asked.

"Yes." Danny never slowed his pace.

"Gude." The ancient black man grinned his rotted grin. "You have a gude Hallereen. You an all da utter kiddies. I know dat I sho will. Trick or treat!" he crowed, his voice cracking as he laughed hysterically. He slapped his skinny knees and rocked madly.

The rest of the journey home passed without problems. Danny took the vegetables to his room on the second floor and put them on his windowsill to finish ripening.

Two weeks later, on a Saturday, Danny's parents went to the grocery store for the week's shopping, leaving Danny home alone. The pumpkins were ripe enough for carving. Danny took a short butcher knife and went upstairs to cut out the hideous faces he had stored in his imagination.

He discovered Voodoo Charlie's trick almost too late.

Halfway across his room, he detected movement from the direction of his window. He stopped and looked. His eyes widened as he saw a figure standing among the broken shards of one of the pumpkins.

The beast was just over eight inches tall and dull orange in color, like the rind of the pumpkin it had hatched from. It crouched on bowed legs, its potbelly tightening and relaxing as it breathed. Leathery wings tipped with small black horns rippled on its back. The hands and feet of the creature all ended in long, curved nails. Danny could see tiny muscles bulging on the small arms and legs. The orange head was about the size of a ping-pong ball; thick lips curled away from lethal yellow fangs. Pointed ears swept back from the side of the head; they twitched as the thing studied Danny. Two more black horns, slightly longer than those on the wings, protruded from the forehead in direct line with the bulbous, tan-colored eyes.

The bat-goblin let out a squeaky battle cry and hopped from the windowsill, its wings flapping. It came soaring through the room toward Danny's throat.

Danny did the only thing he could think to do. He swung the knife as the creature drew close, stepping out of the way at the same time. The knife missed completely, but the step back kept the thing from getting his throat. The needle-sharp teeth sank into his arm instead.

Danny gasped in pain. The knife flew from his fingers. He tried to tear the monster off his arm by pulling on it just below its wings, but the teeth had a firm hold. The creature clawed at his flesh, leaving bloody scratches. Danny released the thing's torso and tugged sharply on one of the legs. The limb tore away from the body with a sound like raw meat on Styrofoam. Yellow goo trailed from the ragged end.

The creature's potbelly swelled with blood. Danny dropped the leg and went into a frenzy. He grabbed at the beast, pulling off the remaining limbs, the wings, and bits of the torso in gory handfuls that he dropped to the floor. Soon all that was left on his arm was the small, horned head, still sucking. Danny could feel the blood being drawn from his arm and watched as it drained out the ragged stump of the monster's throat.

Danny took the monster's head in his hand, squeezing while be pulled upward and away until it was dislodged from his arm. The fangs tore away small ribbons of flesh and the jaw snapped loudly as it tried to get the teeth into Danny's fingers.

Danny dropped the head to the floor. The teeth continued to click together. He stomped on it with his sneakered foot. It made a sound like a chicken bone breaking. More yellow fluid oozed onto the carpet, mingling with the blood dripping from Danny's fingers.

Voodoo Charlie did it! Voodoo Charlie did it!

Danny rubbed his eyes, trying to clear his head. He could smell blood drying on his arm. He let his hands drop to his sides, and his eyes found the window and the pumpkin that had not yet hatched. Danny stepped carefully over the pieces of his vanquished enemy and looked for the butcher knife.

He found it on the floor beside his bed. He took the knife to the window, gripping it tightly. He examined the pieces of the broken womb first, poking at them with the point of the knife before touching them with his fingers. The shards were dry and brittle, cracking and breaking into several more pieces at his touch. Danny noticed that there was none of the stringy pulp or small seeds that were supposed to be inside a pumpkin. He scraped the pieces to the floor and examined the other vegetable.

The orange skin still had several lighter patches on its rough surface. Cracks made dark veins on places where the pumpkin was completely ripe. Danny slid the point of the knife into the top of the orange globe a few inches from the stem and cut a circle. When the cut was complete, he withdrew his blade and lifted the top off the pumpkin.

The green stem continued on the inside of the vegetable, glistening moistly, unlike the dried stub on the outside. It coiled round and round to the small orange body lying in a fetal position on its back at the bottom of the pumpkin. The unborn monster was surrounded in a thin covering of orange pulp speckled with shriveled, tan seeds. The green umbilical cord went through the pulp and between the creature's knees to attach to its stomach.

The monster itself was not yet fully developed, but like the pumpkin's ripeness, its time was very close. The eyes were oversized, puss-filled bubbles, as were the tips of the fingers and toes where the claws would soon break through. The horns on its head were not yet as long as the previous creature's and looked much more delicate; the horns on the wing tips were the same. The thing did not move as Danny peered into the womb.

Danny wondered for a moment about what to do with the monster before he decided on the obvious conclusion. He pushed the point of his knife through the pulp and into the chest of the beast. Voodoo Charlie's creation did not even twitch as the knife sank home. The odor released from the body when the demon was aborted caused Danny to gag. He gave the knife a sharp jab, felt it pin the monster to the bottom of its womb, and then staggered back, the smell making him think of the "dead baby" jokes he had heard in school.

What about the other pumpkins?

Danny thought about the hundreds Farmer Sutton had grown, the thousands the other farmers around Windfall had raised and sent to market? Danny remembered Farmer Sutton telling him that the old Negro had been to all the farms around the town. Would people all over the country be getting a nasty trick courtesy of Voodoo Charlie this Halloween?

What about the unusual pumpkin that had been sitting on the Sutton's kitchen counter?

Danny left the house at a run, not bothering to wash the blood from his arm or even to leave his parents a note explaining where he had gone.

A cold wind blew in his face as he ran along the sidewalk of Ash Street. He pounded hundreds of multicolored leaves beneath his feet, dodging an elderly man raking his front lawn and nearly colliding with a little girl on a tricycle. Soon the town dropped behind him. An extra burst of speed carried him past Voodoo Charlie's shack before the little white dog could even get under the fence to nip at his heels.

Danny turned the corner onto the road where Farmer Sutton lived and the little farmhouse sprang into view. Danny's run became a dead stop, and then a hurried but nervous walk when he saw the bent form of the ancient black man standing at the head of the Suttons' driveway.

Voodoo Charlie was watching the house. He seemed to be waiting on something. *Does he want to hear the screams of the farmer and his wife when their pumpkin hatches?*

Screams, Danny thought, that might be representative of the screams heard all over the nation. He forced himself to take the steps that brought him closer to the bent form of Voodoo Charlie.

Voodoo Charlie must have heard Danny's labored breathing and nervous steps approaching on the road. He turned to face the boy, and for a moment Danny thought sure the old man could taste his fear. The pink tongue licked cracked lips through a hole where the teeth were missing. Voodoo Charlie smiled at him, and Danny looked away.

"Yer jest in time, boy," Voodoo Charlie said. "I think yer farmer friend is 'bout to have hisself a set o'twins." The old man began to cackle.

Danny sidled quickly past him and hurried up the drive. When the screams began, Danny broke into a run. Behind him, Voodoo Charlie laughed harder.

Danny stepped onto the front lawn as Mrs. Sutton ran out of the house, her skirt flying around her knees. The screen door banged against the side of the house and then slammed closed. Heck bounded from the other side of the porch. Mrs. Sutton was screaming and waving her pudgy arms frantically. One of the orange pumpkin-monsters hung from her neck, its body swelling as it drained the blood from the woman. Heck saw the creature hanging from his mistress' neck and tried to jump high enough to tear it away, but Mrs. Sutton's movements prevented him from getting a hold on it. Over the woman's screams and the dog's barking, Danny could still hear Voodoo Charlie cackling.

The monster burst. Danny was still several feet from the struggling group, but he was near enough to see the bloated body of the creature explode, and close enough to be sprayed by the flying goo. He wiped his face and hurried to where Mrs. Sutton had slumped to the ground.

Only the small orange head remained, still clinging to the woman's neck by its teeth, blood pumping from its throat. Heck was nosing at the head.

Danny pushed the dog away and bent over Mrs. Sutton. He carefully pried the sucking head from her neck, but even as it came free he felt the strained pulse in the farmwife's throat flutter and die. Danny stomped the head to mush under his foot while tears leaked from his eyes. He hurried to the house, already sure what he would find.

From the living room, he could see the body of Farmer Sutton sprawled over the kitchen table, the broken pieces of the Siamese twin pumpkin scattered around him. The remains of his killer were splattered around the room; yellow specks, like mucus, clung to the walls and appliances. The head continued pumping a thin trickle of blood from the back of the farmer's neck onto the table, where it ran off and fell to the pool spreading across the linoleum floor.

Danny silently left the house.

It was quiet outside. The cold wind made the only sound. The golden retriever joined Danny on the porch of the farmhouse. Danny absently patted the dog's head and then went slowly down the steps, avoiding the corpse lying a few feet away, and started back up the drive.

The dog followed him a short way, then turned and went back. Danny let him go. Voodoo Charlie was nowhere in sight.

What about the pumpkins? How long before reports start coming in of people attacked by little orange creatures that hatch from their Halloween jack-o-lanterns? What about Voodoo Charlie? Will he be caught and punished?

At the edge of the driveway, Danny found a crumpled heap of clothing— a yellow shirt with black buttons, a pair of almost-worn-out tan pants, and two dusty brown shoes. All that was left of Voodoo Charlie.

Almost.

A gust of October wind rocked Danny on his feet. As it blew past, he heard the dry, cackling laughter of the old black man and the hoarse words, "Happy Hallereen!"

Dining at Sea

Raymond wasn't sorry most of the other men had drowned. He was only sorry that Manuel hadn't gone to the bottom of the Pacific with them. The Mexican, or Puerto Rican, or whatever he was, sat across from Raymond in the yellow inflatable raft, his hairy brown arms thrown out, resting on the sides of the raft, his legs spread before him. Manuel was probably in his late forties and was always grinning—a mean grin that split his raggedly-bearded face and showed off his perfect, gleaming teeth.

"Maybe you should paddle with your hands, no?" Manuel said.

Raymond started to answer, then stopped himself. It was useless to fight with the other man. He had already struggled against his captors and bore the bruises to prove it. Manuel outweighed Raymond by at least a hundred pounds and, if worse came to worst, Manuel still had his long knife strapped to his waist. Raymond was sure Manuel didn't have any qualms about using the knife.

"You don't want to paddle, I think." Manuel nodded.

"There's nothing to paddle with. We couldn't get anywhere with just our hands." Raymond made sure he said 'we.' "Somebody sent a distress call, didn't they? Somebody will find us."

Manuel laughed. "Nobody on the *Lucifer* sent a distress call. We are smugglers. Most of us are wanted men. I am worth one hundred thousand dollars to your FBI." Manuel nodded proudly.

"Smugglers." Raymond rubbed the back of his head where one of his captors had knocked him out before dragging him onto the doomed yacht. "Why did you bring me? What do you do, sell slaves, too?"

"Sometimes the captain, he likes to bring hostages," Manuel said, nodding and grinning again. "Sometimes it is good to have a hostage. I think that is why you are here."

"It was you who hit me outside the bar, wasn't it."

Manuel only grinned. They drifted in silence.

Slowly, the sun sank into the sea, leaving only a pale blush to the sky.

Stars began to twinkle overhead, growing brighter as the blush faded, making the sky a smooth velvet cloth over the rippling silk of the sea, both alive with glittering diamonds.

"Where were we going?" Raymond asked.

"North."

"North? Why north?"

"I am not the captain. I do not know."

More silence. More darkness. Raymond heard his stomach growl. There was no food in the raft—no water, either. Raymond wanted to sleep, but was afraid to do so with Manuel awake. His eyelids sagged. He forced them open. They closed again. He jerked awake and noticed something bobbing in the waves about thirty yards to the northwest of the raft.

"What's that?" Raymond plunged his hands into the water and started paddling in the direction of the object. To his surprise, Manuel leaned over the side of the raft and added his efforts. Raymond watched the Hispanic's muscles bulge and ripple as he paddled. He wondered if he could get the knife away from Manuel if it came to that.

"It's a box," Raymond gasped as they drew closer. The box was about eight feet long and three feet wide. It had two steel eyes on each end; a short piece of thick rope was still tied to one of the eyes.

"I remember this," Manuel said. "Yes, this was on the *Lucifer*. I helped to load it from the dock and put it in the hold."

"What's in it?" Raymond asked. "Is that what you were smuggling?"

"No, no, it couldn't be." Manuel shook his shaggy head. "It is too light, see? I think it is empty. See how it rides high on the water? It must be empty. You are stupid to not see that."

"Why would you carry an empty box?"

"I do not know why," Manuel snapped. "I told you already, I am not the captain." He started to push the box away, but Raymond grabbed the rope and tied it to one of the raft's oar locks. "Why do you do that? I don't want to drag this with us."

"I do."

Manuel's hand raised to his knife but stopped. Raymond acted as if he hadn't noticed, but he tried to prepare himself for the fight. "You are a foolish little man," the Hispanic hissed. "I look forward to eating you and drinking your blood to keep myself alive."

"I would be a very unhealthy meal for you." Raymond hoped he sounded tough. Manuel laughed at him.

They drifted quietly for a while. Raymond kept looking at the box, trying to figure out what was wrong with it. Finally he realized what he'd been looking for.

"There's no nails or screws in the top of this box," he said. He reached out and pushed at the top panel, but it didn't move. "How do you think it's fastened?"

"I don't care," Manuel said. "I am getting hungry. Maybe I will cut a piece at a time to keep you alive until I have to kill you. I like my meat to be fresh. I could cut off a leg below the knee tonight, the other tomorrow, then the arms…"

Raymond couldn't bear it any longer. "Shut up, you damn spick," he shouted. "Shut your fucking mouth. You want to kill me? Go ahead and do it now. Come on. I'd rather die now than have to sit here and smell you and listen to you until we're rescued."

Again, Manuel laughed. He threw back his head so that he was nearly lying in the bottom of the raft and cackled like a woman. Then he stopped abruptly and showed Raymond his evil grin. "I am not so hungry yet," he said. "I will kill you when I am ready. Perhaps when you are sleeping, no?"

Raymond jumped on him. Manuel was ready for him, however, and knocked Raymond aside, then rose to his knees and drew his knife. Raymond threw himself forward, into the Hispanic's body. He felt the knife tear his shirt and heard a sudden hiss as the blade plunged into the bottom of the rubber raft.

"Now look what you've done, you stupid son of a bitch," Raymond yelled.

Manuel didn't answer. He pulled his knife out and jabbed it at Raymond's stomach. Raymond dodged the blade again, but Manuel's empty fist found the side of his head. Raymond fell onto his side. The air escaping from the raft gushed into his face. The knife was coming again. Raymond grabbed Manuel's wrist. He couldn't stop the descent, but he guided it away from his body. The blade slashed across two more chambers of the raft. More air rushed out and suddenly the raft was filling with salty water. Manuel fell sideways as the raft sagged. Raymond used all his strength to shove his opponent off him and into the water.

Manuel yelled something in Spanish as he fell. The knife flew out of his hand and stuck into another of the raft's air chambers. Manuel flailed in the water; Raymond realized the Hispanic couldn't swim, but didn't try to help him.

Raymond grabbed the knife and stuck it into his own belt as the raft became nothing but a dancing yellow stain beneath the waves, the one undamaged air chamber like a bubble on the surface of the ocean. He grabbed hold of the floating box and held on, listening to Manuel's bubbling screams.

The lid of the box flew open and a man sat up in it. Raymond's fingers slipped away and he nearly sank into the ocean at the sudden appearance of the new figure. The man reached out and grabbed Manuel from the water, dragging him into the box as if he were a huge, limp rat.

"Dear God in Heaven," Raymond whispered as the stranger tilted Manuel's head back and lowered his own long teeth to the hairy brown throat. The man rolled his eyes to stare at Raymond as he drank the blood of Manuel. Raymond could see the color draining from Manuel's body as the blood was taken. Then it was over. The stranger, the vampire, pushed the body out of the box and into the sea. With a long-fingered, thin hand, he beckoned to Raymond. Raymond shook his head and turned to swim away.

"Where will you go, my friend?" The vampire's voice was filled with humor, almost mocking, but too silky to be cruel. "Come back. I have fed for the night and you are safe. Come back. Sit in my box with me."

Raymond stopped swimming and turned back to face the vampire. His box—his coffin— still rode high on the waves, the lid standing open so that the vampire, a pale man in a dark, modern suit with a silk tie, leaned his shoulder against it.

"You won't kill me?" Raymond asked.

"Not tonight." The vampire smiled and Raymond saw that his teeth were still stained with Manuel's blood. The vampire beckoned with his hand again. Reluctantly, Raymond swam back to the coffin, where the vampire hauled him into the box just as he had lifted Manuel. Raymond sensed the creature's incredible strength as he was lifted clear of the water.

Manuel's body was bobbing away from them on the dark ocean. Raymond didn't feel pity for the man. He was too concerned with his own safety. He sat up in the coffin, crossed his legs before him, and faced the vampire.

"I heard most of your conversation with the other," the vampire said, waving a hand toward Manuel's corpse. "I think Captain Davis took you onto his ship to feed me on the long journey north. He chose well." The vampire smiled.

"I'm not comforted by that," Raymond said.

"No, I don't guess you would be." The vampire smiled again. "You asked why we were going north. I will tell you. In the far north, the nights last for months during this time of the year. It is always dark. I wanted to see if I would feel the need to retreat to my coffin if the sun did not rise."

"There aren't many people that far north," Raymond said. "I mean…"

"What would I feed on?" The vampire laughed—a low, rippling sound. "There are not many people, no, and there would have been less if I had reached my destination."

"What are we going to do now?" Raymond asked. "What are you going to do with me?"

"This box we are in is sealed against the water," the vampire said. "We will wait in it. Eventually a ship will find us, or we will wash up on shore."

"But…" Raymond wasn't sure what to say. "You're a vampire. I mean, when they open the lid, if it's daylight…"

"A risk, true." The vampire nodded. "But, as you noticed, there are no nails or screws visible on the outside of the box. It latches from the inside. Most people would spend a great deal of time studying the box before risking its destruction with a forced entry. By then, hopefully, the sun will be gone from the sky."

"You said 'we.' Do you mean for me to…to lie in there with you?"

"Yes, I do." The vampire did not smile now. He fixed Raymond with his deep black eyes and held him. "We could be on the sea for a long time. If you were not in here with me, but say, riding on top of the coffin when we are found, you could alert our rescuers to the contents of this box and destroy me. And, of course, I will be hungry again every night."

"Hungry?"

"Your friend spoke of eating you. His methods were crude. I can feed on you night after night without killing or maiming you. I will take only what I need. When we are rescued, I can make you a vampire … or I can kill you, as you wish."

Raymond couldn't answer. He stared at the vampire. Suddenly he sprang to his feet and jumped out of the coffin, prepared to swim away and face drowning rather than the choices of the undead.

But the vampire was faster than Raymond. He caught Raymond by the ankle and dragged him back into the coffin. He forced Raymond to the bottom of the box and lay over him with his own body, like a man mounting a woman. Raymond's struggles were useless against the powerful creature.

"Perhaps you will change your mind before we are rescued, my friend," the vampire said as he pulled the lid of the coffin closed.

The stars were suddenly gone. Raymond heard several muffled clicks and knew the vampire was sealing the box from the inside. The vampire was still on top of him, almost weightless, but Raymond could not move him.

"Be still." The vampire covered Raymond's mouth with a cool, dry hand. "Sleep."

After a time, Raymond did. When he awoke, the vampire was slumped over him like a lifeless corpse. Raymond fidgeted, but the vampire did not move or speak. Raymond raised his hands until he was sure they were over his face and pushed the button that made the dial of his watch light up. He guessed he had slept for close to ten hours. It was daylight outside the box, so the vampire was in his forced sleep.

With the life out of him, the vampire was much heavier than he had been. Raymond struggled to get out from under the body, finally settling with his back against the side of the box, the vampire sleeping beside him.

Raymond slid his hands along the top of the box, hoping to find the latches so he could open the lid, letting in the fatal sunlight. He found one, felt the cold metal, but he could not figure out how to work the mechanism. In the total darkness, he couldn't even study the lock to try to understand it. From touch, he determined it was unlike any latch he knew.

He tried pounding on the lid, hoping to force it up, but that was useless.

Something was pressing against Raymond's thigh. He reached down and found the handle of Manuel's long knife.

It wasn't a wooden stake like they used to kill the undead in movies, but Raymond felt pretty sure the vampire couldn't survive without his head. He drew the knife and felt for the vampire's throat with his other hand while he wriggled his body toward the foot of the coffin to give his arms more striking room. Raymond took a deep breath, then stabbed the knife into the vampire's throat and prepared to saw with the blade.

The vampire convulsed violently. He arms and legs flailed, bruising Raymond as they battered him. The vampire's upper torso and head jerked up and down, banging the coffin as his hands and feet pounded the wooden confines.

Raymond struggled to avoid being hammered, but couldn't get out of reach of the arms and legs. He tried to get into a fetal position to protect his head.

Then he heard the wood crack. The vampire had split the wood of the coffin's bottom with his head. Water rushed into the box. The vampire continued convulsing.

"Stop it! Stop it! Open the fucking box!" Raymond yelled. He reached up and ran his hands along the lid, feeling for the strange latches. The vampire's knee came up suddenly and connected with his hand; Raymond heard the snap as several of his fingers were smashed and broken between the vampire's knee and the coffin lid. He howled with the pain and sea water filled his mouth.

The head of the coffin was tilted down and filling fast. Raymond put out his hands to brace himself against that end of the coffin, the vampire beneath him now, still jerking. The water rose above his arms. Raymond took a deep breath as the water rushed over his head. He felt the coffin start racing toward the bottom of the ocean as the water rose to his feet.

At least no one's going to eat me.

Raymond had one last idea.

He pushed at the bottom of the coffin where the vampire's head had cracked the wood. The bottom of the box was split from end to end. Raymond braced his back against the lid and pushed with both hands and his knees at one half of the split bottom. The wood gave way suddenly and Raymond slipped out of the opening, tangling with the vampire as he did.

He couldn't hold his breath any longer. The air gushed out of his burning lungs. He breathed in, tasting salt water mingled with the blood flowing from the vampire's throat.

Raymond shoved the body away and started swimming toward the surface. A ribbon of the vampire's blood wound around him as he struggled against the water. The vampire rose toward the surface, too, toward the brightening ceiling of light. Raymond thought he could see the body beginning to smolder even in the water.

He never saw the shark that was attracted by the scent of the vampire's blood and the vibrations of Raymond's swimming. He tried to scream as the rows of deadly teeth sank into his right thigh and the shark dragged him deeper into the cold Pacific.

Governing

Tully's Tavern was just opening as Bill Waters parked his Porsche. The digital clock in the dash told the governor it was just after 10 a.m. Bill got out and looked around furtively, like a fugitive, then hurried into the cool, dark room of the tavern.

"Hey Governor, how're you doin'?" Tully asked as Bill took a table in the back, in the darkest corner of the tavern. The governor ignored the question.

"Give me a couple shots of Beam and a beer, Tully," Bill said. "And keep the damn people away from me for a while. Please?"

"Sure Bill, I understand." The short, skinny man with the heavy mustache smiled. They both knew there wouldn't be any other people in the place so early—but the governor was sure the barkeeper could take care of his customers, should any come in and recognize the chief executive of the state having a liquid breakfast.

The alcohol was set before him and Bill immediately downed the first shot of Jim Beam, then took a swig of beer. His belly burned, and he smiled as a bit of relaxation took hold. The smile faltered and fell away as he pulled an envelope from his pocket and stared at it again for a long moment. The handwriting was familiar—a woman's script. The flowing lines of his name were shaped just as a certain woman had done them long ago.

Impossible!

He tore the envelope open and pulled out a single sheet of paper. It was covered in the same neat, impossible script. He read.

> *Bill,*
> *Remember me? Maybe you will by the time you get to the end of this letter. By the way, this letter is coming from a long way off.*
> *I hear you're having some trouble with your career. I like to think I've had a hand in that. I've managed to get intimate with those in power here, just like I did when I knew you so well. I have*

been granted favors here, too.

It wasn't very nice of you to leave me alone, Bill. It wasn't nice at all. Not very manly either. I was cold. That water was so cold. But I'm warm now. Yes, warm.

Our baby says, "Hi, Daddy." He has your face, Bill. He looks just like you. Too bad you haven't seen him yet.

But you will. We're coming to see you, Bill. We're coming to see you real soon. Be watching for us.

Love and kisses,
Connie

"No," Bill moaned. "Not this. Not now."

Of all things, why this? First, there had been the sexual harassment complaint that had nearly cost him the gubernatorial election, then just after the inauguration came the bribery charges. After that, there was the nasty public divorce that so many of the vultures in the media had gotten fat on. Then the tax fraud. Now this. Who could have done it? Who knew?

Connie? Connie Balder? *Dead. Dead for eight, nine years? Something like that. She hadn't sent the letter.* But who had? Who could possibly know? The highway patrol troopers who had kept that little section of road blocked off? *No, they wouldn't do this. They are set for life now. They wouldn't blow their free ride.*

"Need another shot?" Tully's thin voice scratched through Bill's thoughts. The governor looked at the table and saw that both shot glasses and the beer mug were empty. He didn't remember drinking them.

"Yeah, Tully, I think I do." He tried to smile, but only grimaced. The drinks were brought, and Bill put the letter back in his pocket. He drank, re-ordered, drank, and then forced himself to leave. Tully waved him off when he tried to pay.

The streets seemed crowded with blurry pedestrians—fuzzy-edged voters—but Bill was able to weave his Porsche through them to the state capitol building. He decided to ride in the back of the limousine when it was time to go to the courthouse.

The lunch his staff offered him made Bill feel nauseous. He guzzled a couple of beers, then went to the grand jury hearing. He denied everything again and again. Evidence was brought to bear against him. Lawyers argued over details. More evidence was shown, examined, argued over. Bill Waters maintained the smile that had seen him through a tough campaign—and through more than one affair.

Connie...she's dead.

Then the questions and arguing was over. Not for good, not by a long shot, but over for the day. Nothing decided. No verdict. Reconvene tomorrow, the judge said.

Bill let the chauffeur take him home. He rode in the back of the long black limousine, the dark windows raised and his head lowered so he would not have to see the carrion gathered around the gate of the governor's mansion.

Once inside, Bill stripped off his gray suit and didn't bother with a shower. He pulled a bottle of Jim Beam from the drawer beside his bed and lay down naked on top of the covers. He drank until he could no longer hold the bottle steady at his lips, then set it aside.

He slept.

He dreamed of the last time he saw Connie Balder.

She was in a hotel room. She was undressing as he watched, already naked and ready for business. Suddenly, she turned to him and made the announcement, "Bill, I'm pregnant."

"Who's the father?" He grinned.

"Don't be stupid, Bill. You know who."

"Get an abortion," he said, angry that she would call him stupid.

"I...I can't, Bill."

"Why?"

"It's my baby. Our baby, Bill. I can't abort it."

"What? Are you turning into one of those sniffling pro-lifers on me now?"

"It's different. This one's in me. It's mine. Ours."

"Not mine."

"Bill..." She put her arms around him. Her flesh felt warm and soft as it pressed against him. Her perfume filled his nostrils, made him want her so much his balls ached with lust.

"Later," he mumbled. "We'll talk later."

They didn't. They made love. They slept. They made love again. Connie went to the shower, and, when the water began to run, Bill picked up the telephone. He had some good friends in the highway patrol department, men with more greed than conscience. They agreed to give him a favor for a monetary gift that would keep on giving. They knew a winner when they saw one.

Bill joined Connie in the shower. They made love for the last time under the steaming water, and then he offered to drive her home in her car. He had been brought to the hotel by a friend, he lied. He could be picked up from Connie's apartment. Flattered, the woman had allowed him to drive.

She talked about the baby. Bill listened. He said they could work something out. Yes, his wife was a bitch. Yes, he would be happier with Connie. Yes, a little boy would be very nice; they would fish and camp together.

The car passed through a speed trap a few miles outside of town. A highway patrol car pulled out after them, lights filling the night with red and blue flashes. Bill pulled over. It was beginning to snow, big, wet flakes of gleaming white. He and Connie were asked to get out of the car.

Bill hadn't been able to watch when the club came in contact with the woman's forehead, but he saw it now, in his dream. He saw her flesh split and bits of pale white bone suddenly protrude from the gash. Blood ran down her face as her eyes rolled upward.

"Help me get her in the car," the patrolman ordered. Bill did as he was told. They took the car a quarter of a mile up the highway and rolled it off a narrow bridge into the river below. The patrolman drove Bill back to his car in the hotel parking lot.

News reports the next morning said a woman named Connie Balder had been found dead in the river. She appeared to have drowned after her car went out of control and off a bridge; she had hit her head on the windshield and been knocked unconscious before drowning—another case in favor of seatbelt laws.

Bill stirred in his sleep. It was not a pleasant dream. He did not like to think of Connie that way. He preferred to remember the pretty young woman he had met while campaigning for the state senate. She had been so full of energy and enthusiasm for him. When she immediately responded to his first come-ons, Bill had been delighted.

He remembered the times they made love, always secretively, like teenagers in their parents' car. She had been very skilled, with superb muscle control. She could make him come just by clenching her cunt around the head of his dick. He could picture it as he slept—her straddling him, her beautiful legs pressed against his sides. She rode him hard for a while, and then stopped, raising herself up so that he was barely inside her. She smiled as her small hands slid from his chest to her own groin, up her stomach to her young breasts. She cupped them, held them lovingly, wiggled them for him, and then he felt her contract the muscles of her vagina. Bill groaned with pleasure.

He opened his eyes and the dream was over. He tried to scream when he saw the pale, doughy-fleshed thing that was on top of him. Her hands gripped her sagging tits and squeezed a few drops of bloody water from the nipples. The fluid stung where it landed on Bill's stomach. She grinned, and the governor saw mud on her teeth. Leaves and debris hung from her wet hair.

"Connie."

"Give it to me, Bill, just like you used to," she said, her mouth bubbling dirty river water as she spoke. She stopped riding him and he felt her begin to clench around his penis.

"No," he begged. It was too late. He ejaculated an impressive amount, but she didn't relent. Her body continued to contract around him, milking him for every drop he could offer. She finally fell off him and rolled to her back so that she lay beside him on the bed.

He couldn't move. Bill tried in vain to jump from the bed, but he was held in place as if a blanket of lead were laid over him. Not a single finger of his hand would function when he commanded it.

The room grew cold. Bill realized his crotch was covered in a thick, mucus-like substance where the dead woman had sat to fuck him. The rotten, sluggish smell of the river made him want to vomit. He could see his breath as the short, heaving vapor escaped his nostrils. The temperature continued to drop, and the corpse remained beside him.

The clock ticked away the minutes, the hours, and slowly the governor noticed that the side of the bed where the dead woman lay was warmer than his own. He tried to snuggle closer to the water-logged woman, but still he could not move. Only his eyes rolled in his head. The air around the corpse shimmered as the room grew colder and she became warmer. One side of his body was freezing, the other side was near scalding.

Then he heard the first crack. It was loud and sharp, like gunfire. He saw that the woman's chest was sunk in on one side now. Another crack, and the other side of her bosom caved inward, causing her breasts to slosh to the center. More crackling, and then a tearing sound as a rip appeared in her abdomen. Bill could hear crunching, slurping, and sucking sounds coming from within the body.

When the thing inside the woman's corpse tore a larger hole in her belly and lifted a charred black hand into the frigid air, Bill screamed. Steam formed around the hand and smoke rose from the woman's womb. More tearing, more cracking. No sucking or slurping now; the thing was done feeding and ready to be born. Another hand appeared, and then out popped the head.

Bill choked and nearly passed out. It was his own face he was looking into. His own face, except it was flaming red where it was not burned black. Only the eyes, somehow still blue and brimming with enthusiasm, belonged to the mother. The small creature sprang from its mother's womb to stand on its father's chest.

Bill looked into the eyes. The thing was smiling, and it had his smile, the smile that could win confidence and votes. It was only two feet tall, with large feet and claws on the toes. Bill could feel the claws digging into his skin as the monster tried to balance itself. The thing was, beyond doubt, a male. A thick, blackened, sausage-like appendage dangled from its groin.

"Hi, Daddy," the creature croaked. It reached out its long, charred arms and hugged Bill's head to its own burning chest. "I hear Mommy laughing now."

Then·the beast hopped from the bed and, with a waddling gait, ran to the door of the bedroom. It opened the door and faced the bed. "We have hearings again tomorrow, Daddy. Or maybe not." Then it scurried from the room.

The invisible blanket of lead was gone now, but Bill did not try to move. Only a few minutes passed before he heard a commotion at the gates of the mansion. The vultures were being disturbed at their roost.

They would have plenty to report now. Bill smiled as he heard exclamations and screams coming from outside the mansion.

"I have a son," he said to the body beside him.

Aces Over Eights

"You're out of funds, Jimmy-boy." Don smirked as he raked the coins and bills closer to the neat stacks standing before him on the green table.

"Damn you," James grumbled, only half-grinning as he watched the last of yesterday's paycheck move away from him. "You'd take my last dollar?" he asked.

"Only if you're fool enough to gamble it," Don answered. "And it looks as though you were."

"A college man can get kind of hungry hurrying from the university to his full-time job," James reasoned. "Come on, one more hand."

"You have nothing to bet," Don, the meticulous philosophy major, answered.

The two men sat in the dim light of the crowded garage apartment Don had rented for the duration of the school year. Empty bottles and cans stood on the table with the crumbs of a small junk-food feast. The card players each sat hunched over the table, Don in his casual clothes, a dress shirt and Dockers, and Jim in his usual garb, blue jeans and a T-shirt. In the street outside, they could hear the late evening traffic creeping through the slush of wet snow.

James sucked the dregs from a beer bottle and looked thoughtful. Finally, he slammed the bottle down and announced, "Yes, I do." He dug in his pockets until he found a pen and a scrap of yellow legal paper. "Law students are never without legal paper," he joked as he scribbled something onto the parchment. He pushed it to the center of the table.

"I don't take IOU's," Don said.

"Read it, dumbass. It's not an IOU."

Don picked up the paper and squinted at the block letters to see them better in the dimness.

This note binds my immortal soul to the bearer.

It was signed, *James Zigmore.*

"Is this a joke?" Don asked.

"No. It's a contract for my soul."

"You don't believe in that crap, do you?"

"In souls? Of course I do. Don't you?"

"No. There's absolutely no proof whatsoever that such—"

"So you won't take my bet?" Jim challenged. Then, more hopeful, "I really kind of need to win my money back."

Don sat quietly for a moment, then answered, "All right. I'll bet the pot, the pot you lost, against that scrap of paper you seem to think is of some value."

"You deal," Jim invited, his brow wet and his eyes wide. He snatched up the five cards Don flipped at him and eagerly studied each one. When all five were in his hand, his expression fell to one of perplexity. He shifted and sorted the five waxy cards, and finally dropped three of them back to the table. "Three," he croaked as he reached for a fresh beer. Don dealt him three more cards, taking no more for himself. Jim looked at his cards, shifted them, studied them, rearranged them again, and then slumped back in his chair.

"You don't look happy," Don said. "What do you have?"

James put down two fours, a jack, a five, and a queen. He said nothing. Don laid down his own cards, forcing back the sharp remarks he wanted to make in respect for his friend's obvious disappointment.

"Full house. Aces over eights."

"Dead man's hand," James said as he stood up and began putting on his coat. "I better go. Big test tomorrow." He picked up his beer and started for the door.

"Sit down, Jim," Don said, getting to his feet and blocking the exit. "I can't let you leave, we still have beer to drink. Besides, you lost too early. The night's still young."

Reluctantly, Jim sat down, but kept his coat on. The two men talked for a few hours while the remainder of the beer went steadily into Jim's body. Finally, Don got up to go to the bathroom. When he returned, Jim was gone. He checked outside and saw that his friend's car was gone, too.

"Damn fool. He shouldn't be driving." Don shook his head, went back inside and locked the door.

He returned to the table and stacked coins, knocked them over, drank beer and slowly shredded the piece of yellow legal paper with the cryptic inscription on it. He took the ribbons and made a small ball of each, which he dropped into an ashtray and set on fire. There was very little smoke and the odor was soon gone. Don realized he was nearly asleep, so he stripped off his clothes and crawled into bed.

He awoke at about three in the morning. He was shivering though he was covered in a layer of blankets and knew he had left the thermostat turned high. He rolled away from the wall and faced the smoky image of James Zigmore standing silently beside his bed.

"What?" he mumbled. "How'd you get in?"

"I can move through doors now." Jim grinned a sad grin.

"Go home." Don tried to roll back over.

"I guess this is home now," Jim said slowly. "They won't let me go on because I lost my soul to you."

Don was motionless for a moment as the words and the translucent image of his friend sank in. He figured he was drunk, sleepy and feeling guilty for cheating at cards. He sat up and faced the apparition of his guilt. "What?"

For answer, James reached out and put a freezing hand on Don's arm. Don fell back on the pillow, his mind filled with images of a car, a slick highway, and a tree looming up in alcohol-blurred vision. Then there was a crash and a sorrowful voice explaining that he could not enter because his soul was bonded to another. Then the hand moved away and Don was looking at the ghost of his friend.

"What can I do?" he asked, rubbing the blue mark where the ethereal hand had touched him.

"You could sign the contract and give it back to me," Jim answered. "That would free me. But there's something else. It seems selling my soul was a major offense that calls for severe punishment. If you release me, I'll have to suffer the punishment."

"And if I don't?"

"I'll just kind of hang out with you until you die." Jim smiled. "I guess I'll still be bound to you, so then I'll just go with you to whatever punishment or reward you get in The Great Hereafter."

"I…I don't believe in—"

"You kind of have to believe now, Donny-boy," Jim said. "I'm here. You can't deny that."

"I burned the contract," Don said. "Doesn't that release you?"

"No. It doesn't release me. They know. Besides, like I said, I'm not sure I want to be released."

"But I don't want you here," Don said slowly. "I don't want to believe in you anymore. Not if you're dead."

"You really don't have a choice," James said. "You have to believe. Now, like I was saying, I'll be going with you when you pass on. I don't want to suffer. I saw some of that. So, we need to change some of your habits to make sure we don't have to endure that when you...well, when you die."

"You're crazy. I must be crazy. Okay. I'll admit this to my subconscious. I cheated. I had those aces under my leg in the chair," Don said. "When Jim bet his soul, I used them to make the dead man's hand, just to show him how stupid all that crap is. Now I'm going to sleep. You'll be gone when I wake up. And if you're not, a few cups of strong black coffee will get rid of you."

"Go to sleep, Don," James urged. "You'll see it differently in the morning. I won't be any bother. Go to sleep."

Then the icy-cold figure got into bed with him. Don moved as far away as he could, but still shivered uncontrollably. He stared at the ceiling, hoping he was dreaming. Maybe it would be better in the morning, he thought. Maybe he would wake up to find he had kicked off his blankets and the electricity had failed in the storm so that his heater was no longer working.

He would not look beside him.

He stared at the ceiling.

He said he was dreaming as he wished for sleep.

Dawn's New Coat

"It's a guy thing. It's a guy thing. God, I am so sick of hearing that," Dawn Davis said. "We'll just see about that."

Her husband, Bill, lay on the hardwood floor. His sinews glistened in the lamplight. Drops of blood still trickled from his body to join the puddle spreading on the wood. There wasn't as much blood as Dawn had expected. But then, her daddy was an expert in skinning wild game and he had taught his daughter well.

She stood over the skinned body, naked herself, sweat glistening on her brow, her long brown hair hanging limply around her pale face. She held her husband's skin folded over her left forearm. Her eyes were large and bright, her mind filled with echoes of her late husband's voice.

"It's a guy thing. I don't want to be married anymore," the voice said. "I want to be free to fuck around."

"Seven months, Bill," she said. "Seven months of marriage and I come home to find you in our bed fucking that whore from the deli." Dawn wished Bill had died with his eyes open so she could believe he was paying attention. But the rat poison she'd added to his dinner had let him die with his eyes closed. "You told me I wouldn't understand your fucking needs until I stepped into your skin and walked around in it. All right, Bill. All fucking right. Let's just see about that."

Dawn flipped the long coat of flesh out and draped it over her shoulders. It was too long. With the big hunting knife she'd used to remove the skin from its former owner, she trimmed the arms and legs, then tied the flaps of skin around her own limbs with pieces of red yarn. She poked holes where the skin had covered Bill's collarbone and ran more yarn through the holes to fasten the pelt around her neck. She used Bill's discarded leather belt to hold the hide around her waist.

The coverall of skin was still warm from Bill's body, warm and sticky because Dawn had been in too big a hurry to bother wiping all the congealing blood from the inside of her new coat. She found she liked the feel of his skin sticking to her own nakedness.

She went to stand before a mirror mounted on the wall near the bathroom door. She raised the final flap of flesh over her groin and tucked it under the belt. Bill's penis stood erect; she'd stuffed it with cotton after removing his flesh. She wrapped a hand around the penis and squeezed. It felt lumpy and soft but...but good. It felt powerful. It felt like a tool that should be used.

Dawn looked back at the very naked body of her husband. She sighed. She hated it when he was right about something.

"Now I understand," she said.

The Night Cloak

Ten-year-old Jason Wynn lay in his bed, the sheet and one blanket tucked securely under his chin. The night was cool, but the covers and his flannel dinosaur pajamas kept him warm. Jason knew he had a math test in school the next day, a test with double-digit multiplication problems. Still, it was not thoughts of the test that kept him awake.

Someone was calling his name. He listened to the soft, persistent voice. It sounded as if it came from right outside his second-story window.

He didn't want to leave his warm, safe bed to look out the window, but he found his feet being tickled by the carpet anyway as he moved slowly toward his Batman curtains. He moved one curtain aside carefully and looked outside. The night was very dark. Thousands of stars glittered and winked at him. He didn't see anybody—or anything—that could have called to him.

But he heard the voice again just as he was ready to drop the curtain back into place.

"Jason," the voice called softly. "Jason?"

"Who are you?" Jason whispered.

"I'm the man in the moon," the voice answered.

Jason looked out his window again but didn't see any moon.

"You can't see me tonight," the voice said. "It's my dark time. I want you to come play with me."

"The moon isn't alive," Jason said, remembering to keep his voice low so he wouldn't wake his parents in the next room.

"I'm very much alive, Jason," the voice said. "I want you to come play with me. There are many other children here. You'll have fun. You're not really tired, are you?"

Jason thought about it for a moment. He wasn't tired. "How can I come play with you?" he asked.

"Open your window."

Jason did as he was told. The night air was cool but refreshing. "Now what?"

"Come to me," the voice said. Jason felt himself slumping forward, his eyelids becoming heavy, as if he was suddenly too tired to remain standing.

"Welcome, Jason," the voice said. "We've been hoping you'd come play with us."

Jason looked up. He knew he was dreaming...or not dreaming, but not awake like he was usually awake. He was looking at a very tall man who wore a long black coat, or cloak, like in the old movies. The man wore the hood low so Jason couldn't see his face. The cloak billowed around the man and other children played in the folds of the rich, satiny cloth.

"Come play with us, Jason," the children called. Their faces seemed to be a brilliant white against the ebony of the man's cloak. They jumped and hid and squealed in the rippling cloth.

"It's okay, Jason," the hooded man said.

Jason dove into the soft, silky folds of the cloak. He chased other children and they chased him until he became tired. He lay down and snuggled into the soft cloak.

He woke up in his own room, curled on the floor under his open window. It was morning. Jason felt stiff and very tired. He dressed for school and hurried out to catch the bus.

He knew he didn't perform well on his math test. He almost fell asleep during his English lesson. That night, he was too tired to watch television before going to bed.

As soon as he pulled the blankets over himself, he heard the voice outside his window. Reluctantly, he got up and looked outside. A sliver of moon greeted him.

"Come play with us again, Jason," the voice said. It seemed to come from the moon.

Jason opened the window and felt himself falling into the presence of the black-cloaked figure again. This time, the man's hood was arranged so that Jason could see a slice of bone-white face against the black cloth.

"The children have been waiting to play with you, Jason," the figure said. Jason dove into the luxurious black cloak to play tag with the shining children.

The next morning, Jason felt even groggier. Still, he dressed and went to school. He came home, did his homework, ate his dinner and went to his bed. Soon after sunset, he heard the voice calling to him again. He went to play with his new friends.

A week later, Jason was sent to the office for falling asleep twice during a chemistry lesson. His mother fretted over him at home because he had become so lethargic. His old friends stopped asking him to play after school because he only wanted to go to bed.

Each night, Jason answered the call he heard outside his window. Each night, as the moon grew, he was able to see more of the glowing white face of the man in the billowy black cloak.

Each day, he woke up more tired than he'd been when he went to sleep. He knew the man in the moon was stealing his energy. He knew he would get weaker as the moon grew fatter, and when the moon became full of him, he would be trapped in the black cloak like the other children.

Jason told himself he would not answer the call outside his window anymore. When it came, he tried covering his head with his pillow, but he could not block out the soft, commanding voice. He asked to sleep with his parents and they let him, but during the night he was called out of their bed; he woke up under his own window again.

He couldn't go to school. He couldn't stay awake during the day. His mother took him to doctors, but the doctors couldn't find anything wrong with him. One doctor gave Jason's mother a bottle of sleeping pills and told her to give Jason one each night.

The pills didn't help; Jason was always called to his window before he could fall asleep.

Jason didn't want to be like the children trapped in the cloak of the man in the moon—he didn't want to be a twinkling star. If he let the man in the moon grow fat on him, he would be trapped there. Jason thought of that as he stood in the bathroom, the bottle of sleeping pills in his hand.

"If I die before you're full, you can't have me," he mumbled. Jason twisted the cap off the bottle, filled a Dixie cup with water and swallowed seventeen of the pills. He was barely able to get back into his bed before he fell asleep.

"Jason, why did you do that?" the voice asked. Jason looked toward the voice and was surprised to see that the entire glowing face of the man in the moon was now visible in the folds of the black hood. "You weren't supposed to see all of my face for two more nights. You've been very naughty, Jason. But I'm not angry. Come play with your friends. You won't have to leave them tonight."

Jason saw the star-faced children beckoning to him from the soft creases of the cloak. Slowly, he moved to join their play.

New Blood

The basement door opened slowly, silently, on well-oiled hinges. A long-fingered, pale hand reached through to the darkness. There came the sharp click of a switch and electric light exploded into the cellar. The seven naked people below lay unmoving on their cold steel tables.

Luther Cushing carefully planted one foot on the top of the stairs leading to the basement floor. The step seemed safe; he trusted his weightless form to it and glided down the staircase to the earthen floor, then to the bodies on the table.

He checked the slim line connecting the first, a middle-aged man, to the bottle suspended over his table. The fluids that kept life in the brain-dead body were still flowing properly. The bottle was getting low on solution; Luther made a mental note to change it soon.

He lowered his head and slid his long, needle-sharp incisors into the two wounds on the man's neck. He fed silently, not taking much blood, not nearly enough to satisfy himself; he had to leave enough to keep the body alive.

He moved to the next blood supplier and repeated the procedure. And so on down the line until he came to number six. There, he stopped.

He had been expecting the sixth member of his feeding line to expire for several days now. Expecting it, and dreading it. But the time had come. The old man was dead, and a replacement was needed.

Luther went on to the seventh body and drank from it, then returned to the sixth. He pulled the IV line from its arm and lifted the body from the table where it had rested for several months.

He carried it back up the stairs and sat it in a chair in his living room. He took a chair opposite the corpse.

"Why did you have to die?" he asked. His voice was soft, like velvet sliding over ice. "Now I have to find someone to replace you. You know how I hate going into the city. I could be killed going there." He sighed and rose from the chair, straightening the crease in his slacks as he did.

"But I have to go," he continued, more to himself than to the corpse. He donned a charcoal-colored trench coat, buttoned it to the chin, and tied the belt around his waist, though it was a warm night for mid-November, then hefted the naked body in his arms.

Luther went to the front door, opened it halfway, and looked out into the night, his cat-like vision easily piercing the darkness and not seeing anything unusual. He hurried out and pulled the door closed behind him as if he were afraid something might try to slip past him and into his home.

Brisk steps carried him from the porch to the small car parked in his drive. Luther pushed the body into the front passenger seat, then ran around to the other side of the car to slide behind the steering wheel. He put the key in the ignition and turned it.

The engine turned over sluggishly, but did not fire. He tried again. The car still did not start. Luther cursed himself and vowed that he would come outside and start the car at least once a week, even if he didn't go anywhere. He turned the key again and the engine forced itself to life. He backed carefully out of the driveway and started down the hill toward the glittering lights of the city.

As he drove, Luther thought of Thomas, the ancient one who had given him the gift of immortality. "Take it. Drink from me," Thomas had commanded. "You don't have to be the whimpering pup that you are. Be strong. Be a god!"

Luther knew he would have lived his miserable life and died unremembered had Thomas not come to him in the night. Luther remembered how he had gratefully accepted what the ancient one offered. But nothing had worked out right after that. Thomas had been killed by some foolish priest, and Luther was left alone long before he was ready to face the world with his undead eyes.

He stopped only once on his drive to the city. That was on a small, forgotten bridge over the brackish river. He bid his expired blood supplier good-bye, then tossed the body over the rail and into the sluggish water.

Luther drove into the city, not sure where to begin his search. He sat at traffic lights, crouched low in his seat, hoping people could not see his pale flesh through the tinted glass of the car's windows.

The world has changed too much.

Luther had not remained active for very long after the death of Thomas. One of the few things Luther had learned was the ability to hide underground for long periods of time; it was a trick suited to his character. He had tried hunting alone for a while, but the results had been near disastrous. At that time, there had been not only the danger of priests with their wooden stakes and holy water, but the Black Plague. Choosing victims had been such a worry; what if they had the Plague? Could he catch it from their blood?

And today's world was not much better. *So many new diseases.* The new one, AIDS, scared him more than even the Black Plague. He had always suspected he could drink Plague-tainted blood and be all right, though he had never dared try it. But this disease affected the blood itself, killed the ability of the blood to fight other diseases. That, he feared, could be deadly to even a vampire. After all, it was the infusion of fresh blood that held off decay. Luther shuddered at the thought of being exposed to such a disease.

He parked in an area where there were still several stores open so late, mostly sex shops that catered to the perverse tastes of the late twentieth century. He left his car and stepped into the throng of people, pulling a pair of sunglasses from his pocket and putting them on to hide his burning red pupils. He returned his hands to his coat pockets and walked along the street, looking for someone he could lure to his home.

They were watching him, he knew. He could feel their eyes—blue, brown, and green—boring into him. They were looking into his soul, seeing him for the blood-sucking, undead creature he was. They averted their gaze whenever he looked their way, but he knew they were watching him.

Luther tried not to think about it. He told himself he was master here. He was the vampire—that made him superior to the mortals surrounding him.

But which of them has the wooden stake in his pocket? Who has the hammer? Who holds the vial of holy water clamped in a sweaty fist, ready to throw it in my face and burn the flesh from my skull? Who?

"No one," he murmured to himself, hoping it was the truth.

There was not much variety in the types of people on this street. They were hookers, pimps and bums. But worse yet were the people they preyed on—downcast weaklings, scuttling from hooker to whore looking for the best buy on a night of pleasure.

Luther walked past a movie theater without noticing the title on the marquee.

"Vampires don't scare me anymore," a woman's voice shrilled. Luther stopped, stunned. "I think a bite on the neck might be fun. Kind of kinky."

"And when you're tired of 'em," another voice added, "you just shove some wood through their heart and you don't have to worry about 'em anymore. It'd be a lot easier than dumping some of these leeches."

Luther ran. He knew people were staring at him, and now they didn't bother to drop their gaze as he sped past. They knew. He was sure of it. They were not afraid of him; they wanted to use him for pleasure and then kill him. He ran faster, sure the shrill voice of the woman who thought he might be kinky would blare from directly behind him.

He jumped into his car and slammed the door. He started the car and drove away as fast as the congested traffic would allow.

Home.

Luther's heart pleaded with his hunger, begging to go home where it was safe, back to his quiet house on the hill beyond the city limits. But he needed a body to replace the one that had died.

He tried a small bar next, feeling confident he could find a lonely soul there who could be convinced to go home with him. He parked his car behind the building and went inside.

Soft music from a glittering jukebox filled the single room. Couples danced close and slow. Luther made out several people sitting at tables around the dimly lit dance floor. He walked up to the bar and sat on one of the tall stools. The bartender started over; Luther waved him off.

A young man walked bravely up and sat on the barstool next to him. "How're ya doin'?" the man asked in a slurred, drunken voice.

"Fine." Luther knew his voice sounded like that of a kitten. "I'm fine," he repeated, louder than before, if not more confident.

"Can I buy ya a drink, buddy?"

"No, thanks," Luther answered.

"C'mon, I'll buy ya one," the man insisted. "Bartender! A drink for my friend. What'll ya have?"

"Bloody Mary," Luther sighed.

"And another Long Island tea." The bartender brought the drinks and set them before his customers. The stranger began gulping his; Luther faked a few swallows.

"Here alone?" the man asked.

"Yes."

"No date? Just as well. Women are all bitches. Dirty little sluts. That's what they are. All of 'em. And these..." He waved his arm at the occupants of the bar and then turned back to his drink.

"If you say so," Luther agreed.

"Who needs 'em?"

"I take it you're here alone, yourself?" Luther forced the conversation onward.

"Damn right. Bitch said she was too good for me. To hell with the whore." The man drank half his remaining cocktail.

"Would you like to come home with me?" Luther asked. "We can talk about it more at my house. I'm really very interested."

"That's what I'm here for," the man bellowed. "I ain't never made it with a man before, but I'm game. Gotta be better than messing with those bitches."

"What? Made it...?" Luther looked around and it was then that he realized all the people in the bar were men. "Oh, I see." He wondered if the panic was evident in his voice.

"You come here often?"

"No." Luther choked on the word. "No, I've never been here before." He suddenly wanted to leave this establishment as soon as possible. "You've never had a man?"

"Nope, not yet." The man grinned a drunken grin. "Do you want to be my first?"

"Oh, that depends on whether or not you'll come home with me," Luther repeated his offer, rather boldly, he hoped.

"Sure thing. But aren't you going to buy me a drink? I bought you one." He pointed to Luther's full glass.

"We'll drink at my house," Luther promised.

"All right. Let's go." The young man took Luther by the arm and hopped off his barstool, pulling Luther after him. He staggered a little and Luther had to support him. "My name's Chet, by the way. What's yours?"

"Luther." He let himself be led to the door by the would-be homosexual, and then motioned toward the rear of the building. "My car is around there."

He opened the car door for Chet and closed it behind him, then hurried around to the driver's side. Luther drove quickly out of the city and back up the hill to his home as the young man sat and babbled all sorts of nonsense about his ill luck with women.

Once he was home, Luther took the young man into the kitchen and sat him down at the table. He then went behind a counter and mixed a drink, a large quantity of brandy and a small amount of a yellowish fluid—the serum that would render Chet a human vegetable.

He handed the drink to the man and bid him enjoy it.

"Aren't you going to have anything?" Chet asked.

"No," Luther answered. "I've drunk nearly my fill for the night, but perhaps we'll share a drink later. After." He forced himself to wink at his visitor, which won him a smile in return.

Chet swallowed half the snifter's contents in one long draught.

Luther smiled.

"You look awful pale," Chet said. "Do you feel all right?"

"I'm fine," Luther said. "Drink up."

"You don't have AIDS, do you?" Chet asked, a look of alarm creeping over his face.

"No!" Luther answered, appalled that the man would have the gall to ask him such a question. "I assure you I have absolutely no disease whatsoever."

"Good," Chet said. He took another swallow of his drink. "You look almost like a vamp—" His face split into a yawn. His body slumped as if it had been suddenly deflated. The remainder of the drink spilled onto the chair.

Luther moved the glass away, thankful Chet had not been able to finish his sentence. He picked up the man and carried him to the basement, where he laid the new body on the vacant table and removed its clothes. Luther tossed the garments into a corner, then pushed an IV line into one arm and checked to make sure the fluid was flowing into the body.

He was thirsty. He couldn't drink from his new member yet, not until the serum had been absorbed by his system and made harmless. It had been a nerve-racking night, however, and Luther needed some nourishment.

He decided to take another sip, just a small one, from the seventh body. He scarcely noticed when the heart stopped beating and the body died under his teeth.

SKN-3

Children crowded the dirty street, some carrying bags or sacks of treats given by local residents, or stolen from other children in other parts of the borough. Older kids sat on the curb smoking pot or whatever their pusher sold them last. No mothers would call these kids home as the evening grew steadily darker. Screams filled the night, but that was not unusual for this neighborhood. Jack-o-lanterns that had not yet been smashed by the marauding children of the ghetto still glowed dully in the dirty night.

Reluctantly, the trick-or-treaters and drug users and pushers moved aside to let a battered old Mercury chug past them.

The long brown Mercury stopped in front of the house where Dr. Daniel Stillson had set up his medical practice. A tall white man got out from the driver's side and a huge Negro from the passenger side. The black man opened a back door and began pulling another white man from the seat. The driver came around the car to help his companion.

The man they extracted from the car was unconscious. He was well-dressed, in a tailored gray suit, though his silk tie had come untucked from his suit coat and flapped in the gentle breeze as the other two men, supporting him between them, dragged him through the yard to the front door of Dr. Stillson's home office. A scowling jack-o-lantern watched them from inside the window.

Once on the porch, the black man knocked heavily on the front door. A curtain in the window flickered before the door was pulled open and the three men admitted. The door closed quickly behind them.

"Bring him in here," Dr. Stillson said, waving for the other men to follow him. Daniel Stillson was a medium-sized man of about forty-five, though he looked at least ten years older due to life in the city's slums. He was losing his dark hair at the crown, but his eyes still burned with unspent life. Tonight they shone even brighter than usual. Tonight he was a man on the brink of revenge.

The doctor led his guests into his examination room, the cleanest room in the house, and also the kitchen. White linoleum covered the floors, and the many cabinets on the walls were painted white, though in many places the paint was faded and stained. The sink in the corner had rust stains around the drain, and the table where the doctor sat to talk with his patients was propped up by chipped bricks because one of the legs had been broken off by a patient who had gotten angry over a price. The only other piece of furniture in the room was the steel examination table, and it was unremarkable except for the fact that tonight it was equipped with pieces of nylon rope tied to each of the four legs.

"Undress him and put him on the table," Dr. Stillson instructed. "Then tie his wrists and ankles with those ropes. Make sure you get them tight. Stretch him out so he can't move." He stood by and watched as his orders were carried out. When he was satisfied, he tossed a bottle of pills to each of the two men.

"Remember," he warned, "You don't know anything."

"Right," they both agreed.

"Good. Now go." Stillson followed the two and locked the door behind them. He heard the cough and roar as the old Mercury was started and driven away. He peeked out the window again to make sure his visitors had not attracted any unwanted attention.

Just the usual scum, he decided. The little ones dressed in costumes were less monstrous than usual tonight. He let the dingy curtain drop back into place and returned to the examination room.

He stood over the unconscious body on his table for a few minutes, studying the smooth, pale flesh and the peaceful look of the handsome face. Then, smiling to himself, he turned and walked away.

From a corner, he pulled out a small, wheeled cart with a gleaming metal tray for a top. He removed the utensils he would need from a drawer: a scalpel, a syringe, and a new needle in a plastic wrapper. He took a small, corked bottle of clear liquid from a cabinet and placed all these items neatly on the tray of his cart and pushed them to the examination table. He brought a chair from the conference table and put it beside the tray, then sat down to wait for the man to regain his senses.

The wait wasn't long. The man's head began to move, his well-groomed blond hair becoming mussed. He tried to raise an arm, and the ropes held it down. His head snapped up and he found Dr. Stillson's smiling face. The man's eyes widened in surprise.

"Hello, Jeffrey," Dr. Stillson said. "Or shall it still be Mister Davies?

Like it was in the courtroom? No, I think here it will be just plain old Jeff. Is that all right with you?"

"What am I doing here, Stillson?" Jeff demanded. "Where the hell am I?"

"Why, Jeff," the doctor feigned surprise. "This is my new office. Don't you like it? It's the best I can do since you ruined my practice with that nasty lawsuit."

"You killed my wife," Jeff accused, again.

"It was an accident," the doctor said harshly. "I explained before the operation that there was the chance she wouldn't make it through. You didn't hesitate to give me the go-ahead."

"You killed her because she wouldn't have sex with you in the hospital room."

Dr. Stillson's face reddened. "She was mine. She needed me as much as I wanted her. You should have heard her begging me to fuck her that first day she came to me. She said her husband was too busy with his work at the bank to give her the dick when he came home, if he came home. She told me she had heard rumors of homosexual activity between you and a clerk in the vault. Did you like getting corn-holed while you were bent over stacks of hundred dollar bills? Huh, Jeffy?"

"Fuck you! Why am I naked? Where are my clothes?"

"They've been taken care of. Be happy with what you have on.

"I made love to Molly," Stillson confessed. "You never got me to admit that in court, did you? No. But I did. She was a wonderful lover. Exquisite, really. She was going to leave you before we found out the lump was cancerous. I wanted her to leave you immediately then, but she didn't want to go through a divorce until after the operation. We made love in her hospital room several times. Even after her hair fell out.

"I miss her," Dr. Stillson added. "I doubt you do."

"It's none of your business," Jeff said. "Why am I here?"

"I'm going to do an operation on you tonight, Jeff. I've never performed this particular operation on a human before, but I'm sure if Molly were here she would give me the okay, just like you did for her. Besides, you're not that much different than an animal. Are you?"

"You're not going to cut on me," Jeff said. "You can't."

"Sure I can," Dr. Stillson said. He plucked the scalpel from his tray and showed it to his patient. "I'm all ready to go."

"No," Jeff said quietly. "No! Help! Somebody help me!"

"Nobody will help you because nobody cares!" Dr. Stillson shouted over the other man's voice. "We're in the slums, Jeff. The ghetto. The people out there, they've heard shouts coming from this house before. Most of my patients are thieves, gang members and junkies. My neighbors won't care about your shouts."

"Nooo," Jeff moaned.

"Oh, yes," the doctor said in a reassuring tone. He took the syringe and the needle from his tray and fitted them together. He picked up the small bottle and stuck the needle through the cork, pulling the plunger up until the syringe was just over half full. He put the bottle back on the tray and shot a quick stream of the clear fluid into the air.

"Got to get the air bubbles out," Stillson said. "I don't want you dying of a heart attack. I have something much better in mind."

"What is that?"

"This?" Dr. Stillson brandished the syringe. "This is a concoction that I made up. I call it SKN-3. The three is because the first two tries were unsuccessful. It's an amphetamine. Speed. Can you say trick-or-treat? I thought you could."

"Don't…" Jeff whined as Dr. Stillson brought the needle close to his arm. He winced as the steel penetrated his flesh. The plunger came down and the fluid was in his blood. "Now what?" Jeff asked, a tear coming from his eye.

"Now we wait," Dr. Stillson said, dropping the empty syringe onto the tray. "It should be just a few seconds before the drug takes effect."

"Then what?"

"Then, Jeff, I'm going to skin you alive. SKN-3 will keep you conscious for most of the operation. Won't it be interesting to watch as your flesh is peeled off?"

"*No!*" Jeff began yelling for help again. Dr. Stillson let him shout without trying to stop him. He sat calmly and watched his patient, smiling when he saw the drug was working. Jeff's eyes bulged in their sockets and his face turned red as if he were blushing deeply. He trembled slightly. His heart beat rapidly beneath his skin, causing the flesh of his chest to pulsate.

"My hair's crawling," Jeff said. "Are there bugs in it?"

"No, it just feels that way," the doctor told him. "I think we're ready to begin." He stood up, pushed the chair out of his way, lifted the scalpel from the tray, and pushed the cart back beside the discarded chair. He stepped close to the trembling man on his table.

"No. Please. I'll give you anything," Jeff begged, his voice hoarse with fright. "Anything you want."

"All I want from you, Jeff, is revenge," Dr. Stillson said. "And I'm about to have it."

Jeffrey Davies howled when the cold steel of the scalpel touched his super-sensitive skin. Dr. Stillson ignored the noise and concentrated on his cutting. He made an incision from a point a few inches below the Adam's apple to just above the start of the pubic hair. The cut swelled with ripe, red blood that soon spilled from its canal and ran down the man's hairless chest and stomach. Jeff continued to shriek with pain, and the doctor smiled to himself as he made his next cut along the inside of the left arm, then the right, and then the legs. He joined the slits on Jeff's limbs to the first cut on his torso, and peeled the flesh away from the carcass. Jeff's screams became louder and shriller, reaching an octave that Dr. Stillson would have believed impossible from the human throat.

Jeff's ropy red muscles glistened beneath the room's naked hundred-watt bulb. Within moments after his insides were exposed, Jeff passed out. Dr. Stillson looked at his watch.

"Good," he judged. "You stayed awake for the best parts, Jeffy. Thanks to my little drug."

The doctor completed his job, his face a mask of concentration. He cut from the top of his first incision, below the Adam's apple, around the base of the neck as far as he could reach. He untied Jeff and rolled the body over so he could complete the cuts on the wrists and ankles, then, bringing the cut from the man's neck up around the hairline and back to the forehead.

Taking hold of Jeff's blond hair, Dr. Stillson pulled slowly and steadily. The scalp lifted, and with a little help, the rest of the man's flesh came away from his back with a wet, sucking sound. Dr. Stillson lifted the skin away from the calves carefully so as not to tear the trophy, and then spread the dripping hide on his floor, inside up.

Leaving the body on the table for a moment, the doctor went to a cabinet and took out several white rags. He knelt beside his prize skin and wiped away the blood. When the inside was clean, he flipped the hide over and wiped the streaks of crimson from the front.

The skinless body still glistened wetly on the table. Dr. Stillson stood looking at it for a long moment. He smiled. "Happy Halloween, Jeffy," he said. "I love your costume."

He brought a bone saw from a drawer and quickly and expertly cut the body into small pieces, which he put into two Hefty Cinch Sacks along with the bloody rags. He then cleaned up his examination table and the floor around it, added these rags to the plastic bags, and closed them up. He pulled them to the far corner of the room to wait until he could hire a couple of junkies to dispose of them. Happy with a job well done, the doctor looked down at the skin laid out on the floor.

"I feel better, Jeff," he said. "Thank you." He took the small bottle of SKN-3 from the tray and examined the remaining fluid. "And thank *you* for keeping him awake long enough to make my task thoroughly enjoyable." He tossed the glass vial into the air, holding his palm out to catch it.

The bottle went up, tumbling end over end, and began its descent. The fluid within rolled from cork to bottom and back as gravity demanded. The bottle hit Dr. Stillson's upturned palm and bounced up before he could close his fingers around it. Again the bottle sailed through the air. It hit the skin stretched on the floor and shattered on impact with the hard linoleum beneath. Glass fragments flew like sparks in all directions as the liquid spread in a small stain.

"Shit!" The doctor glared at the mess. He stooped and picked the pieces of glass off the skin and the floor, then went for another rag to wipe up the formula. When he returned, the SKN-3 had soaked into the hide, leaving a small stain that looked like a birthmark.

"Oh well," Stillson said, "I suppose I didn't need the rest of it anyway." He dropped the rag onto his table and left the room, turning out the light.

He went to his bathroom and quickly showered, then to his bedroom and lay down, wearing only his underwear. He was asleep within minutes.

In his examination room, the skin began to move. At first the activity was only in the area where the fluid had stained the hide, a small rippling motion. Soon, however, the movement traveled outward until the entire hide was flowing, wave-like, from the headless scalp to the feetless legs and handless arms. The rippling became concentrated, and the skin began to inch its way across the floor toward the open doorway.

In the living room of the house, it rolled itself into a turn and rippled past a worn chair, the outstretched arm brushing the leg of an end table. The jack-o-lantern in the window took no notice. The skin slithered into a short hallway and then over the threshold of Daniel Stillson's bedroom. It crossed the hardwood floor and was soon at the foot of the narrow bed. Snake-like, it raised itself up until the scalp seemed to be peeking over the edge of the bed. The top part of the skin flopped down onto the mattress and pulled the bottom of the torso and the legs up after it.

The skin quickly covered Dr. Stillson's nearly naked body, wrapping the empty husks of its arms and legs around the sleeping doctor. It began to squeeze.

Daniel Stillson woke up slowly, thinking at first that some of the neighborhood heavies had broken in and wanted drugs. He would give them something that would knock them on their asses for disturbing him. He looked through bleary eyes and saw the skin of Jeffrey Davies wrapped around him. He screamed.

The piece of flesh on the top end of the hide flopped forward. Dr. Stillson sucked Jeff's starchy hair down his throat and gagged.

As the doctor fought to free himself from the skin, the empty hide wrapped itself tighter around him, hugging out the small breaths he could draw around the hair in his throat. At last he lay still, his body limp, his gray eyes like specks of polished glass staring at the water-stained ceiling.

The skin continued squeezing for several hours, until all the SKN-3 had evaporated from the flesh.

The Pollination

Alicia Brooks remembered all too clearly the day her life changed. It was just over a month ago, on May 20, 2066. It was the day the shuttle, Probe II, landed a manned unit on a small Venetian moon, VB-13.

It was supposed to be exciting. The moon had just been discovered a decade earlier, and samples brought back from unmanned probes indicated the little moon had the potential to sustain life. Every astronaut in NASA, along with several Russian cosmonauts, had signed up to go on the manned mission.

Alicia was part of the three-person crew who touched down in the shuttle's first landing unit. She was the only woman to make the mission. There had been a barrage of media attention when she was chosen, and as she stepped from the landing unit, she was wondering whether or not she could be on the cover of *Time* magazine twice in one year.

"Look at this." Stan Bowker's voice interrupted her thoughts of headlines and talk-show circuits. Alicia focused her attention on her surroundings.

From space, the moon was tinged a dull orange color, similar to Mars. Now that she was standing on the moon's surface, she knew why. The face of the moon seemed to be completely covered by flowers of various shades of orange, red, yellow and brown. Alicia bent over to get a better look and found that each flower was shaded differently than the one beside it. They varied in length, ranging from twelve to fifteen centimeters tall. The petals resembled those of a daffodil more than any other flower she could identify.

"It's a damn florists' dream," Paul said. "Incredible." He ripped a handful of stems from the ground and held them toward Alicia. "For you, my sweet."

Alicia took the flowers, but didn't smile. She'd been lonely during training exercises, and after an evening of cocktails, she'd gone back to Paul's apartment. He wasn't good in bed and she didn't feel right sleeping with her fellow crewmembers, so she hadn't gone back. He seemed sure that he'd won her over, though.

"Come on, you two. Save the office romance for the office." Stan, the oldest and most experienced of the crew, took command. "Let's move away from here and see what's going on."

The flowers beneath the landing unit were blown to the sides; most of them were laid nearly flat. The air was tinged a dark orange, like a cloud of gas hovering around the capsule. Alicia felt her eyes watering and noticed Paul and Stan both wiping at their noses.

She tossed aside the bouquet Paul had given her and stopped to pluck another flower. She was sure she heard a tiny voice cry out in pain when she broke the stem. A puff of orange dust flew from the center of the flower and directly into her face. Alicia sneezed several times and wished she'd brought her allergy medicines. She sniffed the flower; it had no odor.

Alicia pulled her nose back and looked into the flower's iris. What she saw there made her squeal in delight.

"Look at this," she said, holding the flower toward the men.

The center of the flower was round and of a harder, rougher texture than the petals. What made Alicia squeal was the peculiar resemblance to a human face that she saw in the ridges and marks of the iris.

Paul laughed at her and turned away. "You're being silly, honey. It just looks like a flower."

Stan looked and grunted. "It's strange, all right, but doesn't really mean anything. We'll take samples back, along with the soil, rocks and whatever else we find." He turned and followed Stan deeper into the field of flowers, away from the landing unit.

Alicia fell in behind Stan, still carrying the flower. Soon, she felt something warm trickling down the palm of her hand. She stopped to look and found a dark liquid running from the severed stem of the flower. She called out to the men and told them about the "blood."

"We've heard enough about the damn flower," Stan said, pausing long enough to give her an angry look over his shoulder. Alicia saw that the man's eyes and nose were running.

"Come on," Paul said, reaching for her free hand. "It's just some kind of sap."

It seemed she walked for hours, but Alicia knew it couldn't have been more than two at the most. They found no life forms other than the flowers. She was feeling very sleepy.

At length they came to a patch of barren ground where the flowers had not grown.

Or where they've moved aside to make a place for the invaders.

She turned around, looking to see how far they were from the Probe II's landing unit. The metal capsule was only a speck on the horizon, a miniature monstrosity looming above the flowers. When she turned back, both Stan and Paul had sunk down in the barren patch of dirt and fallen asleep. Alicia dropped to her knees between the two men. She shook Paul's shoulder and got nothing but a groan. She tried Stan; he grunted and rolled away from her.

She felt panicky for only a moment, then she too sank down and slept.

Later, she could never say for sure what had awakened her—some sixth sense or a horrid dream—it was hard to tell. She awoke to a nightmare that was all too real. The patch of ground where the landing crew of the Probe II had fallen down for their naps was now empty except for her and two of the strange flowers. Alicia crept closer to the two flowers that occupied the places where her two comrades had slept.

She pulled back the petals of the smaller of the two—petals that were a creamy white with black swirls running throughout them. She thought of Stan's pale skin and black hair. In the yellow circle that made the center of the flower, among the dots and ridges, was outlined clearly the features of Stan's weathered face.

Alicia shrank back, whimpering, afraid to look at the other flower. She knew she had to do it. If for no other reason than to fill out a NASA report, she had to do it. She crawled toward the waving blossom.

Its petals were dark, with lighter streaks. Paul had a good tan and fair hair. She pulled the petals back to reveal what she already knew she would find. Paul's face looked back at her. The detail was perfect. Alicia could see the blue of his eyes in the dots that made his face.

She began to weep violently, then stopped abruptly and looked around for the landing unit they had left behind. She found it on the horizon, just as she had last seen it before falling asleep.

Delicately, she pulled the flower that was Paul from the ground, trying to bring up the roots with it, but the soil clung stubbornly and the stem of the flower snapped. Once again, Alicia heard a tiny cry of pain and saw the dark liquid flowing from the broken stem. Orange dust flew from the center of the flower and made her sneeze again. She moved to the other flower—Stan— and again tried to carefully remove him from the soil. But again, the stem broke, there was a cry of pain and a puff of pollen.

Alicia held the two flowers that had been her two companions in her hand. She looked at them for a moment, wondering if she wasn't still asleep, then began to run in the direction of the landing unit.

Launching the unit by herself took all her skill, especially since her eyes and nose were running and she was still sneezing. She flipped switches, wiped at her eyes, pushed buttons and blew her nose. Finally, the capsule began to vibrate with life. She flipped a final switch, felt the burners kick in, and the metal pod slowly lifted off the moon's surface. Alicia leaned back in her seat, her head to the side, her eyes on the two flowers in the seat next to her. Watery snot dripped from her upper lip.

She felt tired again. It was all she could do to hold her course and connect with the docking station on Probe II. She was pulled out of the landing unit by other crewmembers. They tried to take the two flowers from her hand, but she wouldn't give them up.

Of course, nobody believed her story. A search party—all men—was sent to find Paul and Stan. The party did not return. Another party was sent in the shuttle's second landing unit. Again, it did not return.

Capt. John Davis, the commanding officer of Probe II, decided there was nothing he could do. There was no radio contact with the missing crewmen. There were no other landing units and it was too risky to attempt a shuttle landing. He gave the order to go home.

Alicia made the journey home strapped to a bed in the sick bay area of the shuttle. She kept the two flowers in a tight grip and cried when she noticed how quickly they wilted in her sweaty palm.

* * *

The shuttle returned to Earth with no problems. The disappearance of the crewmembers and the appearance of the strange flowers had been carefully covered up. Alicia spent two weeks undergoing treatment for her shock. She never believed the doctor telling her that Paul and Stan had simply died in the alien atmosphere and she'd taken the flowers in memory of them

But, to get out, she finally pretended to succumb to the suggestion. Of course, there was still the threat from the government. She would be caught, tried and executed for treason if she ever leaked word of what happened. So, there had been no interviews, no second appearance on the cover of *Time*.

That may be about to change, though, Alicia thought as she hurried through a Houston park, heading for her private physician's office. She'd missed her period. Instead of the usual menses, she was experiencing a recurrence of the allergic reaction she'd felt on VB-13.

She wiped at her nose, dabbed a tissue to each eye and walked on. She was unsteady on her feet and knew that people watching would think she was drunk. She didn't care. All she cared about was getting to her personal doctor as soon as possible.

Surely the NASA doctor had overlooked something in his examination after Probe II returned, some sort of contamination in her body. Maybe he hadn't "overlooked" anything. Alicia walked faster. She had a terrible urge to lie down in the flowers beside the walkway and go to sleep.

Her head nodded, her chin bumped against her chest and she stumbled, falling to her side, falling among the flowers.

They smell so sweet.

She slept.

When she awoke, she felt very strange—very alive. She straightened and tried to look around her, but all she could see was the petals of a white flower with brown swirls rising above her face.

It was almost as if ...

As if I've become a flower.

She tried to move, but could do no more than make herself sway slightly. Her feet would not move.

They are rooted in the ground.

Perhaps it was her swaying motion that caused the little boy walking on the sidewalk to notice her. He came closer and bent over her. Alicia could feel his warm breath on her petals.

"Look, Mom," he called to the lady coming up behind him. "Isn't it a pretty flower?"

"Yes, David," she answered. "It's beautiful."

"I'm going to pick it for you."

"No, David, you can't pick the flowers in the park."

But it was too late. The boy's pudgy hand closed around Alicia's stem. He pulled.

Alicia screamed in pain as she felt her stem break. She felt her bloody sap begin to flow from the broken end. The boy held the flower to his nose and sniffed. Alicia tried to resist the urge. She fought not to do it, but her dying breath was building like an explosion within her.

"Poo!" She spat a could of orange dust into the boy's small face. She died as the first drop of mucus fell from his nose.

The New Disciples

Nathan Jackson lay in his bed, smiling a large jack-o-lantern smile that showed his few rotted teeth. Saliva trickled from the corner of his mouth. The people who took care of him, they thought he was crazy. Mentally incompetent, they sometimes called him. They thought he was a loon, he knew.

Nathan's sightless eyes stared at the white ceiling of his little room. The eyes that looked out onto the world had been blinded by the knowledge he gained, but the single Cyclopean orb that peered into his soul had retained sight, had indeed gained not only the ability to see the past but was now seeing the present—the present in a place far away. What he saw made him smile.

* * *

Four children steered their bikes off the dusty country road to a tall chain-link fence. They dismounted and leaned their two-wheeled steeds against the wire fence while they surveyed the barrier. Their eyes climbed up the small diamonds to the top of the fence and over to the other side and on to the horizon where the ground sloped toward their destination.

"So this is it?" Ken asked, pulling his blue eyes away from the fence and beyond to look at the leader of the group.

"Yes," Lee answered. "This is it." He was the tallest of the gang. His unruly brown hair whipped around his head in the wind. He brushed it away from his eyes and looked his companions over. "Are you all sure you want to come?"

"Yes," Ken answered.

"Yes, I want to," Davy, the youngest, said. Only one member of the band hesitated.

"How about you, Terr?" Lee asked.

"Yes, I'm coming," she answered.

"Are you sure, Terr?" Lee asked. "You don't have to."

"I know I don't have to, but I'm going." She couldn't understand what the big deal was. Over the fence and down the slope there was nothing but the remains of an old insane asylum, one that had burned down years before she was born. She didn't believe the rumors that Satanists met there to worship the devil. She knew that all the boys had penknives in their hip pockets, and that they considered themselves to be her protectors. Boys liked to be dramatic about exploring, she supposed. "Let's go." She started climbing the fence.

When they all had dropped to the ground on the other side, the children looked around again, as if they expected the landscape would have changed as they climbed. The winter-dead grass was taller on this side of the fence; it swayed in the breeze, brushing against the knees of the children. The sky remained dull and overcast. Only a glowing spot in the clouds gave proof that the sun had not deserted the earth.

"Come on." Lee led the band in single file toward the slope.

Terry noticed that Ken had his hand in his hip pocket, probably toying with his knife. At the crest of the slope, the group saw the object of their quest.

A tall red brick wall stood at the bottom, unbroken except for the gates that interrupted the brick. There did not seem to be a single building standing within the confines of the wall.

The slope led down to the north wall—the gate was set into the west wall. A dirt road led away from it toward another country road, but it no longer reached that far; it had become overgrown with grass and small shrubs only about twenty yards from the gates. A few tumbleweeds pounded against the wall. The adventurers started down the slope, angling toward the northwest corner and the gate.

When they came to stand in front of the entrance, they stopped again. They took a closer look at the wall. It looked much taller now that they no longer had the advantage of looking down on it. The red bricks were crumbling in places. Chunks of mortar lay in the grass around the foundation. The gates were made of wrought iron and had long since given way to the dull orange of rust. They creaked gently in the wind. The gates were not locked—they swung open to Lee's push. He stepped reverently inside the wall. Ken followed, his hand still in his pocket. Terry went next, and then Davy.

"Why did we come here?" Davy whispered.

"Because I dreamed about this place last night," Lee whispered back.

* * *

Nathan saw the children and his smile grew broader. The saliva now hung in a sticky rope from chin to chest. They thought he couldn't feel things like that, the fools who looked after him. They thought he did it because he couldn't help it. But he did it because it didn't matter. Nothing mattered. Nothing but faith. He had that. His mind's eye turned inward, to the past now, leaving the children for a while.

Once, the walls the children had just breached did hold an asylum for the insane, much like the one Nathan was in now. The doctors hadn't been so nice in those long ago days. He knew. He had been one of them.

When a patient misbehaved, the punishment might be a beating. Or a bad drug. Or they could be sent into the boiler room, chained to the wall in a corner, shivering and wailing in fear of Barag-Bor.

To the doctors, Barag-Bor was an ingenious idea that Nathan himself had come up with.

The institute had recently switched from heating the asylum with a coal-burning boiler to a natural gas unit. The pot-bellied coal stove still stood on short, squatty legs in the darkest corner of the boiler room, slowly rusting. The pilot of the new gas heater threw dancing shadows on the bulk and filled the glass of the many gauges with blue light. Pipes still sprouted from the belly of the heater in all possible directions and lengths.

To the terrified patients given the punishment of being chained to the wall in Barag-Bor's dim corner—and this had included most every patient in the institute at one time or another—the old heater was a huge, tentacled beast that would devour them if they did not huddle in the corner and beg for forgiveness. They fully believed that the heater was a monster with blue flame in its eyes. Their faith was total. They would press themselves in their corner, as close to the wall as they could get, and wail in terror, sure they would soon be eaten by the beast.

It had been that unshakable faith that eventually caused the real horror.

* * *

"There's nothing here but a bunch of rocks and weeds," Ken said.

He was right, Terry thought. The rocks were actually chunks of concrete. Some of them had rebar twisting from the ragged edges like petrified serpents. She figured the pieces were the walls, floors, and ceiling of the buildings that had been the asylum. But, she thought, there should be more. She felt sure the outer wall must have enclosed several buildings. But there was scarcely enough concrete chunks left to make one medium-sized structure.

When they had entered the gates and not seen any black-robed figures killing babies, the group split up and began exploring separately, kicking at the concrete and looking at the burned patches on the brick wall. Davy had wandered to the center of the compound. He called to the others.

"Hey, there's a hole over here," he said. "With stairs leading down. It's dark."

The other three hurried over to where he stood atop a mound of earth with slightly more concrete chunks around it. He was pointing at a hole, just as he said, with concrete stairs leading down into blackness.

"That's probably where the devil-worshippers meet," Ken said. "Let's go down." He pulled his penknife from his pocket and opened the blade.

"Put that away," Lee told him. "We'll go down and have a look. I don't suppose you'll stay up here, will you, Terr?"

"Of course not."

"All right," Lee said, guessing that it would be useless to argue. "Did anyone bring a flashlight or any candles?" No one had, except Lee. He reached into his back pocket and pulled out a box of household candles and a book of matches.

"How did you know to bring those?" Terry asked.

"I told you, I dreamed about this place last night, and in the dream I had a candle, so I brought these." He took the four candles from the box and tossed the cardboard container aside. He lit one candle with a match and lit the rest from the wick of the first, passing them out as he lit them. When all four explorers had a light, he led them down the steps.

The stairs were old and in bad repair. Many chips of concrete gritted and fell away under their feet. Some of the steps were partially rotted away. The children all kept a hand on the pitted wall as they descended. The steps ended in an empty room about twenty-feet square with an empty doorway on the other side. The children crept to the doorway, tip-toeing unconsciously.

Lee peered through the opening. To the right was a blank wall, to the left was another doorway with more steps leading down. At the bottom of these stairs they found themselves in what appeared to have been a boiler room. Twisted bits of burned metal and pipes lay on the floor. More blackened pipes were suspended from the ceiling.

"The fire started here," Lee said. "The gas heater exploded." He pointed to a spot that was blacker than the rest of the floor. A jagged pipe poked from the floor. Part of the wall behind it had been blown away in the explosion.

"How do you know all this?" Ken asked.

"My dream."

"What else did you dream about?" Terry asked.

Lee pointed to the darkest corner of the boiler room. "The hole over there, and more stairs going down and down." His voice lost its tone and became distant.

"What was at the bottom of the stairs?"

"I don't know."

* * *

Edgar Phillips had been the first disciple of Barag-Bor, after Barag-Bor had come to life.

Nathan thought about that name, *Barag-Bor*. The coal heater had resembled a creature from a Lovecraft tale, and since Nathan had been the one to come upon the idea of using the heater as a monster, he had given it a Lovecraftian name. *Barag-Bor*. Most of the other doctors had thought it a ridiculous title, but it stuck, and in the end it fit perfectly.

Edgar Phillips had asked early one day to be put in the room with Barag-Bor. The doctors had considered that quite strange, but Edgar was a strange man who often suffered from delusions of grandeur. He also was known to have a masochist streak. When asked why he wanted to be with Barag-Bor, whom he admitted he feared, Edgar answered that Barag-Bor was calling him. Permission was refused.

Edgar remained in his padded cell until he tried to kill the orderly who brought his lunch.

It had taken Nathan and three other strong doctors to pull Edgar off his unfortunate victim.

The doctors demanded to know why he had tried to kill the other man. Edgar said he was trying to make sacrifice to the great Barag-Bor. Nathan and another doctor, his name gone from memory, dragged Edgar to the boiler room so he could praise Barag-Bor until he became docile and ready to behave.

When the three arrived in the boiler room and neared where Barag-Bor stood looking with his gauge-eyes into the corner that held the manacles, Edgar cried out, "Oh great one, I bring you sacrifice!" Then he jerked free of the two doctors and shoved both of them forward as he bolted back toward the door.

Nathan had quickly regained his balance and turned to give chase, but the other doctor shrieked with such horror that Nathan turned back.

Barag-Bor was alive. One of his tentacles reached for the doctor, making a creaking sound like an old hinge as it stretched closer. The doctor stood paralyzed by fear until the limb was securely wrapped around his torso. He shrieked and thrashed madly as he was dragged across the floor toward the hulking form with blue, flame-filled eyes.

Nathan watched one of the tentacles reach across the distance for him. He turned and ran.

He ran into mass confusion. Edgar had freed some of the other patients and they in turn had freed more until all the lunatics were loose and trying to capture the doctors. The doctors had given up trying to retain order and were trying to flee. Several had managed to escape into the open grounds outside the building and were running toward the gates. Nathan was among those trying to escape, his white coat flapping around his thighs. They had been about fifty feet from the closed and locked gates when the buildings began to explode, throwing chunks of concrete everywhere. Nathan was struck in the face and fell to the ground.

When he awakened, he knew it only because he could hear the sounds of movement. He was blind. He groaned and called out. Someone dragged him to his feet and shoved something heavy into his arms before leading him away. He asked where he was going and Edgar's voice answered, "Barag-Bor has commanded that we build a chamber deep in the earth. We are still working on the stairs. We must hurry before the people from town come."

Nathan tried to tell them—the lunatics—that Barag-Bor was not real, that he lived only in their imaginations, that if they didn't believe in him he couldn't exist. He had known at the time that it was useless—useless because he himself now believed. He had seen the beast that had once been only an old heater. It had come alive, had devoured another doctor.

The lunatics led him back and forth, putting heavy chunks of the concrete walls of the asylum into his hands so he could carry them to someone else who took them from him to make the crude stairs. He knew that many of the people, both doctors and patients, were being worked to death. He could feel them dying around him, and still the living worked without pause.

Fire trucks and ambulances finally arrived from town. The work had been finished. Only a handful of the people who once occupied or worked in the facility remained alive. They had been taken away. Most—Nathan included—

babbled about a monster in the asylum. All the survivors were put into other asylums to live out the remainder of their lives.

They were all dead now, except for Nathan. He would die soon. He knew that. As soon as the children became believers in the great Barag-Bor, he would be free to die. Faith was all that was required for the god to live. With the children converted, Barag-Bor's life would continue safely.

* * *

The steps were not only jagged and poorly laid, but slick with moss. The ceiling was not even—in places it was only three feet above the steps, while in others it was out of reach of even Lee, the tallest child.

Their candles bobbed in the utter darkness, the only light to fall on the walls of the crude stairwell in over thirty years. The children descended in silence, each concentrating on his or her footing, feeling the concrete stairs carefully before trusting weight to them. How long they endured the darkness none who lived could ever tell. To them, it seemed they went down and down for days.

When they reached the bottom of the stairs, they stopped, staring open-mouthed at what waited for them. There was light in the chamber—or, rather, an illuminate darkness that allowed sight. A slime-coated beast squatted in the far corner of the small room. It appeared to be mostly round, with four short legs beneath it and many tentacles of varying length beckoning them closer. It examined its visitors with flickering blue eyes that were like dancing flames. The children knew that it was grinning. Four candles dropped from numb hands and were extinguished on the frigid dirt floor.

* * *

Nathan closed his sightless eyes and let death finally claim him.

* * *

Excerpt from the Windy Acres News, Tuesday, Oct. 13, 1997:

Two of the four children reported missing late Saturday have been found wandering in the ruins of the old Lahman Sanitarium near the town dump. They are Lee Pritchard and Terry Windslow.

When found, the two were blind, apparently from clawing out their own eyes. They babbled incoherently about their two missing friends, Ken Standridge and Davy Jacobs, being devoured by a beast they referred to as 'Barag-Bor.' They have been committed to Meadowlands Hospital for the mentally insane in Enid.

Going Places

Can't she shut the fuck up?

Tim kept his right arm over his face so he couldn't see his wife as she spoke to him.

"If we pay all the electric bill, we can only pay half the water bill," she said. "We could do that. They haven't sent a notice yet. The gas company has, though. We have to pay the gas company..."

Tim's penis was still wet and sticky. It lay in his lap as if its recent exertion had killed it. He wanted to pull the blanket over himself and go to sleep, but if he did that, the covers would absorb the goo on his cock and develop a nasty, crusty stain.

"...The car insurance is due next month, but we..."

Tim could hear traffic passing along the highway that stretched north and south less than a half-mile from the little house where he and his family lived. Trucks, cars, buses, all filled with people who were going places.

"Are you even listening to me?"

"Yes, dear," he answered automatically. She'd get mad about that. "We can pay the insurance out of my check next month. It'll only be a couple of days late."

"The kids both need new clothes for school. I thought we'd..."

A drop of reluctant semen dripped from Tim's penis and fell into the tangle of dark hair in his groin, hanging to its source in a white strand that glimmered in the soft glow of the nightlight. *Is she still taking her birth control? Are we still able to afford that?*

An airplane roared overhead. *Don't land here!* Tim screamed it in his mind. *You won't like it here.*

He wished he could hear the whistle of a freight train. When he was a boy, he had lived near a major railway and he could lay in bed at night and listen to the trains with the wheels throbbing like a heavy metal heartbeat and the whistles screaming a lonely call to the cold stars.

"We'll only have forty dollars for groceries next week."

"We'll manage," he said. "We always do."

Poor people, like weeds and cockroaches, always find a way to survive.

A sudden commotion erupted outside. Tim lay still as his wife sprang to a sitting position beside him.

"It's a dog," he said. "He comes around four or five nights a week, knocks the trash can over and looks for food. I always clean it up before I leave in the mornings."

"Someone should kill the thing if no one cares enough to feed it," she said.

"You think so?"

"That would be better than letting it run loose digging through trash cans for scraps."

"He's living off the land, taking what he can find. No one's telling him what to do. No one's—" Tim checked himself.

"What?" she asked. He knew her eyebrows were raised.

"No one's sending him notices about his electric bill."

"Um-hmm."

Tim peeked out from under his arm and saw that she was studying her hands, especially her fingernails and their chipped polish.

"I have to pee," she said and got out of bed.

Tim watched her leave the room, then scooped his clothes from the floor and quickly dressed. There was a packed suitcase under the bed—it had been there for over a month. Tim was in his old pickup and turning the key when he saw the silhouette of his wife returning to their bedroom through the drab curtains of their window.

From the deep shadows of a pine tree, the stray dog looked up at the vehicle as it backed out of the drive. Tim waved, glanced at the scattered trash, and headed for the highway.

Barney the Boa

It was near closing time when Sylvester Dominik, commonly known as Sly, entered the zoo's snake house. He quickly and delicately broke the glass of every cage, then hurried back to the door, only to find it had locked behind him.

Sly dry-gulped about a quart of the cool, dry air of the snake house as his right hand tightened to a death-grip on the steel doorknob. His eyes were glued to the small wire-mesh-enforced window set into the steel door. Behind him, he heard a shaking sound, and knew that Rikki the Rattler was warning another snake to get out of his way. Sweat suddenly broke out all over Sly's tanned face. A cow's lick of oiled, black hair slipped down into his face, the end of the lock nearly touching the tip of his nose.

"Please let me out," Sly whispered in a voice much higher than his usual tone. He tried the knob again. Still locked. A moan rose in his throat and threatened to push him into hysteria. Sly closed his eyes, feeling the sting of sweat, and forced himself to calm down.

"I should have just taken my pay and got the hell out of here," he hissed. This morning he had been an employee of the zoo. He had been in charge of the snake house for nearly two months. This afternoon, however, when he had tried to entice the pretty young blonde concession-stand girl into a storehouse for a little fun, he had pushed too far.

Of course, if the zoo super wasn't a woman, I might not have been canned, just bitched at a little.

But, as it was, the pretty young blonde had run to the main office and reported that Sly Dominik had made unwanted sexual advances toward her.

Sly was fired on the spot and told to come back late in the afternoon to receive his final paycheck. He had done that. The check was folded in his back pocket. He also had decided to give the zoo something to remember him. Something like a snake house filled with loose inmates.

Sly heard a thump behind him and knew that one of the bigger snakes had dropped from its cage to the floor of the house. He knew by the heavy sound who that would be. Slowly, he turned to face the serpents.

Dozens of snakes were either slithering happily across the floor or peering curiously from the sills of their broken cages. Most of them, Sly knew, were harmless. Or, rather, not deadly. Others... His eyes quickly found Rikki swallowing a small South American snake. Sly searched out Katy Cobra and found she was raised and looking eagerly from cage to floor.

Then, reluctantly, Sly felt his gaze drawn toward the tallest of the cages set in the corner farthest from the door—the cage of Barney, the eight-foot boa constrictor that was the pride and joy of the snake house. The loud thump Sly had heard was Barney dropping from the limb of the artificial tree in his cage to the concrete floor.

Barney was the only snake that seemed interested in the human. His slitted eyes studied Sly intensely, and Sly quickly turned his face away while behind his back his hand continued to scrabble at the doorknob.

Then something happened that caused his hand to freeze.

Barney was writhing on the floor. His multi-colored, glistening body was twisting and thrashing as if he were in pain. The other snakes quickly slid away from the frantic boa, some continuing to watch, others acting disinterested. Sly couldn't pull his eyes away. Barney's body seemed to split and divide into branches. No, not branches, Sly thought. Limbs. The snake now had two arms and two legs. These continued to split until they had fingers and toes. The trunk thickened in the middle and thinned just below the head, making a torso and a neck. The head became rounder and the face moved in closer to the back of the skull. But the impression remained that the head was too flat and wide to be the human head it seemed to be imitating. The eyes remained golden and slitted, but the humanoid body that Sly was now looking at lost most of its colorful pattern and took on a dusty brown shade. Barney rose to his feet and faced Sly.

"Hello," Barney said in a low, whispery voice. "Thank you."

Sly only moaned again while his head wobbled slowly back and forth on his neck.

"It was the reflection, you know," Barney said. "They arranged the lights in here so that I could always see only myself reflected back in the glass of that abominable cage." He glanced toward the floor while he slid a large piece of glass aside with one of his naked feet. "It's horrible to be confined." He looked back up at Sly. "Isn't it?"

"Barney?" Sly croaked.

"No, that's not my name, friend," the boa-man whispered. "Your poor human tongue couldn't begin to curl itself around the syllables that make my name, so you can call me Barney."

"Are you going to kill me?"

"Yes, friend, I am." Barney nodded his flat head. He stepped forward and Sly tried desperately to push himself into the steel of the door at his back. He wanted to turn around, but couldn't seem to peel his gaze from the eyes of the strange figure approaching him. "You needn't be afraid," Barney promised. Sly felt himself relax involuntarily.

"Why?"

"I need you," Barney answered. "This shape is nearly useless to me now." He held up his hands as if to look at them, but his eyes never left Sly. Sly saw that the fingers of the hands were too long. Much too long, and seemed to have no joints; they bent everywhere, like miniature snakes protruding from a palm-shaped leaf. "I have shed my skin too many times since devouring my last human," Barney continued. "I can no longer take his shape in a convincing manner. But, I suppose you noticed that."

Is that a smile on his face?

"Remove your clothes," Barney ordered quietly. Sly shook his head violently, but still could not break the mesmerizing stare of Barney the Boa. "Please, friend, take off your clothes," the snake insisted.

Are those my hands doing that? Sly wondered as his jeans were loosened at the fly and slid down his legs. His feet raised and his shoes were kicked off, then his jeans and soiled underwear removed and tossed aside. *IS IT ME?* He couldn't tear his gaze away from the slitted eyes of the human serpent before him. *Surely when I pull my shirt off, that will break the hypnotism.* But then the air was filled with the sound of ripping cloth, and Sly knew he was tearing his own T-shirt down the front to avoid breaking the hold Barney had on him. The shirt fell away and Sly stood naked before the thing that had promised to kill him.

"Thank you, friend." The boa nodded without moving his eyes. "You must go in feet first. Lie down, please."

"No," Sly begged. "Please. I don't want to."

"It would be a great help to me," Barney insisted. "I would appreciate your full cooperation."

Sly started to plead with his adversary again, but was cut short by a gasp of pain from Barney's wide slit of a mouth. The boa-man looked away and Sly suddenly felt as if he had been dropped from a high roof. The reality of his danger swept over him. He turned to face the door, screaming for help.

Barney reached down and pulled the fangs of Rikki the Rattler out of his calf. He held the rattlesnake close to his face and spoke lovingly to it. "Your venom, my little friend, only soothes the blood of one such as I. Thank you." Then Rikki began to bubble and run like a toad caught on a highway in mid-summer. Barney dropped the dripping mess to the floor and returned his attention to Sly.

"I'm sorry, but time is short," Barney whispered. "The digestion takes time." He moved to lie with his belly pressed to the floor.

Sly knew the strange creature had not dropped down there, he had just seemed to fold until he was in position. He was not given time to study the situation, however. One of Barney's arms lashed out like lightning and swept Sly's feet from under him.

Sly crashed to the concrete floor, his arms already trying to drag him away from the human-shaped boa constrictor. He saw Barney's jaw unhinge itself. The mouth gaped open like the gate to Hell. Sly tried to get to his feet, but his ankles were gripped by the unjointed fingers of Barney's hands; the grasp was cool and clammy and very tight.

Sly looked back in time to see his bare feet going into the thing's mouth. He screamed again as the clammy hands worked up his legs, like a mountain climber working his way up a rope, Sly thought. His own hands clawed at the steel door until the white paint started peeling off the surface. Soon, he was leaving bloody tracks on the door as the ends of his fingers were worn away. His voice cracked, and then was gone so that he screamed in silence.

His knees, his thighs, his limp penis, tight stomach, hairless chest and finally his straining neck were pushed into the cold, dark mouth of the serpent. Sly continued scratching at the door with his bleeding fingers.

* * *

Tim Beechum had to hurry to do his duties and those of the greasy kid who had been fired yesterday. He finished pitching hay into the zebra's stable and ran to the snake house, digging the key out of his pocket as he approached.

"Damn fool," Tim muttered, thinking how he had been late getting home to dinner last night because he was assigned to take care of Sylvester Dominik's closing duties. He paused before inserting the key into the lock of the snake house door, wondering if, in his haste, he had forgotten to check inside the building to make sure there were no straggling tourists. With a shrug, he unlocked the door and reached for the knob.

The steel door was thrown open and Tim staggered back a step and then fell to the sidewalk, his body holding the door open. He gawked in amazement as Sly Dominik rushed out of the snake house, naked and clutching his clothes to his chest. The greasy-haired kid looked about him frantically for a moment, then darted off down the walkway.

Tim Beechum started to get to his feet when he saw the bloody scratches on the inside of the door. Then he saw the snakes milling about restlessly within the building. He slammed the door closed and ran, making sure he went in a different direction than Sly Dominik.

It was several hours before Barney the Boa was missed.

Summer Offspring

No Relief In Sight; State Swelters

By Aimee Tate
News-Sun Staff Writer

The National Weather Service in Norman predicted Monday that central Oklahoma will break the old record for consecutive days without rain by the end of this week.

"We've been 36 days without rain so far and there's no precipitation showing up for at least the next seven days," said meteorologist Kurt Hammond. "It looks like the summer of 2000 will go in the record books as the longest drought in state history..."

Rash of Animal Killings Confuse Police

By Missy Abernathy
News-Sun Staff Writer

Gayle Wofford bought her pit bull, Sammy, for protection. Now, she wishes she could have protected Sammy.

"He's gone, just ripped to shreds," Wofford said between sobs.

Sammy is just the latest pet to fall victim in a rash of pet killings around the city. Police and wildlife officials speculate that the prolonged heat and drought are driving coyotes into town. They blame the wild canines for the killings.

"I've seen coyotes and dogs go crazy from the heat before," said police spokesman Sgt. Nathan Singer. "It just gets so hot, and their water holes dry up..."

Record Heat, Drought Continue to Keep People Indoors

By Aimee Tate
News-Sun Staff Writer

As Oklahoma continues to wilt under the triple-digit temperatures and record-setting drought of Summer 2000, residents are staying inside near their air conditioners.

"I haven't even been going to work," said Jim Richardson, an asphalt spreader with the city's traffic department. "It's just too hot. I'm using up all my sick leave and vacation, but that's better than dropping dead from the heat."

Finding something to keep them busy while they stay inside hasn't been a problem for most residents.

"I eat a lot of ice cream and watch Pokemon on TV," said Mattie Hayes, 4.

Ron Tibbits said he and his wife have found other ways to stay busy.

"Well, it's really hot and our air conditioner isn't very good, so we don't wear a lot of clothes," Tibbits said. "Being half naked all the time, we find things to do…"

Water Treatment Center Up and Running Again

By Stacey Weidner
News-Sun Staff Writer

Nearly 15,000 residents were without water for about 16 hours Thursday when a rodent clogged the intake system of the city's water treatment center.

Bill Lowe, plant superintendent, said one of the 12-inch pipes that moves water through the plant became clogged early Thursday morning. That caused other pipes to back up and eventually burn out a pump in a treatment plant that was already straining to meet customers' needs during this summer's drought.

The cause of the clog turned some stomachs, Lowe said.

"It was the biggest damn rat I've ever seen," he said. "I don't know how the thing got into the pipe, but there it was, dead and wadded up against one of the filters with about 50 condoms and other pieces of solid waste.

"It was the nastiest thing I've seen in a long time," Lowe said.

Girl Missing from Local Apartment

By Missy Abernathy
News-Sun Staff Writer

The frantic cries of a mother filled the shimmering evening air outside the Rolling Oaks apartment complex late Tuesday.

Tamara Pritchett, a resident of the apartment complex, said she was playing ball with her daughter, Monique, in the apartment parking lot when the ball rolled into a storm drain. Tamara Pritchett went to find a friend to see if he could get the ball out of the drain. When she came back, her 6-year-old daughter was gone...

Report Says Not to Anticipate Spring 2001 Baby Boom

From Associated Press Reports

A recent Guff Company survey has found that condom sales have risen by 38 percent in the states affected by this summer's unseasonably high temperatures.

"When people stay indoors because of the heat, they are more likely to use condoms or some other form of birth control," said Joyce Horn, professor of sociology at North Central Oklahoma College. "It seems couples are more open to the idea of starting a family when it's cold outside. When it's hot, they're just looking for pleasure..."

Two Boys Missing

By Missy Abernathy
News-Sun Staff Writer

Tommy Powell and David Denton, both 12, often rode their bikes on N 19 Street. Neighbors say the boys also would build ramps to jump the storm ditch that ran beside the road, or crawl through the culvert where the ditch passes under E Ash Avenue.

Saturday afternoon, the boys' bicycles were found near the north end of the culvert, but they boys haven't been seen since late that morning.

"We think they might have gone in there and then crawled into the smaller tunnel that empties into this ditch," said police spokesman Sgt. Nathan Singer. "So far, we haven't found them…"

Murder Suspect Released; Authorities Apologize

By Kevin O'Connor
News-Sun Staff Writer

Dale Washington was released from the city jail Wednesday morning. District Attorney Kathy Maddox said the two first-degree murder charges against Washington have been dropped.

"It has been determined by forensic investigators that the bite marks on the two victims could not have been made by Mr. Washington," Maddox said in a news conference Wednesday. "DNA evidence confirms that Mr. Washington's wife and son were the victims of some kind of animal attack."

Washington, who has become known as "Ratman," spent 21 days in the city jail, accused of murdering his wife and their infant son in their apartment. Police reports state that, upon his arrest, Washington was hysterical. The report says he was holding the bloody body of his three-month-old son. There were large bite marks on the child's body and blood on Washington's mouth.

"I told them I didn't do it," Washington said during Wednesday's news conference. "I was just trying to give my son CPR. It was the rats that killed him…"

Homeless Man Found Mauled to Death

By Stacey Weidner
News-Sun Staff Writer

City police and state wildlife officials are examining the death of a homeless man found in a Burlington-Northern railroad switching station Friday afternoon. Police reports say the man was apparently mauled and partially devoured by some kind of animal.

"We don't know what kind of animal it was," said Gayleen Babbs, a spokeswoman with the state Wildlife Department. "We do know that there was more than one animal involved."

A report from the state medical examiner says the unidentified man appeared to have been overwhelmed while intoxicated and asleep.

"His body is covered in bites of varying size from head to foot," Babbs said. She added that the bite marks do not match any known animal…

City Plagued by Animal Attacks

From Staff Reports

What began with the killing of outdoor pets has become much more serious. Police and wildlife officials have linked the pet slayings to the deaths of 12 people in the metro area, and suspect the disappearance of several others—mostly children—to also be the responsibility of wild animals.

"The bite marks on most of the pets that have been killed recently match the patterns we've found on several humans that have also been killed and partially eaten," said department of wildlife spokeswoman Gayleen Babbs. "Unfortunately, we still can't confirm what kind of animals we're dealing with. All we know is that there are a lot of them and that they attack at night."

Police officials say they believe the animals are living in the city's sewer system by day and coming out in search of food by night.

"From what we've been able to learn from when people are reported missing and from lab reports to determine time of death, it does appear that the animals kill at night," said Sgt. Nathan Singer, a police spokesman.

Singer said he has asked the governor to provide National Guard assistance to create a task force to venture into the sewer system to find the animals responsible for the deaths.

"Based on what we've learned from lab reports, we think there are just too many of them for our department to handle," Singer said.

A spokeswoman for the governor said a decision on whether or not to activate the National Guard should be made public later today. Even if approved, it could be two to three days before troops enter the city's sewer system.

In the meantime, residents are urged to remain indoors after dark and to keep their doors and windows locked. City Manager Mike Hughes said he plans to call an emergency meeting of the city council Monday to discuss further action.

"I will ask the council to pass a mandatory curfew on the city," Hughes said. "I don't think anyone should be allowed out after dark until we can solve this."

Resident Kills Rat-like Creature

By Kevin O'Conner and Missy Abernathy
News-Sun Staff Writers

Mildred Williams, 68, knew it was no ordinary burglars scratching at her window late Sunday night. What she didn't know was that she would be the first resident to survive an attack by the strange creatures that have been stalking the city by night.

"I grew up on a farm out by Tuttle," Williams said. "I've drowned skunks, shot coyotes and trapped coons. But I ain't never saw nothing like those varmints last night."

The "varmints" Williams saw numbered about two dozen, she said. Six of them weren't able to leave her home on the city's north side.

"I blasted the hell out of them," said the grandmother of four.

But the question remains: What are the strange animals? The shotgun-riddled bodies of the six animals shot by Williams have been taken for examination by state wildlife officials. Williams said she's never seen anything like the animals.

"They look like little kids, except they're rats," she said. "They walk on their hind legs, but are about as tall as my youngest granddaughter. She's a pre-schooler. They're covered in hair and have a face and tail just like a rat. Damned if I know what they are, but they come messing around here again, I'll sure as hell shoot some more of them…"

Police Admit Knowing of Rat-like Creatures

By Stacey Weidner
News-Sun Staff Writer

Local police admitted late Monday that they have known for over a week that the animal attacks plaguing the city have been from some kind of rat-like creature.

"We have known, but we chose not to make that information public," said police spokesman Sgt. Nathan Singer. "We felt it would incite a public panic."

Now it seems panic is mixed with outrage as many residents work to turn their homes into fortified sanctuaries. Local lumberyards are being hard-pressed to meet the needs of customers wanting material to board-up their doors and windows. Grocery store shelves also are under attack from customers stocking up as if for a siege. Many residents say they are closing their homes against the rat creatures and the police.

"I can't believe they would withhold that kind of information," said Karen Dandridge as she filled a grocery basket with supplies. "Who can you trust? My husband is at the sporting goods store right now buying ammunition. We'll shoot anything that comes scratching, gnawing or clawing at our house…"

National Guard Enters City

By Kevin O'Connor
News-Sun Staff Writer

The Oklahoma National Guard came into town late Monday night and are expected to enter the city's vast sewer system at around 3 p.m. today.

"We're studying blueprints of the system now," said Lt. Dan Coffey.

Coffey said his troops will be armed primarily with flame-throwers and handguns. Each guard will be equipped with lighted helmets and orders to kill.

"This isn't a rescue mission," Coffey said. "We're going in to kill them."

That has sparked a new controversy with animal rights activists who have descended on the city since it was learned the National Guard would be coming to town.

"We don't know exactly what these animals are," said Michael Hart of People Against Animal Cruelty (PAAC). "We have no right to go into their homes and exterminate them."

Protesters and residents have already clashed in several skirmishes around city hall, forcing the governor to activate even more National Guard troops to keep the peace and patrol city streets.

"I can't believe these whack-o people," said Oliver Haslett, a resident who came to city hall to get a building permit and was confronted by several PAAC members. "What do they think is going on here? These animals are breaking into our homes and killing us.

I'd like to see how many of these freaks stay out here carrying their signs after dark..."

DNA Experts Say Rat-creatures are Half Human

By Aimee Tate and Missy Abernathy
News-Sun Staff Writers

State forensics experts released a report late Tuesday saying the vicious animals preying on the city are half human and half rat.

"We didn't dare to believe it at first, although when you see them, it's pretty obvious," said Cindy Kline, a forensics expert with the Oklahoma State Bureau of Investigation. "They have several human characteristics, such as walking on their hind legs and, we believe, the ability to use tools. They have the incisors common to rats, but their back teeth are very similar to human molars."

Kline could only speculate on how the creatures came into existence.

"The only theory we have is that normal rats living in the sewer were exposed to condoms flushed down city toilets," Kline said. "Ordinarily, semen would die long before it ever got that far into the sewer. However, because of the long heat wave and lack of rain to really flush the sewers out, it's possible the sperm in the condoms didn't die and somehow entered the body of a few female rats. One female rat can spawn dozens of offspring in a very short time, so it's easy to see how we could have such a high population of these things very quickly.

"From there, it's really just a logical evolution to the animals we're dealing with now," she said.

City leaders were skeptical of the report.

"It sounds like some kind of sick Stephen King-type trash to me," said City Manager Mike Hughes.

National Guard troops had already entered the city's sewer system when the report was released. Operation Sewer Sweep commander, Lt. Dan Coffey, was contacted via radio from a command post established at city hall. He wasn't impressed by the report.

"I don't care if it's a race of midgets living down here," Coffey said from the sewer. "They're killing Oklahomans and my orders are to kill them. That's what I plan to do."

Residents are shocked by the DNA report, but most still support the National Guard effort to exterminate the creatures, regardless of their origin...

PAAC Protesters Killed, Missing; National Guard Suffers Casualties

From *News-Sun* Staff Reports

Sixteen members of People Against Animal Cruelty (PAAC) were found mauled and partially eaten around city hall Wednesday morning. The remaining 12 members of the group, who had come to town to protest National Guard plans to kill the animals preying on the city, cannot be found, police say.

"It's pretty obvious the rat-creatures got to the protesters," said police spokesman Sgt. Nathan Singer. "The evidence is all there, just like in the other cases. We ordered them off the street, even escorted many of them to their hotel, but we got a report a few hours later from the mayor saying they had come back to city hall and were marching again."

The animal-rights activists were not the only ones to suffer casualties.

Seven National Guard soldiers are currently in All Saints Hospital being treated for bites sustained in the city's sewer system Tuesday night. Three others are reportedly dead, killed fighting the sewer-dwelling animals that some experts say are half-human...

National Guard Says Mission a Success

By Stacey Weidner
News-Sun Staff Writer

Operation Sewer Sweep was a complete success, according to commander Lt. Dan Coffey.

"We spent about 36 hours down there and killed probably over 1,500 of the beasts," Coffey said. "We killed all of them we saw and explored every route shown on city blueprints. They had nowhere to go. We got them all."

Not all his troops share the commander's confidence or brashness. One private who asked to remain anonymous said he had never been as scared as he was in the city sewer system.

"There were thousands of those red eyes staring at us, just about waist-high," the soldier said. "We just turned loose with the flame-throwers and side-arms, but those things weren't scared. They came right at us."

National Guard casualties total 23 dead, 52 injured and nine missing, Coffey said.

"The loss of my men is tragic, but considering that it was one hell of a tough mission down there, I still say it was a total success..."

From the *News-Sun* Editorial Page:

The following letter was received in our office on Nov. 1. At first, we were inclined to believe it was a sick hoax. Still, we turned it over to the police for investigation. They, in turn, sent it to the state Bureau of Investigation. Cindy Kline, the DNA expert who proposed the theory that the rat-like creatures that preyed on our city during the late summer months were half human, said the stains on the original letter were made by semen from a creature such as she had examined. She said she believes the following letter is authentic. In the interest of public safety, we have chosen to print the letter.

—Steven E. Wedel, executive editor of the *News-Sun*

Dear Readers,

You have destroyed hundreds of my brothers and sisters, but you failed to kill just as many. We won't forget your efforts to exterminate us. We are busy now, as you can see from the stains on this paper. You will see us again.

Woman Trains Mutant to Speak, Tries to Protect Pet from Government

By Louis DeValcourt
Associated Press Writer

PHOENIX—A local woman has a very unusual pet. The creature stands nearly four feet tall, is covered in long gray hair and has all the facial characteristics of a common rat. However, it walks on its rear legs and has learned to speak a few words in harsh, broken English.

"I found him beside the road when he was just a baby," said Sharilyn Hubbard, who lives in a small house she built in the desert just outside Phoenix. "He was no bigger than my hand just six months ago."

Keeping the animal, named Harvey, is forcing Hubbard into the fight of her life. Government officials claim Harvey is an escaped half-human, half-rat creature like the ones that reportedly killed numerous people in central Oklahoma last year. Hubbard says she has already been ordered to turn the animal over to authorities, but so far she has refused to comply. She has turned to the public, hoping for support.

That may be hard to get, however. Since going public with her cause, FBI officials have released a video they say Hubbard has been selling on the Internet. The video shows Hubbard copulating with her pet...

Soul Trap

The afternoon sun was hidden behind a heavily overcast, dull-looking sky—a sky that threatened rain at any moment. A light wind that would have been only briskly cool elsewhere was nippingly cold to Michael Moore as he sat in a rowboat on the small lake. An early frost had turned the grass around the water's edge a premature brown. A gnarled elm tree still clung stubbornly to a very few dried-up leaves. The leaves rustled in the wind, promising that they, too, would soon leave their sleeping benefactor.

At the top of the slope leading to the water, but hidden from Michael's sight, an occasional car or truck would whiz or roar by on the old highway that had come to look like a tattered gray ribbon. Most vehicles now took the newly completed interstate that ran parallel to the old highway about a half-mile to the east.

Michael was thankful for the weather and the new interstate. He could be alone with his task. It was a task he feared and welcomed at the same time.

A fishing pole was fastened to the left side of the boat, just in case somebody was to see him, but he didn't think it was too likely. It was not a day that would attract fishermen to the lake, and the lake was too small to attract any tourists. There was no bait on the hook he had cast into the water— a bite would have been annoying. The bobber danced choppily on the small waves created by the wind.

Michael sat in the boat, hunched against the cold, watching the bobber. His task would not take long, but he wanted to complete it as soon as possible. He huddled down in the boat, trying to find a more comfortable position. His hands and feet had gone numb. He rubbed his hands together, more out of habit than for warmth; heat was not what they needed. He closed his eyes and somehow managed to find peace enough to doze.

* * *

A blue Chevrolet Impala sped down the highway. Its occupants, Michael

124

and his wife, Janet, talked happily. They were on their way to her mother's house for the evening meal and perhaps to spend the night, if any persuasion was offered. They were both in their late twenties and were still considered newlyweds, having been married for just over a year. They had reason to be happy; life had been good to them thus far. He worked for a law firm that put them in a comfortable financial position, enabling her to stay at home during the day.

A light rain had just begun to fall from the overcast sky, but it went relatively unnoticed by the couple. Michael unconsciously flipped on the windshield wipers.

They continued talking. She slid across the bench seat of the car to be closer to the man she loved. Michael reached an arm across her shoulders to give her a sideways hug. The steering wheel slipped from his hand and the car swerved to the side of the highway. He quickly jerked the wheel right. The tires slid on the film of old oil and fresh water that coated the asphalt. The Impala skidded sideways, straddling both lanes of the highway. He jerked the wheel again, causing the car to straighten momentarily, then skid to the other side of the highway and head straight for a metal guardrail and the hill beyond.

He slammed the brake pedal to the floor. The tires screeched, but to no avail. The car crashed into the guardrail, jerking both passengers violently forward. Michael heard a thump and the sound of glass breaking. Janet was screaming and looking at him through a river of blood where she had hit her head on the windshield. Glass sparkled from the gaping wound in her forehead. Her hair was matted into dark, thick strands that hung limply around her face.

The car began to roll down the hill. Michael glimpsed a small lake at the bottom.

* * *

Michael awoke with a start, making the boat rock dangerously. He was sure he had been splashed by water from a car crashing into the lake. A light rain had begun to fall; the drops splattered on his face. He realized he had been dreaming. Again.

His vision was fuzzy, as if a mist had settled over his eyes. His hearing, too, was muffled by a low buzzing sound, like bees had built small hives from his earwax.

125

Not much longer.

He settled back down in his boat to wait for it to end.

* * *

A man and his teenage son had been fishing at the lake the day the car crashed through the guardrail at the top of the slope where the highway was. They had stopped fishing when the rain began and were putting their equipment into the back of an old farm pickup when they heard the skidding and the crash. They stood and watched, paralyzed, as the blue Chevrolet rolled down the hill and into the lake. Only when the car splashed into the water did they begin to act. The man told his son the get on the citizen band radio on channel nine and call for help; he ran around the shore of the lake to the place where the car had entered the water.

When the car had settled into the water and started to sink, Michael realized the danger he and his wife were in. He had been thrown across the front seat and was now lying on the passenger side, his legs trapped under the steering wheel on the driver's side. He tried to sit up and pain shot from his right leg, making his entire body go limp. He looked for his wife, fearing she had been thrown from the car.

He saw one sneakered foot sticking up from the backseat. He called her name, but there was no answer.

He heard a gurgling sound and looked at the bottom of the door. Water was rushing in under it. Michael panicked, trying to sit up in the seat. After several painful attempts, he gave up. The water had nearly reached the bottom of the dash; the velour seat was under water. Michael looked up at the window and saw that the water level on the outside of the car was nearly halfway up the window. He tried desperately to pull his legs free. The pain made him dizzy, then blackness claimed him.

Sometime later, Michael realized he was in a room that seemed somehow familiar, though he could not remember ever having seen it before. It was a hospital room. He was leaving the room, but some nagging portion of his mind screamed that the door was the other direction.

But I don't need the door.

That was an odd thought. He decided to use the door and turned around to look for it.

Several doctors were huddled around a table. A large machine was visible at the head of the table; a line on the machine's computer screen seemed to be making a sharp humming sound.

"He's dead," one of the green-coated doctors proclaimed. Michael thought the doctor pronounced it too flatly and without any emotion, considering that a human life had just expired.

Who died?

Michael decided he probably shouldn't be here. He wondered how he'd come to be here in the first place.

But who died? I was here when it happened. I should at least see who it was.

The doctors had begun scurrying around the patient. One of them stepped aside and Michael saw the figure lying on the table. He moaned, realizing the truth of the situation. The figure on the table was his own, his hair wet and matted to his forehead. His sodden shirt had been removed and was laying in a heap beside his stomach. He remembered the car, the lake, the water.

Michael reeled, but still the doctors didn't seem to notice his presence. They continued to move frantically, one pulling another machine to the side of the table, while others took wires from this machine and put them on the body.

Michael felt himself being pulled toward the doctors and the form on the table. He tried to resist, but couldn't. He was pulled closer, and then blessed blackness overcame him again.

The next time he awoke, he was lying in a bed. A hospital bed. He remembered the vision of himself on the table. He looked around the room. A doctor sat in a chair beside the bed. He was young, as far as doctors go, with short blond hair and a pointed chin.

"Hello, Mr. Ross," the doctor said. "How are you feeling?"

"My wife," Michael groaned. The doctor's face became creased—the face of an older man. "She's dead?"

"I'm afraid there was nothing we could do."

Michael tensed as if slapped. Dizziness led him back into the darkness.

He awoke again. He didn't want to, it just happened. There was another doctor in the room with him. This one was older than the earlier one; his black hair was streaked with thick bands of gray, but his blue eyes were still clear and sharp.

"How do you feel, Mr. Ross?" He had a gentle, kind voice. He was the perfect TV doctor.

Michael noticed for the first time that his leg, which was now bound in white, was hanging from a bar above the foot of the bed. Waves of pain were coming from the leg, but not as bad as when it had been trapped in the car. Michael was hungry, too.

There was also a pain in his chest. It throbbed, but not in rhythm like the pain coming from his leg. It was more like something was being held inside him, pounding on his chest, trying to get out. Michael groaned and turned back to the doctor. He pried his gummy lips apart to speak.

"Janet," he rasped.

"I'm afraid she is no longer with us," the doctor said quietly.

Warm, salty tears slid down Michael's face. He turned away from the doctor as sobs shook his body.

"I'm going to leave, Mr. Ross," the doctor said. "I'll send a nurse in with some food and medicine in a little while. After you eat, I want you to get some more rest." He rose from his chair and silently left the room.

Michael cried in silence for a long while. Soon, a dark-haired woman in a white nurse's uniform brought him a tray of food. He picked at the tasteless meal, finishing only the glass of water that accompanied it. He slept again.

He awoke staring at the ceiling. He felt a little better, the pain in his leg and head had subsided a great deal, but the feeling in his chest remained. He felt terribly alone. The tears began again.

"Feeling better?" the older doctor asked.

"A little," Michael answered, not surprised that the doctor had entered the room unnoticed.

"That's good." The doctor sat down in the chair beside the bed. "You were lucky."

"Janet," Michael began, but he couldn't finish. "Tell me what happened. How did I get here?"

"Are you sure you're ready to hear that?"

"Yes."

The doctor told him about the rescue made by the fisherman and his son. He also told how Janet had been dead on arrival at the hospital. He finished by saying, "We thought we had lost you too, there for a few seconds."

Michael thought about what he had seen in the other room, but didn't say anything about it to the doctor.

He was released from the hospital three days later and returned to a home that seemed too empty without his wife. His leg was still in a cast and he walked with the aid of a crutch, but his insurance at the law firm had paid nearly all the hospital expenses. He also received fifty thousand dollars from a life insurance policy Janet had taken out a few years earlier.

He went to his wife's funeral that afternoon and wept openly in the arms of both her mother and his own. He returned home after the services to a lonely house where he sat and stared at the walls.

He returned to work the following week, but the depression was too much; he took an extended leave of absence, and soon quit the firm altogether. He lived on the insurance money and the small amount of legal work he could do from his house. Two months after his release from the hospital, he returned to the kind-voiced doctor to have the cast removed. He was told he would walk with a limp for the rest of his life.

Through it all, that feeling of having something trapped within his chest remained. It was now only a low, dull ache most of the time, but occasionally it flared up into a violent pounding—a lunatic pounding the padded walls of his cell.

Then one day the depression and feeling of loss had been so great that he decided to return to the place where his happiness had ended. He drove down the highway to the dirt road that branched off the side and followed it to the deeply worn ruts where a countless number of trucks had made their way to the side of the little lake. Once there, he parked his new car and went to stand by the water's edge.

He looked across the surface of the water. There was no wind and the water was like a dirty mirror, reflecting only the afternoon sky in its murky depths. Michael looked up the slope, toward the highway, and noted that the guardrail had been repaired. He walked around the lake to the place where his car had entered the water.

As he walked, he felt his body change. His hands and feet became numb. The feeling soon spread up his limbs to his torso. His vision was fuzzy and his hearing muffled. Then the pounding in his chest began, more violently than ever.

When he reached his destination, he looked out over the lake again, and the pounding stopped.

Standing on the flat surface of the water a few yards from the shore, approximately where the car had sunk, was an image of himself. It wore the same clothing he had worn on that fateful day; its hair was wet and matted to its head. Michael tried to rub the sight from his eyes, but the figure remained. He stared at it, transfixed.

The specter beckoned to him, and Michael felt his feet moving toward it. He took several steps, feeling the water soak through his shoes. He could feel the soft mud at the bottom of the pond, then he tripped over something beneath the water and fell headlong into the cold lake.

When he pulled himself, shivering, onto the shore and looked back at the water where the phantom of himself had been, it was gone. His sight and hearing were normal, and the numbness had left his limbs. The dull ache was back in his chest. At last he knew what the pain meant.

* * *

Michael rubbed his eyes and focused on the bobber bouncing on the waves of the lake. He pulled himself out of thoughts of the past. The pain in his chest was gone. He lifted his gaze from the yellow and red bobber.

His own ghost was there, waiting for him to act.

Janet is waiting.

"I'm coming," Michael said. He leaned over, tipping the boat until it spit him out like a bit of rancid tuna. He splashed into the cold water and sank. Michael tried to stay under the surface, but he lacked the will. He rose to the surface, his head breaking through the waves and the breath exploding from him.

"Help me," he sobbed.

The ghost approached him, its face impassive. It knelt on the choppy surface of the lake and placed a freezing hand on Michael's head.

Michael became still as the waves closed over his head again. He breathed deeply, welcoming the cold, murky water into his lungs, letting it flood his body, letting it shut down his vital organs so that they would release the spirit above.

So he could rejoin his Janet.

Grandpa Frost

NOVEMBER 12, 1999
Running for three days now.

NOVEMBER 13, 1999
Still running.

NOVEMBER 14, 1999
Ace and Thunder died today. The sled is light, but I know the other dogs won't last much longer.

NOVEMBER 15, 1999
Tired. So tired, but must keep going. Jock died late yesterday.

NOVEMBER 16, 1999
Hector is the only dog left. I had to abandon the sled. A polar bear ran past us today. I could count his ribs as he ran, but he never gave us a second glance. So cold. Must keep running. I'm sure Grandpa Frost is catching up.
The beard I had such a tough time growing is frozen so hard I can barely open my mouth to eat the tasteless, dried food I have left.

NOVEMBER 17, 1999
My toes have turned black with frostbite. Food is practically gone.
I'm afraid I'll never live to see my wife or son again. I can't warn them of what's coming. Linda, Monte, I'm sorry. I can't—Dear God, help them.
Must keep going.

NOVEMBER 18, 1999
I'm so cold. And hungry. I'm rationing the food, but even with just myself and Hector, we only have a couple days of eating left. That's allowing one meal a day. I'm wearing so much clothing I can barely move, but it's just not

enough. Nothing will be enough.

At this point I have to assume I will never make it back to civilization. I feel like I have to leave some record of what happened; I may be the only one left of the crew that was there. I'm sure of it, really.

I can see the clouds of a blizzard that seems to be running ahead of Grandpa Frost. They're massed up behind me like the Dallas Cowboys' defensive line. Oh yeah, they're ready for the blitz. I'm camped beside a lake, or maybe it's the edge of a bay. I don't know, but it's already beginning to freeze around the edges as Grandpa Frost gets closer.

I hope this pitiful diary will be of use someday.

I wish I had the records that were lost. I didn't understand much of the stuff the scientists said or wrote, but I caught the gist of the matter. A dog trainer doesn't need to understand the geometry involved in the measurement of the Earth's axis or the angle of a meteorite's impact. If humanity survives this onslaught, the research would be helpful; it would provide some scientific proof to a mad tale. But I don't have it, so I have to record from memory. And speculation.

The beginning may really be in the Ice Age, but the beginning for me, for the modern world, was October 11, 1999.

I was in Alaska. I wanted to run a team in the next Iditarod race. Linda came with me, and of course Monte, too. I'd only been out of the Marines for five months; I was in charge of a K-9 Corps in Texas. I love dogs, especially working dogs, and having a sled team has been a dream of mine for years.

I was training my team when it all began. When I learned the United Nations was sending an international coalition of scientists to the North Pole to investigate the cause of the disasters, I volunteered and was accepted as the civilian commander of the K-9 division for the unit.

I'm glad I sent my family home to Texas. Maybe, just maybe, they'll have a chance to run farther south and possibly escape. I can only hope...

NOVEMBER 19, 1999

The clouds are closer and I'm even colder today than yesterday. I can't stay here long. Grandpa Frost is catching up, and I don't want to be sitting here, my story half done, when he catches me. Just a short rest, and then we'll run some more.

Back to the story.

October 11, 1999. Something like a month before that, I think it was, a major disturbance was recorded in the asteroid belt that is between Mars and

Jupiter. Most of the scientists I worked with at the Pole actually witnessed the crash in the belt. Anyway, there was a major collision between some exceptionally large meteors, and the debris from that crash was sent flying through space. I was told this has happened before, but never with such a large amount of debris.

What is believed to be several hundred tons of meteorites crashed into the Arctic, very near the North Pole. Immediately, things changed on Earth.

I have to jump ahead here to tell some of what was learned in the short time our crew was on the site. What was suspected was proven to be true; the angle of the Earth's axis had shifted when the space debris crashed. I can scarcely imagine such an impact. Not even a string of cobalt bombs could produce that kind of an effect.

Because of the shift in the Earth's axis, the balance between planet and moon was thrown off kilter, causing abnormal tides worldwide. Also, many icebergs drifted farther south, where they melted and added their water to the oceans.

Melting. Oh, but that won't last. No. Grandpa Frost will re-freeze them soon enough.

Gotta move on now. Is Hector asleep or dead?

NOVEMBER 20, 1999

Hector is still with me. I feel sorry for him. I know he's suffering even more than me. His feet would be bleeding if I could chip the ice away from his worn-down pads.

What happened next? Oh, yeah, the earthquakes.

New fault lines were created from the impact of the space junk, and old lines were aggravated. Earthquakes rocked the globe, finally proving the pessimists right; California is now just a series of little islands off the Nevada coast. China gained a canyon that surpasses America's Grand Canyon for size. Of course, they lost a few million citizens in the trade. Most of Vietnam is gone, and what is left is a salty swamp. A lot of the old coastal countries and states are like that now.

But then we have new land to make up for it. The Hawaiian Islands, for instance, are now a small continent. I heard on the international news before leaving for the Pole that there was talk of Atlantis returning to the surface. They'll never find it. They won't have time.

The meteorites that found their way to Earth had burned into the ice, which then re-froze. That sounds familiar to sci-fi fans, I know, but this is worse. The ice was very thick. Most of the meteorites were about twenty-five feet below the surface, and still glowing pretty good when we got there. The scientists, led by an Englishman named Penobst, thought they were sinking deeper.

A hasty village was built near the place where the largest pieces of the debris were sunk, a cluster of huts around a gasoline-powered generator.

I have to sleep. Just a couple of hours. Not too long. No, that wouldn't be good.

NOVEMBER 21, 1999

When I woke up today, the snow was falling. Just flurries. I outran them, but they'll catch me again. Is Monte warm and snug in his crib? Does Linda have the fireplace roaring? Do they have any idea what's happening?

Digging began as soon as our camp at the Pole was set. We were trying to get to the meteorites before they sank any farther.

Nobody paid much attention to the ice around the meteorites. At first it wasn't considered odd, especially in the excitement and confusion. The ice in about a ten-foot diameter around the meteorites was normal, but beyond that it was blue.

Dark, deep blue. Like a baby's eyes. And the blue moved, inch by inch, toward the meteorites.

By the time we had dug down five feet, the blue matter had closed around the glowing meteorites. The light caused by the space junk's heat was still visible, but muffled, like we were seeing it through a fog.

Oh, yeah, though I was the dog trainer, I was still called upon to do manual labor, such as digging. That's why I was there to see what was happening.

Everyone noticed the blue stuff closing around the rocks, but nobody thought it important enough to bother with; just an effect of the fast melting and re-freezing of the ice.

We continued digging. Penobst said he thought the meteorites had stopped sinking.

The glow of the meteorites faded and died. It wasn't a slow process. One minute they were still glowing red, then they flickered and became nothing but cold, dead rock.

And the blue in the ice was rising to the surface.

To be continued...

NOVEMBER 22, 1999

No out-running the snow now. It's still falling pretty light, but I know it'll pick up soon. I wouldn't mind so much if the food wasn't gone. Hector's given up sniffing my empty pockets.

Penobst was a very curious man. It was right and proper he died first. He stood in our hole in the ice, watching the blue matter rise to the top like a whale needing air. By the time he realized the ice was softening, his feet had broken through.

He should have gone completely under, but he didn't. Only his feet went, and them not even to the top of his boots.

Then, the ice re-froze.

Two of us, me and a French scientist, tried to pull him out, but he was stuck tight in solid ice.

Then, the ice opened under the Frenchman—I think his name was Limly. He became stuck, too, his screams mingling with Penobst's. I'm afraid that the screams of those two men will ring in my numb ears forever.

I jumped back before I was trapped, too. I was still holding the gloved hand of Penobst, and when I jumped back I felt his fingers break inside his gloves. They shouldn't have broken, but when they did, it was more like icicles snapping apart than the bones of fingers.

I didn't have time to think about Penobst's fingers. The blue under the ice was moving. It was coming toward us. We panicked and ran like rabbits.

Rabbits are delicious to eat. Oh, what I wouldn't give for a hot, spitted brace of hare right now. Oh God, I'm rambling and I still have so much to write.

NOVEMBER 23, 1999

No time for chit-chat. And definitely no time for stupid rambling. The snow is falling as fast as the temperature, and my fingers hurt when I try to curl them around my pen. I have one match left. Maybe tomorrow I'll use it.

We gathered in one of the buildings. Those who had not seen what happened were quickly filled in.

Suggestions as to what the blue thing was began to be thrown around. At first, it was thought it may be a form of alien life that had crashed with the meteorites, but that idea was dropped when someone reminded us how the blue had closed around the hot debris. It was coming to them, not away from them. Somebody else mentioned how the blue mass had seemed to suck the heat from the space rocks, and I related how Penobst's fingers had broken.

An American named Mitchell thought maybe it was a remnant of some one-celled animal that evolved in the primordial seas at the dawn of creation and was then frozen as the Earth's crust solidified and the first Ice Age came, about 570,000,000 years ago. Then, when the ice retreated, these creatures, who had adapted to such extremes, retreated to the polar caps with the ice. He said they went with the ice because they had learned to move through it by melting it ahead of them. Mitchell went on to say that these creatures lived by drawing the body heat from fish they caught under the ice. I don't know. A month ago I would have roared with laughter over his idea. Now, I'm just not sure. Mitchell claimed to have evidence to support his theory in a Virginia lab, evidence he found while core drilling in Greenland.

Then our Russian cook, whose name was Borg, spoke. He told a tale I don't have time to recap in much detail, but I'll try to convey the heart of his story tomorrow.

NOVEMBER 24, 1999

Too tired to write much.

Borg said there were legends dating back to the times of Odin and Thor, of something living in the ice of Siberia. Something that lived on warmth. He said that there were tales of campfires being sucked into the snow and ice, as well as the people who sat around them. When he started talking about frost giants, he was silenced with harsh words.

His tale was, of course, dismissed as folklore.

I guess the more they talked, the less the men of science believed what they had seen, and then there were those who hadn't seen. By now, nearly all of them had become unbelievers. They decided they wanted to go back out and look at the bodies of Penobst and Limly. Most of the rest of us went, too.

Grandpa Frost had retreated and seemed to be gathered around the spot where the meteorites and the two men were frozen in the Earth.

Penobst and Limly were still standing. Both were dead, their blue faces frozen in ghastly screams. I looked from their faces to the mass under the ice. I thought of a cat, crouching, ready to spring.

The scientists, the fools, walked boldly over the ice, only one or two looking down nervously. I and a few of the others stayed back, just watching. Someone tried to pull Limly from his place in the ice. A sound like breaking sticks filled the air and Limly fell forward, his back and lower legs broken.

Tune in tomorrow for the bone-chilling conclusion, folks.

NOVEMBER 25, 1999

This is it. Tonight is to be my last night. The snow is so heavy I can no longer see two feet in front of me. I've found shelter, of sorts, in a tiny ravine—a Texas pothole. I've used my last match to build a small fire. That should give Grandpa Frost incentive to hurry this thing up.

Hector knows this is the end.

The thing under the ice attacked before the sound of Limly's breaking bones had died on the frigid air.

The men of science saw it coming, but in their hurry, one of them slipped. They fell like dominoes. Some were trapped completely under the ice and frozen as they struggled. Others were caught as they tried to rise, half in and half out of the ice. None of them escaped.

The rest of us broke and ran toward the two helicopters that stood just outside the ring of huts. My feet got tangled up with someone else's and we both came down. Only us two saw what happened with any perspective.

The screams of the trapped scientists were fading, and as the men became blue and brittle in their parkas, the mass under the ice grew.

Then it stretched. I thought of a cat again, a cat just waking from a long nap.

The thing reached the helicopters as they prepared to take off. It melted and re-froze the ice. One of the choppers was sunk to where only the whirling propeller was visible, the other just so the doors were sufficiently blocked. Inside, people pressed against the glass like trapped flies.

I was already moving. I ran to the kennels and hitched my dog team. We took off at a run, with only the emergency supplies that were kept on the sled at all times. No one tried to stop us; not many were left by that time.

The blue mass gave chase at first, but the dogs were fresh and strong, and I suppose Grandpa Frost wanted to finish with those he already had trapped. Maybe he knew he would catch me later.

I ran. And now here I am, with only one dog left and both of us too exhausted to go any farther.

What is the mass under the ice?

I've thought about that. I call it Grandpa Frost, but maybe Count Frost would be a better title.

I think both Mitchell and Borg were right in their theories. After all, most folklore evolved from what can be proven to be a base of scientific fact.

He's close now. The snow under my fire is starting to turn blue. Bring it on, Gramps. Get it over with. Hector is growing agitated, but he still won't leave me. He really is man's best friend.

We all know of Jack Frost, the little elf that paints the leaves bright colors in the fall and glazes frost on our windows.

But what is he really doing?

Stealing the warmth. The life.

What about the frost giants of Nordic myth?

I think both are mythological descendants of this thing under the ice, this thing Mitchell thinks has been living on Earth since the planet was formed.

I think it has tried to conquer the Earth before, in those times we call the Ice Ages. What stopped it? I don't know. I think maybe the young planet shifted as it became more solid, more mature, so to speak, and the sun's warmth turned it back.

And now, the Earth has shifted again.

He's all around us now. I'm not sure, but I think the ice I'm sitting on is softer than it was a few minutes ago.

My campfire isn't warming me anymore.

Hector has lain down to accept his fate.

I will too. I'll wrap this pitiful diary back in its oil skin and throw it away so Gramps won't swallow it with me, then I'll lie close to Hector so that we can share our warmth to the end. He's all the family I have now.

I wish I was home in Texas with Linda and Monte. I wish I knew they would be safe.

Good luck, world.

—Guy Olsen

Digging Up the Past

Levi pitched the shovel aside and stood up. He reached behind him with his right arm, his only arm, and held his back as he stretched to relieve the cramping. Digging the hole hadn't been easy. The on-going drought made the ground as hard as cement.

The sun was setting. The old house on the horizon was only a haunted black silhouette. No one lived in the house any more. The farm was leased to a tenant who grazed cattle on the land, leaving the house to slowly decay. Levi didn't care.

He squatted beside the small grave and brushed dirt off the lid of a pine box.

"Twenty-three years," he whispered. "Long time."

He cleared dirt away from the box. There was no moisture, not even this deep. The dirt smelled dry and dusty. Levi snorted to clear his nose.

Getting the box out of the ground would be tricky. "Shoulda wore the damn prosthetic," he mumbled. Using the shovel blade as a wedge, he dragged the box into the high brown grass.

"Gotcha." He knelt beside the container and pulled a hammer from his belt. Years of continued farm work after the combine tore away his left arm had made him adept at using tools one-handed. Rusty nails screamed and emitted tendrils of reddish dust as he pulled them from the lid.

The nails out, Levi sat quietly. The lid was about to fall off. The hammer slid from his dusty fingers. Levi reached for the lid, then stopped. He heard himself swallow. His fingers trembled. With a sudden flick of his wrist he flung the lid aside.

His father had thought the whole affair melodramatic and took part only after an argument with his wife.

The bones were gray and hard in the deepening gloom. Very carefully, Levi lifted the partial skeleton out and held it before his face.

It felt no different than the bones of cattle that had died and decomposed on the land. The long bone of the forearm was smooth except for some pockmarks.

"Worms been at me already," Levi said. "Damn worms."

He was shaking. The tip of his index finger rattled and fell away from the rest of the skeleton. Levi winced as the particle hit the ground.

The joints—fingers, wrist and elbow—were stiff and did not move as he held the arm; they had rusted like any other piece of neglected farm equipment. The severed end was ragged and sharp. Levi remembered his father cursing as he bound his son's gushing stump with the same red handkerchief in which he blew his nose.

"Coulda died," Levi told the passing wind. "Worms coulda had all of me."

He put the arm down and stripped off his shirt. Another deep breath. Levi raised the skeletal remnant of his childhood until the ragged edge butted against the rounded knob six inches from his shoulder.

"I've outgrowed it." He tossed the bones back into the box and reached for his shirt.

Souls In Motion

"Are you the exorcist?"

Startled, the old woman behind the counter looked up from the Carolyn Wheat mystery novel she was reading. Her face registered mild surprise at the sight of the man in the dark blue shirt and faded Levis looking at her over the cash register. "Yes, I perform exorcisms," she answered.

"Good," the ghost said. "I need an exorcism. I've been possessed."

It had started out as a normal day for Rosa McVera, owner and operator of LADY MAGICK'S. She had served five customers during the day; three of them bought ceremonial candles, one a book of spells to relieve minor body pains, and the last had merely looked around for a while and then left without buying anything. Rosa had decided that he was probably a skeptic.

Now, a half-hour before closing time, she had felt another presence in her store. She hadn't heard the bell over her door ring and she had been deeply involved in a quest with Cass Jameson, so she ignored the presence as hallucination. Then the ghost had spoken.

Rosa looked from the ghost to the large display window at the front of her shop; twilight was beginning to press its shadowy face to the glass. Once the window had displayed used items such as small appliances or musical instruments, but that had been before William McVera died of a heart attack and his widow turned the store from a pawnshop into LADY MAGICK'S. A piece of cardboard propped in the window read "Fortunes Told, Tarot Read." Another proclaimed, "Exorcisms Performed." Besides the signs, only a few spell books, the bigger sellers, were in the window, standing on end, the covers fading.

In the six years since William's death, Rosa had performed only two exorcisms. The first had been a success, of which she was justly proud. The second had been a case of pure schizophrenia, and though she went ahead with the exorcism procedure (and collected her fee), nothing had happened and she'd finally been reduced to giving the kind of advice that was stock-in-trade for people like Ann Landers and Dr. Ruth: "Get counseling."

Rosa turned back to her customer. "Usually an exorcism is performed to banish a demon or unwanted spirit," she explained. "Are you trapped in this world and trying to get to the next?"

"No," he answered. "I have been driven from the body that was mine, and I want you to help me to reclaim it. Can you do it? If not, say so and I'll leave."

"I don't know," Rosa said, finally putting her book aside and standing to face the man. "Can you pay for it? Exorcisms aren't cheap, and I have bills to pay." A lot of them, she added mentally, looking at the stack under the counter.

"If you succeed, I can pay you well. Any price. If you fail," he shrugged to show that failure would mean no payment.

Rosa thought for a moment. "I'll need to hear what happened," she said. She checked her watch—still twenty minutes until closing time—but she decided to lock up early. She didn't suspect she would get much more business anyway, and the chance of an exorcism fee would more than make up for a missed candle sale. "Go in there." She motioned to a small room in the back of the shop that was used primarily for fortune reading. A thick black drape hung in the doorway. "I'll close up and then come and hear you out."

The figure turned and drifted toward the other room. He looked like a blue silk scarf blown by a gentle but persistent breeze, Rosa thought. The ghost moved his feet as if he were walking, though it was clear that putting one foot before the other was no longer a necessity of motivation. *Old habits die hard.* The ghost went through the curtain without so much as rustling the fabric.

Rosa closed and locked the front door and turned the sign that said OPEN around so that it read CLOSED. Then she went to hear a ghost story.

She sat in one of the two folding chairs at the card table in the dim room. Two white candles provided the only light. There was electricity in the chamber, but Rosa had removed the bulb. Candles added atmosphere, and customers liked atmosphere during fortune readings. The ghost stood on the other side of the table, his arms folded on his chest.

"Okay, I'm ready," Rosa told him.

"My name is Stephen Gallager," he said, then paused. "Perhaps you've heard of me. I own several oil wells around the state."

"The name does sound familiar..." Rosa said. Her face suddenly brightened, "Oh yes, I've heard of you. Everyone has. What happened? I thought you were alive and well."

"Yes, well, in a way I am," Gallager told her. "About two months ago I was out on one of the rigs. It was late in the evening and most of the men had gone home for the night. It was only me and a few others. There was a storm coming and the wind was blowing like all hell. Me and one of my foremen, a guy named Jack Nixon, were tying down a stack of steel pipes with some cable." He paused in his narrative and looked away, remembering. Rosa waited. "We were tying those pipes down and Jack's foot caught in the cable. He tried to jerk it loose and when he did, all those pipes came down on us.

"I was lucky. I got hit on the shoulder and thrown to one side before they all came down. When I hit the ground, I blacked out, but I saw what happened to Jack first. He was knocked over by the pipes, and then one of them came down on his head. I saw his brains leaking out his busted skull. I saw it. He was dead. Then I blacked out. It was dark, I remember that, and then something, something like a blast of cold, compressed air shot into my mouth. I saw Jack again then, but he was inside my head, like a dream." Gallager shook his head as if still unable to understand what had happened.

"This thing that I thought was a dream, it wasn't," he said. "I know that now, but while it was happening I thought it was just a dream. I remember Jack yelling at me to get out. He said he deserved to live more than I did, then he started to fight me, pushing and shoving, all the time yelling at me to get out. I was so surprised that I didn't put up much of a fight. The next thing I knew I was standing up, looking down at my body. But I was...the real me that is...was just like you see me now. A ghost.

"About that time, the other guys came running over. I guess they heard the pipes fall. One of them stopped and checked on Jack's body, even though it was obviously dead. The rest ran over to me. One of them ran right through me. He shivered, but other than that he didn't even notice me there. They managed to bring my body around, and that's when I fully realized what had happened. Jack Nixon's ghost is living inside my body." Gallager stopped again. He began to pace around the small room while he continued talking, occasionally flinging his arms to add emphasis to his words.

"He's taken my body and my identity. That bastard is pretending to be me. He's living in my house, collecting my money, sleeping in my bed. If I was married he'd be fucking my wife!" He threw his arms wide this time, one hand brushed through a candle, the flame flickered and died, throwing the room into further darkness, making Rosa nearly invisible in her chair.

"I've tried to fight him myself since then," Gallager continued. "I sneak into my own house while he's asleep—he does that a lot, hardly ever goes out to the jobs anymore. He fired all my household help, too. You'd think someone would realize that there's something wrong. But anyway, I go in and try to take my body back. I enter through his mouth—my mouth, I mean—but he forces me out every time."

He stopped pacing and turned to face the old woman again. "I guess I've gotten a little carried away with my story," he said. "I'm sorry. I just don't understand how he could have done that—take my body, I mean. Can you help me?"

Without answering, Rosa left her chair and walked slowly to the extinguished candle. She took a match from a nearby shelf and re-lit the candle, then returned to her chair.

"Apparently, when he died, this Jack, his soul became free from his mortal body," she explained. "It should have gone immediately on to the next plane of existence. He must have been a strong man—strong-willed. Very strong. He managed not only to keep his soul on this plane, but also to force you out of your natural body. You, on the other hand, are not so strong. Plus, you were still under the limitations of being connected to your mortal body, not being dead yourself. That gave him a big advantage. He had nothing to lose, while you still had your mortality, something that we all try to hold onto as long as possible, at any cost.

"Do you understand now?"

Gallager looked at her in a way that made her think he resented being called inferior to any of his employees, but it passed quickly and was replaced by a look of tired resignation. "Yes, I think so." He paused thoughtfully. "If he was to be killed while in my body, could I take it back then?"

"No," Rosa answered. "If he was killed as he is now, you would both pass on to the next world. Unless he took someone else's body." Now Rosa paused to think. "You could take the body of someone that has died a natural death, but you would become them rather than yourself, and if it was an old person, your life would be short."

"No, I want my own body back."

"Yes, I thought you would. I was just thinking out loud."

"Do you think you can do it?" Gallager asked.

"Oh, yes, I can do it."

"Good." The ghost smiled at her. "I'm glad you're willing to try. I was afraid you'd be a fake or something and back out when you saw that I was a real ghost. I can't tell you how much I appreciate your help."

"Strange jobs keep me in business," Rosa said. "This will be a challenge

144

though." Especially if the plan that was crystallizing in her mind worked out well. "And besides, I need the money."

"How much do you usually get for an exorcism?" Gallager asked.

"Oh, we'll talk about that later," Rosa answered. "It depends on how long it takes and what I have to use. Believe me, you'll be able to afford it easily."

"How soon can we start?"

"How about tomorrow?"

"That's fine. He usually naps at about three. I could meet you at my house at, say three-fifteen?"

"All right. But how will I get in?" Rosa asked. "I doubt you'll have any trouble, but I can't walk through doors."

"Yes, being a ghost does have certain advantages. There's a key under a brick in the flowerbed. I'll show you where. I used to lock myself out, and hiding a key was less embarrassing than having the maid let me in every time."

"Fine. I'll see you tomorrow at three-fifteen at what we commoners call the Gallager Mansion."

"All right, I'll see you then." Stephen Gallager drifted through the fabric closing off the room.

Rosa felt him leave the shop and smiled to herself. She sat in the candle-lit room and worked over the details of the next day in her head. When she believed she had developed a foolproof plan, she rose from her chair, her joints creaking, and blew out the candles that had now burned low. The hour had grown late; twilight had fled and in its place was the deep dark of night in the run-down area of town.

Rosa went behind the counter and lifted the stack of bills from its place on the lower shelf. She sorted them out, studying each one for a moment before returning it to a new pile. After each had been examined, she picked up the stacks and dropped each into the wastebasket. Then she turned off the lights and went home to get some sleep.

* * *

Rosa McVera pulled her battered Volkswagen Bug into the tree-lined circular drive of the Gallager Mansion and killed the sputtering engine. A low stone fence surrounded the property, broken only but the entrance of the driveway. She parked in front of the house and got out, a red tote bag over one shoulder.

145

She surveyed the house quickly. It appeared to be modeled after the Southern mansions of pre-Civil War times—rectangular and gleamingly white with tall windows that reflected the afternoon sun.

The ghost was sitting in a porch swing. He got up and came down the steps as she looked at the house.

"Do you like it?" he asked.

"Yes, it's very nice," Rosa responded. "Very nice."

"The key is right over here," Gallager said, unable to hide the excitement in his voice. He walk-floated to a brick footpath leading though the dazzling flowerbed. He led her to the middle of the path and pointed to a brick. Rosa ignored the ache in her back as she bent, turned the specified block over, and picked up a brass key. She straightened, grimacing, and followed Gallager to the front door of the house.

The heavy oak door swung open on a huge living room, lit only by the sunlight streaming through the windows, causing the many furnishings to cast odd shadows. A wide stairwell curled up to the second floor. Gallager was already halfway across the living room when Rosa quietly closed the front door. She hurried after the ghost. They went to the top of the stairs and turned down a corridor, passed three closed doors and stopped at the fourth.

"This is it," Gallager whispered. His ghostly face was drawn in anticipation.

"All right, just a minute," Rosa said. She reached into her red bag and took out a vial of chloroform and a white cloth. She opened the small bottle and poured half its contents onto the cloth, then recapped the vial and put it back in her bag. She nodded at Gallager.

He vanished through the door. Rosa turned the knob and pushed it open. She strode quickly into the room and to the side of the bed where a man who looked exactly like the ghost of Stephen Gallager lay sleeping on top of the covers. She plunged the cloth over his face. He struggled only minutely, then lay perfectly still. Rosa put her bag on a table beside the bed and pulled out four lengths of nylon cord. She used these to tie the wrists and ankles of the body to the bedposts. The ghost stood beside the head of the bed, watching.

When the body was secured, Rosa stepped back and surveyed her work. She felt sure that even if he woke up, the man would be unable to free himself. She took a deep breath, raised her arms, and began to chant.

A look of puzzlement came over the face of the ghost. "What are you doing? What are you saying?" he asked.

"I'm exorcising this soul from your body," Rosa replied, irritated at being

146

interrupted. "I'm using Latin; it adds a little class. Now, please, do not interrupt me again. I have to concentrate very hard."

Without waiting for a response, she began to chant again, her voice rising and falling in unmelodic cadences, her hands swooping down at intervals so her fingers could waggle over the sleeping man's face. The body in the bed began to jerk and convulse, pulling the restraining cords taut. Rosa's chanting became harsher. Sweat beaded on her forehead. Finally, the struggles of the man's body began to lessen; the bindings became slack and the body was still.

The mouth of the body fell open and a translucent figure burst from between the teeth, visible for only a moment—a man who looked nothing like the body he had just left. The apparition let out a shriek, then vanished with a quick pop. Exhausted, Rosa sat heavily on the bed and watched as the true soul of Stephen Gallager entered the mouth to fill the body.

The man remained motionless on the big bed. The chloroform would last for probably another hour. Rosa left the room, leaving the body tied. She went into the next room down the hall and fell onto the bed she found there. She was asleep within moments.

She awoke to calls from the other room. Gallager was awake and wanting to know where she was and why he was still tied up. Rosa dragged herself off the bed and went to him.

She stood at the side of the bed, looking down on the bound man. She smiled. He smiled in return.

"You did it," he said. "Thank you. I don't know how to repay you. Money doesn't seem enough."

Rosa's smile broadened. "This is a very nice house you have here, Mr. Gallager. In fact, this is a very nice life you have. Wouldn't you agree? No wonder Jack Nixon wanted to keep it."

"You can't possibly want my house?" Gallager asked.

Rosa picked up the white cloth she had tossed beside her bag. She took out the vial of chloroform. Her eyes remained on Gallager as she emptied the small bottle into the cloth.

"That's just part of my fee," she said as she shoved the cloth into the man's face.

When the body was still once more, she put the cloth aside and took the final item from her bag—a long dagger. She cut the cords binding the man's limbs, then leaned over the body, put her open mouth over his, and plunged the knife into her own chest.

Her soul found his in a dark, swirling place. Rosa raised her spirit arms and began to chant in Latin again. Gallager fought. He tried to find some anchor to hang on to, but there was nothing but the spinning blackness. Rosa chanted, watching as Stephen Gallager's soul was pushed farther and farther away by her words.

"It isn't fair," he shouted. Then he was gone.

Later, the man on the bed stirred to life. He pushed the body of the old woman off him; it thudded to the floor. Rosa looked at her old body, and for just a moment thought she might miss it.

But this one will be so much better, she told herself. "I'm a rich man now."

Last Trick

Mary Beth closed the door and faced her last customer. Not just the last one for tonight, this one would be the last one of her life. She had made a decision. Her days of being Daddy's little moneymaker were over. She could feel the seed of her previous customer, grown cold and crusty on her thigh, as she walked toward the bed where her final lover waited for her.

She didn't greet him, though he winked it her. Perhaps his wink was only a trick of the thread of light shining through the curtains of the room. She didn't know, and it really didn't matter. She slipped out of her clothes and reached down to the bed and began stroking her lover.

She had seen this one before—a friend of her father. She knew her father called him Mag. She whispered the name as her hands caressed his hardness. He didn't respond, only lay motionless. She lifted him from the bed and sank to her knees before him. She took him into her mouth, her hands continuing to fondle until they squeezed his butt and held. Her tongue toyed with him for a few moments, and then she began to bob her head slowly along the length of his shaft.

Her father wouldn't be happy about this. She knew that, but didn't really care.

She had decided to do Mag, and make him her last, about a week ago. The problem had been getting him away from her father. They had been close as long as Mary Beth could remember. This one, her last, would be free of charge.

She bobbed her head a little faster as she felt the hardness in her mouth getting warmer.

She had heard that the human mind began storing information almost from the time of birth. Her own earliest memory was of a family get-together when she had been two years old. Her mother had already departed from the family, leaving her little girl with her father. Mary Beth could remember sucking the last drops of milk from a dirty bottle. She remembered crying for more.

A man who called himself Uncle Dick asked, "Why do you still let her suck that thing?"

"It's good practice," her father had answered, laughing.

"Oh, yeah? Let's see about that," Uncle Dick said. He pulled the bottle from her hands and opened his pants at the fly. "Here you go, Mary Beth," he said as he pushed his already hardened member into her face. She had cried harder.

Her father scolded her. "Take your new bottle, Mary Beth. I promise you'll like it."

She took the thing into her mouth and began to suck. She remembered swallowing the salty juices that spurted out.

Tears ran from her eyes as she continued to move her head back and forth along Mag's barrel. Her hand began moving again, ready for the vital moment. He trembled in her hands. It was time for the climax. Her finger found the trigger.

The .44 magnum exploded in ecstasy and Mary Beth's brains splattered in red and gray streaks on the grubby wall of her childhood bedroom, staining the faded images of Raggedy Ann and Andy at play. Mag fell to the floor, Mary Beth's hands still locked on his butt as her final tears rolled off his dark barrel.

Phaethon Reborn

Sam Reece leaned over the handlebars of his bicycle and pumped furiously at the pedals. Evening was coming fast, darkening the fields and woods on either side of the narrow dirt road in north-central Oklahoma. In the brush beside the road, raccoons, possums and other nocturnal creatures stirred. Sam panted and clutched the rubber handgrips of his dirt bike, determined not to let Gene Russell get any further ahead of him.

"You're crazy," Sam huffed. He knew Gene couldn't hear him, and it wouldn't have mattered if the other boy had heard him. Gene would have just smiled and said he wasn't crazy at all.

Sam wondered how far they'd gone since leaving home. They'd left from his house in Ponca City, crossed the Salt Fork of the Arkansas River on the Old River Bridge and then left the paved road for this dirt one. He guessed they were a couple of miles from his house. Finally, Gene veered off the road, onto the rutted trail of an old oilfield lease road, and stopped. He dropped his bike to the ground. Sam came up behind him and stood his bike on its kickstand.

A huge oil pump stood silently in a worn clearing. The dull black metal glinted under the rising moon like the cast-iron bones of some immobile dinousaur.

"Here we are," Gene said.

"Yeah, but where are we?"

"Nowhere. Nowhere that anybody will notice what we're doing."

"And what is it we're doing?"

"First, we're going to build a fire."

"Oh man, this isn't your fire thing again, is it?"

Gene only gave his friend an exasperated look. "Come on, man, start gathering up some firewood."

Sam followed Gene through a field of wheat that was nearly waist-high on the boys and into a nearby stand of trees. They gathered an armload of old oak, maple and sycamore branches. They carried the wood back to the hard-packed dirt around the silent oil pump.

"Go get another load," Gene ordered. "I'll get the fire going."

"Do you know what you're doing?" Sam asked.

"Of course. If there's one thing I know, it's fire. Go on. Hurry."

When Sam returned, Gene had a decent fire going in a pile of old limbs. The smoke curled and danced like smudged ghosts over the flickering orange flames. There was no wind tonight, not unusual for late evening during a hot Oklahoma summer. The smell of the wood fire hung in the clearing. Sam dropped his firewood.

"Now what?" he asked.

Gene didn't answer right away. He carefully chose a few more sticks of wood to feed to the fire. He stirred it a bit, blew on struggling flames here and there, then looked up at Sam and grinned, his face lit like a demon in Hell.

"Now for my greatest work to date," he said, his eyes as bright as the fire.

Sam watched as his friend stood up and began to remove his T-shirt and shorts. When Gene pulled off his underwear, Sam turned away.

"What are you doing, man? Put your damn panties back on. I don't want to see your thing."

"Shut up, Sam. I don't want my clothes to catch on fire. Are you gonna watch this or not? Don't be a girl."

Sam turned around. "Are you sure about this? I mean, this ain't no birthday candle."

"I'm sure."

Gene reached forward and put his hands into the fire. When he drew them back, he held a dancing flame in his cupped palms. He shifted it to one hand, the way another kid might have shifted a blob of Jell-O.

Sam watched, fascinated. He'd seen Gene do this kind of thing before. However, the other times, the fire had been smaller. The first time he'd seen it was at Gene's last birthday party, his thirteenth. Gene had reached out and gathered the flames from the tops of his birthday candles, holding them in the palms of his hands, then balling them up into one bigger flame. He shaped the ball into a thick-bodied dog and was elongating the penis when his mother stopped him.

It had been no big deal to Mrs. Russell. She'd told Gene to wash the fire off his hands in the sink and come back and eat his cake.

The next time Sam saw it, Gene had reached into his father's barbecue grill and pulled out two handfuls of fire. He shaped one into a short bow and the other into an arrow, then fired the arrow at the house. He ran away, pulling Sam after him, as the house caught fire. Mr. Russell had put the fire out before it caused any real damage, but Gene had been grounded to his room for a week after that trick.

"What are you going to make?" Sam asked.

"A chariot."

"A what?"

"A chariot. Like they had in ancient Greece. I've been reading mythology. I'm gonna make a chariot and a Pegasus. You know, a horse with wings."

"Can you do that?"

"Yeah, I think so. I'll need a bigger fire. Wanna find some more wood?"

Sam looked across the dark wheat to the darker stand of trees. He didn't want to go for more wood—but he wanted to see if Gene could really build a chariot and winged horse, so he did.

Finding wood in the dark wasn't easy, but Sam filled his arms again and made his way back to the fire. The clearing was very bright now and at first he thought the fire had gotten out of control, but as he approached he saw it was because Gene's chariot was already shaping up nicely.

Gene had created two spoked wheels that were as high as his chest. The chariot had a floor of dancing fire and the sides were about half finished. The creation was a marvel. Sam put his wood on the ground and watched Gene lift wriggling handfuls of flame from the fire and shape them along the top of what he had already placed, smoothing the fire and creating curves like most boys do when building a fort made of mud or snow. This was, by far, the most complex fire creation Sam had seen his friend attempt.

Gene's face glistened with a sheen of sweat. His eyes were glassy and seemed focused far away as he worked. Perspiration ran down his hairless chest. His feet were covered in gray ash and his hair hung limp and wet around his face.

"Keep the fire going for me, will you?" Gene asked without looking at Sam.

Sam poked at the fire, moving some half-burned limbs closer to the hotter parts of the flame. He added a few more sticks, made sure they began to burn, and turned his attention back to Gene.

It took Gene about thirty more minutes to finish the chariot. He paused then and went to his bike. He pulled a water bottle off the frame post under the seat and took a long drink, then replaced the bottle and came back to stand beside Sam.

"How's it look?"

"Great," Sam said.

"I burned my hands. I haven't done that since I was a little kid. I got distracted, thinking about how much fun it's gonna be to ride in it." He held his hands out for Sam to see.

Sam saw that Gene's palms and several of his fingers were blistered. The blisters were small, white and mushy looking. The skin around them was red from the heat of the fire, but not burned.

"You okay?" Sam asked.

"Yeah. I just have to stay focused. I'm gonna start on the horse now. That'll be the hard part."

Like the dog he'd made from the flames of his birthday candles, Gene's winged horse was blocky and lacked in detail. Unlike the dog, the horse didn't get any sex organ. Sam kept the wood fire going, barely able to provide enough fire to keep up with Gene's busy hands as he scooped out fistfuls of flame to shape the horse. Two hours later, Sam was thinking he'd have to go back to the dark woods to find more fallen limbs when Gene plopped down on the ground, his face streaked with ash and sweat.

"Done," he said. "All done. What do you think?"

Sam knew his friend was no artist, but then, he didn't know of anybody who'd ever tried to make a horse and chariot from fire, either.

"It looks great," he said. "Do you think it'll really fly?"

"Let's find out. Come on."

"Me?"

"Sure."

Sam approached the chariot carefully. The heat was nearly overwhelming. He couldn't understand why it didn't bother Gene. He lifted a hesitant foot and put it on the floor of the cart. Gene jumped past him and took up the fiery reins. The smell of melting rubber hit Sam's nose a moment before his foot registered the heat. He jerked back.

"I can't get on there," he said.

"Bummer," Gene said. "Well, I have to try it out. I won't be gone long." "Whatever."

Gene turned around and flicked the reins. "Giddyup," he called, clicking his tongue.

The horse took a stumbling step forward, not all his legs being the exact same length. The wheels of the chariot rolled. The horse adjusted himself to his handicap and broke into a trot, unfolding his long, pointy wings as he moved. He flapped his wings as he increased his speed.

"Up, up and away," Gene shouted, slapping the beast with the reins.

Sam watched, his mouth open, as the burning horse and chariot lifted off the earth. The horse's hooves pawed at the air; its wings sent waves of heat pounding onto the ground, scattering sparks from the wood fire. Sam jumped around, stamping on the burning embers as Gene circled the old oil pump.

Sam looked up in time to see Gene wave to him once. Even from the ground, Sam could see the wild light in his friend's eyes. Gene looked as if he was so happy he had gone insane.

"I am Apollo, god of the sun," he shouted as he forced the horse higher into the air.

Sam watched as the glowing contraption ascended into the night sky. He wondered if anyone from town would see it and report a UFO sighting. How high could Gene make it go? What was it like to be up there, riding the night? Sam sighed and shook his head. He went to Gene's bike and took a drink from the water bottle.

He heard the jet approaching and didn't think anything of it at first. Small jet airplanes flew into town fairly often. He put the water bottle back on Gene's bike and looked up for the chariot.

He saw the blinking red lights of the jet first. The plane was moving fast, coming from the southeast. Sam looked around and finally found Gene. He clutched at the bicycle seat and almost screamed.

The horse made of fire seemed to have broken free of the chariot. The horse was flying north, very high—higher even than the descending jet. Sam saw the chariot and he knew it was falling, tumbling end over end, coming to crash onto the earth like a tiny comet.

The tail of the jet ripped through the fiery fabric of the chariot, shredding it into dozens of tinier flames and scattering them across the heavens like dying stars.

Sam did scream then. He screamed and screamed as a shadow fell from the sky. As the shadow fell toward the glow of the city lights, Sam was able to see flailing arms and legs.

Then Gene disappeared from sight. Sam, however, kept screaming.

Ghosts

"Damn woman!" Rick Hilliard spat a mouthful of green toothpaste into the sink and jammed the toothbrush back into his mouth. He scrubbed furiously, spat, rinsed, and turned off the water. "Watch your TV if that's what you want. You don't have to talk to me. You don't have to act like you care. I try to talk to you. I try to do all the things you say you want, and I'm lucky if you only ignore me. Fine!"

He left the bathroom and went into the adjoining master bedroom, tore the covers down on the bed, and flung himself under them. He took a book from the night table, opened it, but couldn't read. He slammed the book back onto the table. "That magic box! That television means more to you than I do. Fine. I don't even care anymore. I can be just as cold as you can. Why did I ever marry you? If I had it to do over again, I'd do it different. I could have had—"

The words died a sudden death. A man stepped from the bathroom Rick had just left. The intruder approached the bed slowly but deliberately. Rick scrambled to a sitting position and reached for the drawer of the night table, hoping he could get his hand on the .38 Special before the stranger killed him.

"Don't bother, Rick," the man said. His voice was familiar. Rick hesitated, his hand poised over the handle of the drawer.

"Who the hell are you?" he asked. The man sat down on the bed. The light from the reading lamp revealed his face. Rick felt his insides sag, then clench. "Who are you?"

"Who do I look like?"

"You look like..." Rick didn't want to say it. The word stuck in his throat, coated his tongue, and crashed against his teeth. Finally it fell from his lips. "Me. You look like me."

"Amazing, isn't it?" The familiar face smiled at him. There were some differences: the man's hair was shorter than Rick wore his, the crooked tooth was straight and the scar Rick had received from a jagged piece of metal a year ago was missing. "Not exactly the same, are we?"

"Who are you?"

"Call me Melinda's Husband."

"Melinda? Melinda who?"

"What were you saying before I came in?"

Rick groped back to his anger and remembered what he had been thinking. "I...I was saying I could have married someone else. I could have had—Melinda."

The man's smile grew broader. "Yes, Melinda Graves. I'm her husband."

"Bullshit. She married a guy named Jim. A short guy with a dark complexion."

"You don't understand, Rick. I am you, as you think you would be if you had married Melinda."

"What?"

"I brought some friends with me." Melinda's Husband waved his hand and Rick saw that the room was crowded with misty figures bearing his own features. Three figures more solid than the others approached them. Rick pressed himself against the headboard of his bed. His blood chilled and seemed to have stopped moving, though his heart pounded as if ready to explode. He felt as if he were looking into a multi-faceted mirror, facing himself, except the eyes of the four men now standing near or sitting on his bed all seemed empty, sad. One of the new men wore a uniform with a patch that read *Foreman*. Another had long hair and black fingernails. The third also wore a uniform, with a number stenciled on one breast.

"Who are they?" Rick asked.

"This is Foreman." Melinda's Husband pointed to the first one. "He is what you think you would be if you had taken that job offer in Kansas City. That's Rock Star, who you might have become if you had stuck with your guitar lessons. And Convict. Remember when you thought about killing your boss at that retail store?"

"But I didn't do it," Rick said. "Who are you people? Why do you look like me? Why do you look...hollow?" He glanced back at the crowd standing silently between him and the bathroom door. "They look like ghosts."

"We're all ghosts," Melinda's Husband said. "Some of us are just stronger than others."

"I don't understand," Rick whispered. "What—?"

"Do you remember November third, 1982?" Melinda's Husband asked. "Your friend Bryan had Melinda on the phone. She said she'd go out with you if you'd ask her yourself. Bryan handed you the phone, but you couldn't ask. You couldn't decide between Melinda and Janet. But finally you decided on Janet and handed the phone back without saying anything."

"How do you know that?" Even over his shock, Rick could hear Melinda's voice as it had sounded coming through the phone that day when Bryan passed the receiver to him. *I'll go out with him, but he has to ask.*

"I was born in that moment," the shade was speaking again. "We are all ghosts of decisions you made and later wondered if you had made the right choice. If you had chosen Melinda instead of Janet, you may be talking to Janet's Husband tonight."

"But I didn't. I married Janet. She's downstairs right now, watching television. You can't exist."

"But I do exist. And I will continue for as long as you wonder what would have happened if you had dated and married Melinda."

"And them?" Rick looked at the other three men standing beside his bed.

"You have given birth to a lot of us," Melinda's Husband answered, waving toward the silent, staring crowd. "Many of them are already dead. Many others are dying. They are all weak. These are three you have not allowed to fade yet. Soon, I think Convict will be a shadow like those others. You don't think much about that man you wanted to kill anymore, do you?"

"No."

"Rock Star seems to come and go. You're not sure you made the right decision in giving up the guitar lessons. Sometimes you think you did, other times you really want to be on the stage. Foreman is new to us."

"I could have been a foreman in Kansas City, but Janet wouldn't move. She didn't want to live in a big city. She never wants to do anything."

His burst of emotion seemed to give a spark of energy to the figure named Foreman. The man leaned forward and reached out as if to take hold of Rick's pajama shirt. "Let me die," he said.

"What?" Rick's anger vanished and he pushed himself away from the grasping hand of the ghost.

"It isn't an easy life," Melinda's Husband said. "We can do next to nothing if you're not thinking about us. I'm lucky, I suppose, because you give me so much energy. Sometimes I think I'll live as long as you do. Maybe longer."

"Would I…" Rick looked at Rock Star. "Would I have made it if I stayed with the guitar lessons?"

"I don't know," Melinda's Husband answered. "You think you would have. But you discarded him."

"I wanted to be him." Rick felt something near shame as he looked at the image of himself as he had been a few short years ago.

"You wanted to be all of us, if only for a moment."

"So? I can't go back and become any of you. I can't do anything for you. What do you want from me?"

"We came so you would realize what you just said." Melinda's Husband smiled again. "You really can't go back and become any of us. You have to let us go. Let go of your past and accept who you are and what you've done. You haven't done as poorly as you like to think."

"Can you show me what would have really happened if I had asked Melinda?" Rick leaned forward and looked eagerly at the shape sitting on his bed. "Would we have gotten married?"

"What good would it do you? Your decision was made."

"But you could show me?"

"I could show you one thing with definite clarity," Melinda's Husband answered. "The one thing you already know. I could show you talking on the phone. I could let you hear yourself asking Melinda to go out with you, and you could hear her voice saying yes. That is all. From that moment I could show you nothing. You would have had to decide where to go, what to wear, what to say. Each decision would prompt more decisions."

"More of you would be born?"

"Yes."

"You would die, because I might not become you, and then I'd know it. I'd have to accept it."

"I would die." Melinda's Husband nodded.

"Is that what you want?" Rick looked from Melinda's Husband to Foreman.

"Your wife is turning off the television. She will be coming up the stairs in a moment. My life or death is not for me to decide."

"If I had married Melinda, would I be talking to myself as Janet's husband?"

"Maybe. Maybe you would have been as happy as you like to think you'd be. Maybe you'd never think back to what life might have been like with Janet."

"Maybe—" Rick could hear Melinda's feet on the stairs.

"We must go." Melinda's Husband looked toward the bedroom door. The footsteps were approaching along the hall.

"You'll come back?"

Melinda's Husband shook his head slowly, a smile still on his face, and then he and his shadowy kin faded from sight. Rick started to reach out, to touch the air where his own specter had sat, but didn't—couldn't—do it. He shrank down in the bed and turned off the light just before the bedroom door opened and Janet entered. He didn't move as she got into bed and put an arm around him.

"I'm sorry," she whispered. "I know you put a lot of effort into the dinner and everything. I like the lingerie. I was just wound up from work. Will you forgive me?"

Rick took her hand in his and remembered why he had married the woman. He opened his mouth to answer, to forgive her and offer his own apology. Something caught his eye and he strained to see in the dark room. A shadowy image of himself, angry, grabbed a suitcase and walked quickly toward the bedroom door. The figure vanished as it reached for the door knob.

"Of course I forgive you." Rick squeezed the small hand held in his own. "If I didn't, it might come back to haunt me."

Nocturnal Caress

Last night I visited the Baker house—Pam and Allison Baker of Oklahoma City. I was already under Allison's bed when mother and daughter came home in the evening. I am ancient and I have learned to be patient. I can wait a long, long time before caressing my victims.

I only had to wait a few hours before Allison was mine.

They brought food home with them—hamburgers and fries from a chain restaurant. After eating, Allison came into her bedroom, picked up a ball and a jump rope and went outside to play. Pam stayed in the living room; I could hear the television playing a rerun of *The Simpsons*. Allison was back in the house an hour later. Darkness comes early in the winter.

Sweet, sweet darkness.

Pam went to take a shower. Allison changed the channel on the television and became fascinated by a program about a young woman and her friends who slay vampires. I knew this would happen. It was this premonition that drove me to hide under Allison's bed. Seven-year-old little girls are not meant to watch such shows.

That's exactly what Allison's mother said when she came back from her shower. She changed the television program and sent Allison to get ready for her bath. Allison was sulking when she came into her room to prepare for her bath.

I watched from the safe darkness under her little bed as she took clean pajamas from a dresser drawer. I tingled with pleasure as she removed her shoes and began rummaging in a toy box, searching for something to play with in the bathtub.

Slowly, stealthily, I reached a hand from the safety of the bed. Between her rolled-down pink sock and the cuff of her purple pants a strip of smooth white flesh was visible. Gently, oh so gently, I stroked that little flash of soft skin.

She jumped. They always jump at first. I am ancient and I have learned to be quick. I was back under the bed before the child turned to see what had brushed her ankle. Of course, she didn't see me. She left the room without a toy. She returned to her mother. I heard the conversation.

"Mommy, something grabbed my leg."

"What? When?"

"Just now. In my room. I think it's under my bed."

Yes, they're always sure where I am. They just can't find me. I am ancient and have learned to hide myself well.

"There's nothing under your bed, honey. This is what happens when you watch those scary shows. Now go take your bath."

Allison did as she was told. By the time she returned to her bedroom to brush her long blonde hair, she'd forgotten about me. But I was still there. I was still waiting. Her slight weight settling onto the end of the bed was nothing to me. Her little bare feet dangling three inches above the carpet were everything to me.

Her toes were like little beans. Her feet smooth and still stubby with extreme youth. Her ankles were dimpled and sweet and her calves smooth and round where they vanished into a blue nightgown.

Again, I reached for her. Yes, my touch is cold and dry and I know that it is not a pleasant sensation when I make contact with my human victims. That is of no concern to me. I touched little Allison's right ankle, skimming down the red bottom of her foot to spread her toes.

I should not chuckle at the way she jerked and jumped off the bed. The hairbrush she'd been using fell to the floor and bounced twice on the carpet. Allison, poor dear, was almost crying as she explained to Pam that there really was something under her bed. Really, really.

I saw them coming toward me. Two sets of bare feet, four naked ankles. They paused at the end of the bed. Pam's lovely toenails were painted a soft blue with sprinkles of glitter in the polish. Her hand came down, her long fingers—with nails painted to match her toes—came down and scooped up the dropped hairbrush.

"There's nothing there, Allison," Pam's voice said again.

Then Pam settled to the floor, folding her long bare legs under her—her nightgown was much shorter than that of her chaste little daughter, coming only about halfway down her silky thighs. She raised up the edge of the bedspread and her face looked into mine.

She could not see me, of course. I am ancient and I have learned to become invisible. I studied Pam as she gazed half-heartedly under Allison's bed. She had soft pink lips and large brown eyes. Long blonde hair.

I wanted to touch her, but I knew it was best to wait. I had to finish with Allison first.

"See honey, there's nothing there."

"But something touched me. I felt it," Allison argued.

"There's nothing. Come and look."

"No. I don't want to."

"Come on and get in bed. I'll tuck you in."

I watched Allison's pudgy little feet move around the bed. She didn't let them dangle as she settled onto the bed, but pulled them up quickly. Oh, it was hard not to reach out and touch Pam's lovely ankles with my cold caress. Her very toes came under the shadow of the bed, but still I refrained.

Finally, the mother walked away. She turned off the bedroom light and pulled the door so that it was almost completely closed.

I was alone in the dark with little Allison.

Few children have the ability to lie still when they sleep. Even when they do, it is no matter to me. I am ancient and have learned to control my temperature, which in turn affects the temperature of the air around me. I made myself hot. Very hot. Soon, Allison was tossing around on the bed above me, trying to get out from under the blankets in her sleep.

And then…her little foot flopped over the side of the bed and hung before me. Tiny blonde hairs were backlit from the sliver of light coming into the bedroom through the space between the door and the jamb.

With trembling fingers, I touched the smallest of her toes, plucked at it like a boy in a berry patch. She twitched but did not pull away. I leaned from the dusty darkness under her bed and softly kissed her ankle. My dry, withered tongue slid between my parched lips and caressed the softness of her instep.

She woke up screaming. I laughed softly and withdrew to the darkness under the bed where I could watch her little feet hit the floor and run from the room.

There was no way, she explained to her mother, that she was going back in there as long as the monster was under her bed. Pam gave up the fight.

"Come on, Allison, you can sleep in my bed with me."

I am ancient and I have learned to move quietly. Allison was already in her mother's bed when I entered Pam's bedroom. Nobody saw me move through the open door. Pam sat on the side of the bed, setting the time on an alarm clock. I scuttled between her soft naked feet to the safety under her bed. She screamed and raised her feet.

"What was that?"

"What happened, Mommy?"

"I thought I felt something run between my feet. Like a cat. Only...only it didn't feel hairy."

"It's the monster!" Allison yelled.

I laughed until my ancient eyes each produced one single tear.

"There's no monster," Pam said. "Maybe it was just a draught of cold air."

"It's the monster."

"Hush, Allison. Hush. There's no monster. I'll look under the bed."

"No, Mommy. He'll get you if you do that."

"Let me go, Allison. I'm going to look."

She did. Pam knelt on the floor and leaned over to look under her own bed, just as she had looked under her daughter's. I was having fun. I reached out with an invisible arm and quickly, lightly traced a finger along the soft line of her jaw.

Oh, she screamed and jumped so high. I laughed and laughed. Allison screamed and I laughed some more.

Pam jumped into the bed and pulled the covers up.

"What happened Mommy? Did you see the monster?"

"Go to sleep," Pam said. "There's nothing under there. I didn't see anything. There's nothing."

Oh no, there's nothing under the bed. Nothing but me. Nothing but Fear. The women remained awake until morning, finally slipping into a light sleep after the sun began lighting the bedroom windows. I slipped away, my work finished, my fun over. Pam and Allison will not forget me for a long time. They may never let their lovely feet linger near the shadows under their beds for fear I will reach out and caress them again.

No matter. There are others. So many other beds, so many other feet.

Tonight I will be in Newport, Oregon. A boy named Daniel McComb is reading a scary story despite his mother's warnings.

I am ancient, and I love disobedient children.

Particles

The town of Buzzard, Oklahoma, was dead. Once, it had been a contented little village beside a moderate-sized lake renowned for its population of big mouth bass and crappie. People came from as far away as Virginia and Wyoming to fish in Buzzard Lake. The town sustained itself on tourist dollars. Then the lake died. The town soon followed and, like fleas leaving the cooling corpse of a dead dog, those residents with means left Buzzard to its decay.

Missy Goldblum remembered the day the lake died. She had been six years old and one of the people who went to the beach early that July morning—she went to the beach early every day she was not in school, looking for objects left behind by fishermen and sunbathers. That day, the beaches had been covered in dead fish. By 10 a.m., the fish were baking in the summer sun, filling the town with the rotten stench of watery death. Fishermen reported that there didn't seem to be a single fish left alive in the lake; nothing was taking the bait they threw into the water.

That was two years ago. The dead fish were gone, but Missy knew the lake was still dead—it was truly a "body" of water, she often thought. Still, every morning when she did not have to go to school, Missy went to the lake and roamed the deserted beaches; even sunbathers did not come to Buzzard Lake anymore. Usually, nobody came but Missy. That's why she was the first to find the dead heart of the lake.

She left the crumbling blacktop road that led from the town to the lake and pushed her way through the trees and weeds toward the beach. When she stepped out of the brush and faced the lake, she saw the thing resting in the sand.

The object was roughly one hundred feet long and about half that wide across its middle. It was about ten feet tall at its highest point, tapering toward the ends. The thing was gray-black in color with patches of thick, liquid-looking black. As Missy watched, one of the smaller wet black spots shrank, hardened and began to turn gray.

Missy walked around the thing to stand between it and the lake. It reminded her suddenly of a giant slug. The sand of the beach was packed smooth where the thing had come out of the water. Missy reached out and touched the side of the mass. The gray-black matter crumbled like dust beneath her fingers, floating in the still air. She breathed some of it and her asthma immediately kicked in, making her hitch and wheeze.

Frantically, Missy shoved a hand into the pocket of her jeans and pulled out her yellow inhaler. She took a puff of the medicine, remembering her mother telling her to use it sparingly because she couldn't have another one until the first of next month.

Missy thought about touching one of the darker, wetter spots, but decided they just looked too slimy. She backed away from the thing and stepped into the water. She quickly jumped out and turned to look at the lake.

She could remember how the water used to be clear at the shore, growing to a blue-green as the lake deepened, the waves sparkling in the sunlight. Now, the water seemed thicker, blacker. Even on an August afternoon the water remained deathly cold and it took a good stiff breeze to produce even the slightest waves on the water's surface. A stone tossed into the water vanished with barely a sound or splash, swallowed forever.

Missy looked back to the monstrous thing the lake had vomited onto the beach. She walked around it again, noting that most of the wet-looking places had dried up. She started back for the road, back to town to tell her father.

She passed bait shops and gas stations that had been closed for a long time, their windows boarded over, the boards bearing messages from teenagers who were angry about living in the dead town. Missy began to run as she neared the convenience store, the first business establishment that was still open. A few men sat outside the store sipping beer from brown bottles. She felt their eyes on her but ignored them.

A black cat jumped out of a trash dumpster and ran past her as Missy reached the post office. She tripped and fell. An older man with long, greasy brown hair cackled and pointed from his place on the post office steps. Missy got up, brushed off her clothes, and continued up Main Street.

She turned off Main and walked past houses with chipped and fading paint, some with half-dressed, dirty children playing in yards that were lucky if they were dotted with a few green weeds. At her own home, Missy jumped over the missing steps of her front porch with the sagging roof. The wooden screen door slammed behind her as she went into the house.

"Missy, is that you?" her mother called from the kitchen.

"Yes," Missy answered. Another asthma attack was squeezing gently at her chest but she fought off the urge to use her inhaler. She took deep breaths—in through her nose, out through her mouth—and the wheeze faded slowly from her breathing.

"Are you okay?" Her mother had come to the doorway between the kitchen and living room, a half-peeled potato in one hand. Her red-and-white striped maternity blouse was stretched tight over her belly.

"Yes," Missy said. "Where's Dad? There's something on the beach."

"He's out back."

Missy found her father in his work shed. He was painting a flowerpot. Once, his decorated pots had been just a hobby. Now, painting them and carrying them to various flea markets was his way of supplementing the checks the state sent to help provide for his family. Missy watched as he carefully finished the curve of a vibrant green leaf on a rose stem.

"Dad?"

He gently put the flowerpot down and turned to her, reaching out a hand and gathering her onto his lap. "What do you need, Muffin?" he asked. His tired eyes and unshaved cheeks made him look twenty years older than his real age of thirty-one.

"I found something on the beach," Missy said. "Something weird."

"What is it?"

"I don't know," she said. "It looks like a giant slug, or maybe a huge liver. It's great big and gray, but I think it used to be black because there's black spots on it. Those are shrinking away, though. When you touch it, it crumbles like ashes in a fireplace."

"How big is this thing?"

"I don't know...about as big as two school buses, I guess."

"Now Muffin, where do you think something like that would come from?" His sad, smiling eyes said he didn't believe her. "I think maybe you've been watching too much TV or reading too many scary books. Why don't you go help your mom clean the house?"

"But Dad, there's really something there. Won't you come look at it? Please?"

He sighed and glanced back at his flowerpot. "There's really something there?" he asked. He sounded hopeful. Missy nodded, and he nodded in return. "Let's go," he said. "We'll take the car."

They parked the smoking, coughing Pontiac in the lot near a boat ramp and walked through the woods to the beach. Fred Goldblum let out a low, slow whistle when he saw the thing laying on the sand under the noon sun.

"I'll be damned," he said.

Together, they walked around the mass. Missy noticed that the black splotches had completely disappeared. Her father carefully touched the surface, causing a chunk of the thing to fall off. It exploded into a cloud of dust when it hit the ground. Missy and her father both began sneezing. Missy pulled her inhaler from her pocket and had to take two deep puffs to get her breathing under control.

"What do you think it is, Dad?" she asked when she was able to get her breath.

"I don't know, Muffin, but we better get you away from it. You'll use up all your inhaler if any more of that thing falls off." They started back toward the car. "I'm going to take you home, then I'll go by the police station and tell Chief Payne. He'll probably have to call in some state people…"

"Do you think that thing is what killed all the fish?" Missy asked.

"I don't know, Muffin. I don't know. Maybe."

Missy's asthma had returned with a vengeance before they got back to the house. She hurried inside, pulling her inhaler from her pocket as her father gunned the little Pontiac back toward Main Street.

The inhaler did little good. Missy couldn't help her mother with the housework; any exertion left her gasping for air.

"Why don't you go lie down," her mother suggested.

Missy went to her bedroom but couldn't lie still. The inability to draw breath caused her to thrash and roll on her bed. Her mother came to the door and leaned against the frame for a moment, a worried look on her face. She went to Missy's closet.

"Okay, honey, I'll get the oxygen," Laura Goldblum said. She pulled out a large green cylinder on a wheeled cart and pushed it to the head of Missy's bed. "Hold still." She put the clear plastic cup over her daughter's mouth and nose, then turned a valve on the oxygen tank. "Okay Missy, breathe deep."

Missy did. After a few deep breaths, she felt her airways relaxing somewhat. Laura turned down the valve on the tank.

"Thanks, Mom," Missy said, her voice muffled by the mask. She knew the oxygen was expensive. She took the mask off. "I'll be okay now."

"You sure?"

Missy nodded and watched as her mother closed the valve on the tank. "It makes me tired. Can I go to sleep?"

"Yes, for a while," Laura said.

Missy woke up an hour later, her mother shaking her gently. "Missy, I'm going to the lake with your dad. We're going to go look at the thing you found. Everyone's going. Do you want to come?"

Missy thought about it for a moment. She knew she'd be treated special because she found the thing first. But the thought of how the dust from the object affected her asthma decided her.

"No," she said, shaking her head. "It hurts me to breathe around it. I'll stay here."

Her parents had been gone for about forty-five minutes when Missy heard the wind pick up outside. It began to howl suddenly. She knew from the smell that came in through the open windows that the wind was blowing over the dead lake. She decided the heat would be better than the smell, so she went through the house and closed all the windows.

A few minutes later and her neighbors began returning home. Some walked, others came in old cars. All of them were sneezing and holding hands over their faces. When Fred and Laura Goldblum came home, they were also sneezing. By that time, Missy was back in bed, her oxygen mask over her face, the tank's valve cracked just a little as she drew greedily at the gas.

"What happened?" she asked through the mask when her parents came into her room. They were both wiping at their eyes and noses.

"The damn wind came up and started blowing that thing apart," Fred said. "It's blowing all that dust—or ash or whatever the thing was made of—right into town." He stopped, looked at his daughter's heaving chest and at the green tank. "You going to be okay, Muffin?"

Missy nodded. She breathed deeply, wishing she could turn up the amount of oxygen she was getting, but not daring to use so much.

Hours crept by. Despite the closed windows, the dust blowing through the town crept into the houses. Laura and Fred continued sneezing and wiping their eyes and noses. Missy kept her oxygen mask clamped firmly over her face. There was no sound except the wind outside—no children playing, no cars moving on the street.

Night came. Sometime during the darkest part of the night, the wind died as suddenly as it had sprung to life. About an hour later, Missy was jerked out of a light sleep by the screaming of her father.

"Laura! Laura!" he called. "Come here!" He was in the bathroom. Missy heard her mother run from their bedroom to the bathroom. She heard her mother gasp.

"What is that?" Laura asked.

"I don't know what the hell it is," Fred answered, his voice shrill.

Laura screamed suddenly. "It's on me, too. It's on me!"

"Oh my God," Fred shouted.

"Missy!" Laura yelled. They both hurried to their daughter's room, flicking on the light and blinding Missy in the sudden glare.

Before Missy could ask what was happening, her parents had stripped the blankets off her and were pulling at her pajamas. Then Missy saw that the left side of her father's abdomen was a mass of dark green gelatin—so green it was almost black. He was only wearing his briefs. The rest of his skin was shiny with perspiration. Missy turned her wide eyes to her mother and saw that Laura had a similar growth spreading from her right armpit and disappearing beneath her nightgown.

"What—" She pointed.

"I don't know," Fred snapped. "Do you have any of it on you?"

Missy helped them tear off her pajamas until she sat before them in nothing but her thin underwear. She didn't have any patches of the jelly-like substance growing on her.

"You can't wipe it off?" she asked.

Fred shook his head. Missy saw that the stuff had spread up her father's side to his armpit and the underside of his arm.

"It looks like the wet patches I saw on that thing by the lake, before it dried up," Missy said.

Her parents looked at her, their eyes large and scared, but before they could speak, a woman screamed outside. Fred and Laura started for the front door. Their movements stirred up the dust in the room, triggering Missy's asthma. She retreated to her oxygen mask. A few minutes later, Laura returned.

"That was Dawn Warren. She has it, too. So do her kids," Laura said. She sighed. "I feel so tired." She got up and moved away, back toward her bedroom. Missy could see that the gelatin had spread up her mother's shoulder blade to the nape of her neck.

Missy hunched under her thin sheet, listening to the voices in the night. People were screaming and wailing all around the house. Her father returned. She saw him for a moment; he had put on a robe, but she could see that his chest and the insides of his thighs had turned to jelly. He went to his bed and was quiet.

Morning came silently. Missy slipped out of her bed and crept toward her parents' bedroom. She stopped in the doorway, her hands clamped over her face. Her mother and father were gone, replaced by one pulsing mass of green-black gelatin that lay on the bed in the shape of a man and woman snuggled together—a large lump protruding in the front of what would have been the pregnant woman. Missy ran back to her room and hid under the bed.

Soon, she heard squishy noises coming from her parents' bedroom. She peeked from under the bed and saw the thing that had been her mother and father lurch past her bedroom toward the front door. The screen door slammed behind it. The porch creaked under its weight. Missy scooted from her hiding place and went to the living room window.

The thing was joined in the street by her neighbors, all of who had also become walking blobs of deep green gelatin. They shuffled along the street, all heading toward Main Street, where they turned and directed their steps for Buzzard Lake. Missy saw two of the figures bump into one another; they stuck together, melded into one another and becoming one larger, lumbering mass.

She sank down to the floor. She sat there for a long time. Finally, she climbed to her feet and looked out the window again. There was nothing moving outside. Missy put on her clothes and left the house, moving slowly toward the lake.

The weeds and trees between the road and the lake were flattened. Streaks of blackish goo showed that the residents of Buzzard had joined to form one huge mass and had simply crushed anything that came between them/it and the water. Missy followed the trail to the edge of the lake.

The dead thing she had found the day before was gone without a trace. Water lapped the sand like gentle laughter. Missy looked down into the clear fluid and let her gaze travel outward, toward the center of the lake, where the water deepened and turned dark green. She felt tears on her face. She thought of the flowerpot her father had been working on and how it would never be finished now. She thought of the baby brother or sister she would never know and how she would never get to make pancakes with her mom again. She turned around and went home.

Missy returned to the beach every day, hoping the lake would give her parents back to her. She knew it was a foolish hope. There was never any sign of other people. She ate all the food in her house, then timidly entered the town's only grocery store. There was no one in the store. She took only what she needed and hurried home.

A week after the people of Buzzard disappeared, a pickup stopped on the road near where the trees and brush had been flattened. Missy was sitting on the beach. She stood up and turned to watch the uniformed man walk toward her from the pickup. The man looked at the broken trees with great interest. He stopped beside her.

"What happened here?" he asked.

"I don't know," Missy answered.

"Why is there no one in town?"

Missy only looked at him. She was young, but she knew enough to know the man wouldn't believe her if she told him the truth. A patch on the man's shirt said he worked for the state Wildlife Department.

"Everyone just left," Missy said.

"Even your folks?"

Missy nodded.

"Why didn't you go with them?"

"I have asthma," she said. "I was breathing from an oxygen tank, so I couldn't go."

The man's face crinkled and Missy knew she had probably said too much. "They just left?" he asked. "You don't know where they went? When did they leave? I talked to the police chief last week. He said something had washed up out of the lake."

"It's gone now," Missy said.

The man started to say something else, but was interrupted by a loud splash. Missy looked out over the lake just in time to see a young bass flop back into the water.

"I'll be dogged," the man said. "It looks like this old lake might be coming back to life."

Success

The wind had gusted around the two figures at the side of the Choctaw Creek train depot in northern Oklahoma. Dust devils ran down the road, sending most people dodging to the safety of building interiors. The two people on the depot platform stood face to face, clasping each other's hands.

The boy wore a faded flannel shirt under sun-faded and patched denim overalls. When the wind allowed, his black hair hung limply in his face. His feet and ankles were bare and dusty.

The girl wore a white dress, white leather shoes with gold buckles and a pink sun hat held on by a pale blue ribbon tied under her chin. Her entire outfit had been ordered from the Sears and Roebuck catalogue. The wind whipped her skirt wildly around her knees. Her wheat-colored hair blew behind her like a flag. There was a suitcase on either side of her.

"I wish you wouldn't go off and leave me here, Liz," the boy had said to her.

"Call me Elizabeth, please, Henry." Her voice was resigned. They had been through this conversation before. "I'm going to Chicago because I want to. I want to sing and dance and be famous."

"I want you to stay here with me, Liz—Elizabeth. Ain't I good enough for you?"

She had ducked her head and turned away. "It isn't that, Henry. I…I just can't stay here and be nothing. I want to be famous. Can't you understand that?"

"No. I want you to stay here, to marry me someday. Won't you do that, Elizabeth?"

"No! Henry, I can't. I just can't. You didn't even finish school. You can barely read or write. Henry, all you can do is farm. I want to be more than just a farmwife."

Henry stepped back as if he had been slapped. His brow knitted together and his eyes dropped to the platform floor. He reached a hand to his face, as if the wound were visible, then dropped it, but could not look at the girl.

173

"If I…if I do something with myself—"

"You can't, Henry." She faced him. Tears ran down her cheeks, leaving pale tracks in her makeup. She rubbed her eyes and sniffled.

A whistle split the air and she jumped.

"I have to go now, Henry."

She picked up her two suitcases and gave one last long look at the illiterate farm boy she had known, and maybe even loved, all her life. She kissed him quickly on the mouth, then hurried away to where the conductor was helping the last passengers board the train.

Henry stood where she had left him, two shameless tears running down his dusty face.

The train whistled again, then chugged to life. As it passed the side of the depot, Henry saw her in a window seat. She didn't look at him, but he saw the tears running down her face.

The train rumbled out of his life, taking her with it.

* * *

The man in the gray business suit pulled his thoughts back through the picture window of his sixth floor office. Once again, two shameless tears ran down his face. Above his desk, a gold-embossed plaque read:

Henry Logan, President
Oklahoma Grain, Inc.

He returned his attention to the hand-written letter that had brought the painful memories of youth flooding back.

> *Dear Henry,*
>
> *It's been so long since that day at the train depot. I was a foolish little girl with stars in my eyes. But worse, I made you feel like a fool. I'm very sorry. I wish I could tell you just how sorry I am.*
>
> *That was nineteen years ago, and this is the first time I've even written to you. I'm so ashamed of how I've acted.*
>
> *I'm writing to tell you that I'm coming home. You probably know that I never became anything, just another candle trying to be a star. I hope you can forgive me, but if you can't, well, I wouldn't blame you.*
>
> *I hope you will meet me when I come in on the train. Please*

Henry, be at the depot when I come home.
   Love,
   Liz

Henry looked at the envelope again. It had been sent to his parents' address in Choctaw Creek. His mother had forwarded it to his Oklahoma City office, along with another envelope. He reached for the second envelope, his hand quaking.

Inside was a short note in his mother's handwriting. And a newspaper clipping. He read the note first.

   Henry,
   I was so sorry to hear this news. I almost didn't send it to you,
   but I knew you'd want to know.
   Mom

He reached for the newspaper clipping. It was a tiny obituary from the *Choctaw Creek Daily Times.*

   Elizabeth Sue Bartley will be brought home for burial services on June 3.
   Born December 16, 1938, Miss Bartley died of an overdose of sleeping pills while in an obvious state of deep depression on May 30.
   She is survived by her mother, Charity Bartley.
   Miss Bartley will arrive by train in Choctaw Creek at noon, June 3. Services will be held at the Church of God on June 4. Burial will be at Faith Memorial Cemetery.

Henry returned his tear-filled eyes to the window. "I'll be there, Liz," he murmured. "I promise."

A Change of Clothes

It was just after 10:30 p.m. and the clothes were coming to life.

Walt Higgins stood behind the door leading to the cleaning room, watching the garments through a small triangular window. He enjoyed this spectacle regularly, as he had since his father first showed him the clothing and how it had a life of its own, residue from the people who wore the garments. Walt had come back to the dry cleaning shop after hours at least once a week ever since. The clothes had never minded.

But lately something was different. Walt's hand toyed with a small butane cigarette lighter.

A brown suit, tailored to fit Mayor Russell's ample paunch, shrugged itself off its hanger and fell to the floor. Quickly, it gathered itself and stood upright, the empty sleeves of the arms adjusting the vest and straightening the crease in the pants. The sleeves also reached up to adjust a tie, not seeming to notice that the tie was absent. The suit walked toward a switch on the wall close to the door where Walt hid. The garment moved with Mayor Russell's casual swagger, reached up and turned the switch to the ON position. Soft instrumental music filled the shop.

Other articles of clothing pulled themselves from the hangers. Business suits, conservative dresses, sport coats and slacks, leather mini skirts and formal dinner gowns all came to life. Even the blue jeans and blouse of the young girl who worked in the drug store across the street from Higgins' Cleaning were getting off their hangers and shaping themselves to the contours of her absent body.

Walt couldn't help but grin as he watched the mayor's suit walk nervously past the rack where Mrs. Russell's latest designer dress was delicately sliding off the paper-covered hanger. The mayor's brown suit went to where his secretary's low-cut red dress was tangled in the hook of its hanger. The suit helped the dress free itself, and after standing facing each other for a moment, the two began to dance slowly to the wordless music. One of the mayor's suit arms was resting on the curve of the dress's empty ass.

All around the room, the garments collected themselves into small groups, some dancing as the mayor and his secretary did, others apparently in conversation. Some of the clothing bounced as if the unseen occupants were laughing. The white wedding gown brought in by the mother of a young girl jilted at the altar stood alone in a corner and shook with the memory of its owner's sobs.

Then Walt saw it. The thin black suit of the traveling evangelist who had come into town about a week ago was the last to leave its hanger. It majestically walked to the switch on the wall and turned the music off with a smart click.

Every garment in the room stopped what it was doing and looked at the minister's suit. Walt pressed his ear to the door, hoping to listen, but he heard only the soft whisperings of cloth. The other garments seemed to understand, however. They rustled in return. They seemed to be objecting to something by the quick, sharp sounds of the fabric. The evangelist's suit hissed back, and even Walt could feel the authority of the garment.

What could it be saying?

It didn't matter. Walt had seen the outcome of the sermons delivered by the empty suit. He flicked the switch of the lighter, but let the flame die out. If he could only hear...

Since arriving in town, the evangelist had brought his suits for Walt to clean. One every day. The preacher sweated tremendously during his orations.

And every day after that first time, things had been happening to Walt's customers. Strange things.

Ben Hurley, one of the few customers who brought neck ties in with his cleaning, had been found hanging from a rafter in his basement, dangling by one of the ties Walt had cleaned the first day the evangelist brought in a suit.

Louise Duncan had actually burst into flame while wearing a polyester dress she had picked up just the day before. Dr. Duane Benson, an old friend of Walt's, had examined the body and said it was one of those strange cases of human combustion—unexplainable.

Leroy Nicklas had been strangled by his starched shirt collar while walking from his office to his car. He had fallen on the sidewalk, clawing at his throat. A passerby had seen him fall and rushed to help, thinking Leroy was choking on a bit of food. By the time they had the collar open, it was too late.

All strange deaths, and no explanation found for any of them. Walt suspected the cause of the deaths was originating in his shop.

He had gone to one of the evangelist's tent revival meetings. The minister's name was Thackery Stick. He had exuded a magnetism that Walt found nauseating, though other townsfolk had acted as if they were in the presence of God himself. Much as he hadn't liked the man, Walt had been unable to leave the meeting until it was over. The minister was like a cobra, holding his audience spellbound as he danced before them, waiting to strike.

Walt decided he couldn't let the killings go on any longer. He didn't know why or how the garments were killing their wearers, but he knew he was maybe the only person in town who understood that the clothing retained some life after it was removed. It was up to him to do something.

He banged open the door leading from the front of his shop to the cleaning room and charged inside. He shoved his fist into the dark fabric of the evangelist's suit and flicked his thumb on the lighter. His hand was sweaty and his hold on the switch that sent butane to the flame slipped. He tried to flick the lighter again, but didn't have the chance.

The arms of the suit coat enveloped him and squeezed. Walt heard the rustling of cloth as the suit's congregation moved forward. *Will they help me?* He tried to crane his head around to see. He could feel the menace coming from the haunted clothes. Their anger was directed at him.

Walt redoubled his efforts against the suit, but soon realized it was useless to fight; he was too old and weak to tear the cloth to shreds and he wasn't even sure that would solve the problem. He remembered Mickey Mouse and his broom in *Fantasia*. Walt lifted the hand with his lighter to the back of the suit coat and flicked the switch, ready to burn with the garment.

The fabric ignited quickly, and it seemed to feel the pain. It released Walt, and he fell to the floor, gasping for breath. The suit tried to beat out the flames on its back, but only succeeded in catching the arms of the coat on fire. The congregation of clothing fell back, afraid to help their newfound leader. The suit collapsed to the floor and quickly became smoldering ash.

Walt got to his feet, fully aware that for the first time in his life he was standing among the haunted clothes. He looked at them, unsure how to behave.

The garments advanced on him. A crowd of roughly thirty sets of clothing, empty clothes he had watched dance and play for over forty years of his life. The empty arms of suits, dresses, blouses and jackets lifted toward him, wanting him.

What will they do with me?

He didn't stay to find out. Walt dropped his butane lighter among the ashes of Thackery Stick's burned suit and ran for the front of his store. He pulled the door open and rushed into the chill night.

Crowding the streets were the garments of the town's people. Horrified, Walt saw that some of the outfits still held the dead bodies of their occupants. Walt saw his brother, Phil, among the garments—his eyes popped and his thick tongue protruding between swollen lips. There were others, but Walt didn't have time to count friends. The clothes had noticed him, and were moving toward his store.

Walt started to retreat, but found the clothes inside his store had reached the front door and were trying to pull it open. He turned back and was faced with two fresh terrors.

Thackery Stick was standing about two feet in front of him, dead. The thin body seemed to be crushed within another of the black suits. Only the face was undamaged, except for a look of fear and a trail of dried blood that had run from his mouth. The head hung loosely and rolled as the garment motioned its followers to surround Walt.

There was no need, however. Walt's corduroy pants were beginning to feel very snug.

The Halloween Feast

The air in the car was growing chill. Lewis Robertson stopped the tapping noise he was making with the envelope on the steering wheel. Angrily, he tore the card from the envelope and re-read the words of the invitation.

On the front was a cartoonish picture of a ghoul. In the voice bubble above his head were the words, "Come to a Halloween party!" Inside was an address. Lewis checked for the hundredth time to be sure the address inside the invitation matched that of the building he was parked before; they were the same. He tossed the invitation to the passenger seat of his car.

He stared at the front of the building for a while longer. It was one of many abandoned warehouses along the waterfront, though not in as bad repair as most. Still, there were no other cars here and he had seen no sign of other people in the half-hour he had sat in front of the old building.

Is it a joke?

He hadn't wanted to come to any damn party anyway. He hadn't wanted to do anything for the past month except stay in his dark house and be left alone. He didn't need to work anymore; Beth's life insurance had paid the mortgage as well as all the other bills they had accumulated in their five years of marriage. And the policy they had taken out on little Brandon only two months before had been enough to pay the funeral expenses for both of Lewis's loved ones.

Lewis stopped that train of thought, afraid if he stayed on it he would begin crying again. He didn't want that; recently it had become too hard to stop the tears once they began. He thought instead of his mother and how she had nearly forced him to come to this nonexistent party.

"You haven't left the house in weeks," she had scolded. "This is a golden opportunity to get out and mingle with friends. You need that."

"How do I know this party is being given by any of my friends?" Lewis argued.

"Why else would you have been invited?" she countered. She had nagged until Lewis finally gave in and agreed to attend the party. He knew his mother was only concerned about him being shut up alone and brooding over the accident. She had made the red devil costume he was wearing.

"Shit!" he muttered as he suddenly threw open the car door and stepped out of the vehicle. "Might as well be sure it's just a damn joke." He slammed the door, then straightened his wiry tail behind him, pulled the red mask over his face and charged toward the door of the warehouse. A brisk wind brought the gooseflesh out beneath the thin material of his costume. From the other side of the warehouse, Lewis could hear the steady rhythm of the river slapping against the pilings. Thin fingers of fog drifted toward him, curled around his legs like lovers, then broke apart to reform behind him.

Knock? Or just go in, if the door is unlocked? Lewis reached out and jerked on the door's handle. The wooden door opened with a groan of protest. Lewis quickly stepped inside and let the door close behind him. He was in an office. Another door faced him from the other side of the room. Lewis stepped to it and pulled it open as well. It led into the warehouse itself, and as it closed behind him, Lewis realized he was alone except for two tables in the center of the vast, dimly lighted storage area. He reached behind him for the door handle, ready to leave, angry at himself as well as his mother.

"Lewis, there you are." A hand came down on his shoulder and held him. The grip was cold and heavy. Lewis turned his head to face a tall, muscular man dressed as a Greek warrior. The man smiled, a twinkle in his eyes.

"Do I know you?" Lewis asked.

"Not yet," the man answered. "But we'll have a while to get to know one another."

"Am I the first to get here?" Lewis tried to grin.

"No, you're late. But you're the guest of honor, so it doesn't matter. As long as you're here."

"But I don't see anyone else," Lewis protested.

"Your eyes will adjust."

"Who are you?"

"Who do I look like?"

"I don't know," Lewis answered. "Hercules, or Achilles maybe."

"Odysseus, my friend. Odysseus."

"Okay, fine, but who are you really?"

"Does it matter?"

"I'd like to know."

"You'll know later, though by then I doubt you'll care about me."

"But—"

"Come, Lewis, let's have some punch." The man took him by the arm and led Lewis toward one of the two tables. Lewis could now see that there was a large punch bowl and a single glass on one table. The other was empty.

"One glass?" he questioned.

"Do you need more?" The man picked up the small glass and began stirring the sweet-smelling red punch with a ladle he held in the other hand.

"You miss your wife and child, don't you?" asked the man dressed as Odysseus.

"You know...?" Lewis eyed the man more suspiciously than before.

"We all know." Odysseus nodded. He filled the glass and handed it to Lewis.

Lewis lifted the glass and held it near his mouth, suddenly not sure he should drink. His host sensed his hesitation and laughed.

"It's not poisoned," he said. "Would you like for me to drink some, too?" He lifted the ladle and sipped from it, swallowing loudly.

Grinning sheepishly, but still unsure, Lewis took a small drink from the cup. He swallowed, and then noted the aftertaste: a thick, coppery, salty taste.

"There's blood in here!" He dropped the cup to the table, where it overturned and spread its contents in a shining puddle. "What the hell are you trying to—" Lewis choked on the words as he looked up from the spilled fluid.

"It is Halloween," he heard Odysseus say, but Lewis barely took notice of the words.

The warehouse was filled with people. They stood in bunches and talked amongst themselves, or flitted from group to group carrying news and gossip. Children scuttled among the adults, playing tag, laughing and shouting. Everyone kept glancing toward the table where he stood, Lewis realized, dumbfounded by what he was beholding.

"Your eyes have adjusted?" asked the voice of Odysseus.

"I...But...Where did they come from?"

"The Realm of Death, of course." There was a smile in the man's voice. "Here comes someone you will recognize."

Lewis turned, and his eyes widened as he saw Beth part from the crowd and move toward him, her arms outstretched. He ran to her and they embraced, her cold lips finding his and kissing him passionately.

"I missed you," Beth whispered.

"How can this happen?" Lewis asked, but before Beth could respond, the voice of Odysseus was ringing over the throng.

"Ladies and gentlemen," he called, "Our guest has arrived and tasted the drink we offered. Let the festivities begin." He clapped, and from somewhere came soft, urgent music.

Beth grasped his arms and began leading him in a dance Lewis did not recognize. All around them, other couples paired up and began moving with the rhythm of the music.

"I don't understand," Lewis whispered.

"You don't need to," Beth answered. "Just be with me, dance with me and love me."

Lewis pulled her closer and they danced to the unending music, tears of happiness running down his face.

Finally he was able to ask, "What about Brandon? Is he here?"

"Yes, he's playing with the other kids," Beth said. She looked around, and then pointed. "There he is."

Lewis followed her finger and found his four-year-old son tossing a ball to a girl of about the same age. Brandon's eyes met his, and Lewis saw his son mouth the familiar words, "Hi, Daddy." Then the child waved to him before returning to his game. There was a lump in Lewis's throat and he buried his face on the cold shoulder of his wife.

They danced again for what seemed only moments, but Lewis knew might actually be hours, before the music stopped and Beth put her lips to his ear.

"It's almost midnight. Halloween is almost over, and it's time for you to make a decision."

"Lewis!" Odysseus called from the center of the warehouse. "Come over here, and bring your lovely wife." Arm in arm, Lewis and Beth walked toward the tables.

The punch bowl and spilled glass remained on one table. The other table was still empty, but now Lewis saw that beneath it was another bowl, larger than the punch bowl, and empty.

"Lewis," Odysseus began speaking when the couple stood before him, "We are allowed to return to this world only one day every year. On that day, we must have sustenance, or the next year we may be too weak to return.

"Every year we must search among the living for one willing to help us," the man continued. "One who will feed us."

There arose a murmur from the assembled spirits.

"You have tasted the blood of all those who have gone before you, Lewis. The others who have helped us. It allowed you to see those you believed lost to you. Will you help us, and stay with us now, or will you return to the world of the living?"

"What...what is it you're asking me to do?" Lewis asked as he clutched Beth's arm tighter.

"Feed us from your living veins."

Another murmur from the crowd.

"Kill myself?"

"Yes, slay your body so that your soul may join us," Odysseus answered.

Lewis looked to Beth, and then down at the shadowy image of his son, Brandon, who had come to join them at the table. Brandon smiled up at him.

"It's for you to decide," Beth said quietly. Lewis turned back to her and looked intently into her large, soft eyes. "You can join us now, or wait until your natural time comes. You'll be with us again eventually. But you need to decide now."

"Yes, Lewis, we need your decision now," Odysseus concurred. The horde of spirits murmured once more. He motioned to the table and the bowl, and now Lewis saw a long, curved knife laying on the table. He knew he was supposed to put the glittering blade to his throat, let out the life, and join his family in this shadowy world of death. He reached for the knife.

The crowd shifted and Lewis could feel their excitement, their hunger for him. The knife was cold and heavy in his shaking hand.

"Lie on the table, with your head off the edge so the bowl can catch your offering," Odysseus instructed.

Lewis stepped closer to the table and then stopped. A shudder ran down his body as he considered what he was ready to do. *Suicide.* Slice his own throat open with this razor-sharp blade. His eyes shifted to find Beth and Brandon; their faces were impassive and their thoughts unreadable. He would join them, Lewis thought, just as Beth had said, if not now, eventually.

"I can't," he whispered as he dropped the knife to the table. The spirits became angry, frustrated. He felt something cold being slipped into his right hand, and then his left arm was taken in an equally chill grip. Beth was holding his arm and Brandon had come to hold his father's hand. Lewis felt the warm tears running down his face.

"We'll wait, Daddy," Brandon promised.

"Yes, we have nowhere to go." Beth smiled at him. Lewis nodded. No words would come through his throat.

"But you have somewhere to go, Lewis." The voice of Odysseus was stern and angry. "You must leave here immediately. Go."

184

"Good-bye," Beth whispered. She was fading from his sight as Lewis watched. He reached for her, trying to hold her to him, but she was like a wisp of steam that slipped through his desperate fingers.

"Bye, Daddy." Brandon was already gone, leaving only a cool place in the palm of his father's hand.

Lewis turned and ran from the warehouse as the other ghosts faded. He ignored their curses as well as their pleas. He fumbled for his keys as he ran, then he was in the car and driving, not caring where he went or what route he took.

He drove for hours, and eventually found himself parked on a narrow gravel road that ran beside the river a few miles outside the city limits. It was a favorite spot for fishing. He had brought Beth and Brandon here many times for picnics beside the water. Brandon had caught his first fish, a small, slimy catfish, from this place.

"I should have done it," Lewis said to himself. "I'm weak. I was given the chance to be with them again and I didn't take it because I was scared. Scared of a little physical pain. The damn knife was so sharp I probably wouldn't even have felt the cut. *Damn!*" He slammed his fist against the steering wheel, then rested his head on the balled hand. He was still wearing the red mask, he realized. He pulled it off and tossed it to the floorboard, where it lay with the fallen invitation.

What if it isn't too late?

He restarted the car and swung it around in the road, throwing gravel and dust high and far behind him as he spun the tires and raced back toward the highway.

The eastern horizon was just beginning to turn gray as Lewis reached the warehouse again. He jumped from the car and ran to the door. It was locked. Lewis pulled until his arms ached, but to no avail. He returned to the car and fetched the tire tool. Within minutes, he had splintered the wood around the lock. The mechanism broke loose and fell to the floor inside the building. Lewis hurried through the office and into the warehouse area.

The vast room seemed darker. Only the pale light of the fading stars crept in through dirty windows set high in the walls. Lewis could barely see the tables. He started toward them.

"I'm back," he called to the empty chamber. "I've come to feed you. I want to be with you. Beth! Brandon!" There was no answer. Lewis felt his pointed tail swishing behind him as he walked. He was now close enough to see that something large was laying on the top of one table.

It was the body of a man. A derelict, Lewis guessed by the shabby dress and stench of stale, cheap alcohol that came from the corpse. In the pale light, Lewis could see the long gash in the man's throat. Not a drop of blood remained on the wound. Beneath the man's head, which hung over the edge of the table, just as his own should have done, Lewis saw the large punch bowl, now overturned. Only the faintest smear of crimson gave evidence of what had been contained therein.

Lewis began to weep again. "It should have been me," he moaned. "It should have been me." He began hitting the corpse, pounding the lifeless body as if the tramp were the one to blame for his failure.

Beth and Brandon, his own wife and son, had been forced to take sustenance from this nameless bum, he thought. *Forced to feed from society's waste all because their husband and father was too weak to give them what they needed.* He threw his head back as a sob tore from his body and tears ran from his eyes.

A powerful beam of light hit Lewis full in the face and he staggered back, his arm raised to ward off the illumination. "Hold it right there, buddy!" A man's voice echoed throughout the warehouse. Lewis saw the gun in the man's hand and a glint on the badge pinned to his chest.

Was there an alarm system activated by the breaking of the lock?

"What is it, Bill?" Another man entered the building.

"Somebody dressed as the devil," the fist cop answered. "And it looks like a body on the table there."

"You! On the floor." The second policeman approached Lewis, motioning with his gun for him to lie down.

"You don't understand," Lewis began. *Why bother to explain?*

"On the floor, now!" The cop was moving closer.

"I'm coming, Beth," Lewis whispered. He could feel the chill spot in the palm of his hand where Brandon had held him. Was the hand there again, pulling him forward, begging him to play, to run, to go fishing?

Lewis broke into a run, a smile on his face, the image of a small, green catfish splashing in a river as it was pulled to shore urging him on as he heard his wife's laughter and squeals of delight ringing in his ears.

He didn't hear the exclamation of surprise from the policeman barring his exit. He didn't feel the impact of the bullets as they slammed his body to the floor.

"Hi, Daddy."

He heard Brandon's voice and felt the warm, soft, loving touch of his wife as she helped him up and into a new world of shadows.

Elijah

The small white card read only, "My name is Elijah. I am 367 years old." The card itself was only an ordinary-size business card, the text neatly printed in heavy black letters on a bone-white surface. There was not a word on the card explaining who had sent the caged demon into the young woman's life, or why.

The bird itself would give no explanation. He sat in his gold-wired cage and stared at the woman with small, black, piercingly evil eyes, cocking his head from side to side to utilize both orbs. Then, as if he had lost interest, he began to preen his feathers.

Judy Myers watched as the snow-white parrot combed the underside of first one wing and then the other, drawing his curved black beak slowly through the feathers. He sat on a wooden perch that ran length-wise across his prison. The cage stood in a corner of her living room that only moments ago had been blessedly empty. Judy wished the wooden rod would suddenly burst into flames and charcoal the bird. He looked up from his preening as she thought this, studied her for a moment, then resumed his vain task.

She worked as an interior decorator with her college friend, Suzie. They had recently opened their own office on the seventh floor of the Franklin Tower downtown. They were currently working on a design for Suzie's brother's new law office; it was their second job since beginning the new business.

The day Elijah came into Judy's life, she had just come home from her office. As she stood on the front porch of her side of the rented duplex, Mr. Curtis, the man who rented the other half of the building, emerged from his own front door. When he saw Judy, Mr. Curtis told her that something had come for her while she was at work; he had accepted the delivery on her behalf. He hurried back into his apartment to retrieve it for her.

When Mr. Curtis came out again, Judy felt her heart clinch, skip several beats, and begin to race. He was carrying the birdcage on a tall stand, the black cover thrown back and the evil parrot balancing on the perch, looking around excitedly. When Elijah's small black eyes met Judy's gray ones, they locked there and the two stared at each other for several moments.

Mr. Curtis, smiling, said, "Someone really likes you. This must be an expensive bird." George Curtis was a rather squat man, nearly bald, with only a halo of white above his ears and reddish age spots on the dome of his shiny scalp. He worked as a night watchman at a local bank. Mr. Curtis was a good neighbor, and Judy felt better knowing that he was around the building while she was at work, even if he did sleep most of the day.

"Yes," she stammered in answer to his comment. Judy found the key and opened her door. Mr. Curtis carried the cage inside and put it in the corner Judy pointed out to him. Politely excusing himself, Mr. Curtis left for work.

Now Judy sat on her couch, reading over and over again the words on the card Mr. Curtis said had come with the delivery. *Who would have sent me this bird?* She hated birds—any kind of bird. She loathed them. She feared them. They could fly, could defy the laws of gravity. They could swoop from the sky and strike their victims. She dropped the card onto the coffee table, its white surface now stained with sweat from her fingers. She looked at the birdcage. Elijah was watching her.

"Three hundred and sixty-seven years old," she said, her voice quavering. She didn't believe the bird was really that old. *But parrots live a long time, a very long time, indeed.* She had read that once in a children's encyclopedia. Judy looked away, a shiver running down her spine.

Elijah had not spoken. Judy hoped he had never been taught to speak. *Perhaps his tongue had never been split to allow speech.* Judy wasn't going to get close enough to the curved beak to check the tongue.

She got up from her place on the couch and went into the kitchen to prepare her supper. She couldn't do anything about the bird now; she would take care of him tomorrow. She put a pan of water on the stove, and when it came to a boil she added a box of macaroni and waited for the pasta to soften in the water. Judy didn't really have much of an appetite after finding the parrot in her house, but eating after work was routine. It was, if nothing else, normal.

"Maybe," she told the bird, looking from the kitchen to the living room, "Suzie would take you. Or I could put an ad in the paper to give you away. Surely somebody would take you if I gave you away for free."

Elijah, who had been preening his feathers again, looked up at the sound of her voice. He studied her for a moment, snapped his beak several times, emitting a loud clicking sound, then continued his grooming.

189

Judy could not eat the macaroni. She scraped the congealing glob into the garbage under the sink. The parrot's food and water would have to be checked, she realized.

Her heart beating double-time, Judy crept quietly up to within three feet of the cage. She stretched her neck to peek in at the containers fastened to the bars. The food container was still over half full, but the water was nearly empty. Judy knew that she could never put her hand into the cage with the bird, and yet it would be cruel not to water him, or, in time, not to feed him. She returned to the kitchen and pawed through a drawer of cooking utensils until she found a long-stemmed funnel. She took the funnel and a glass of water back to the cage.

Elijah sat on his perch and watched as she pushed the tip of the funnel through the bars and into the water dispenser. Judy tipped the glass over the funnel, letting the water run through it until the dispenser was full. With a sigh of relief, she turned to put the funnel and glass away. A slow ticking sound came from behind her. Judy jerked her head around, sure the parrot was escaping. Elijah had moved along the perch to get a drink of water; the clicking had been his long talons on the wooden rod.

Judy went to bed early that night, and though she thought sleep would be long and hard in coming, she slept almost instantly. She remained so, sleeping soundly and still beneath her single blanket, until she was startled into wakefulness by an unfamiliar voice screaming in the darkness. She sat up in bed, listening intently for the sound to be repeated. All she could hear was a sharp, staccato tapping.

"Elijah wants your soouuul!" the voice screamed again.

Judy nearly choked on the panic that rose in her throat. She sat in bed, trembling for several moments, fearing to get up and knowing she must. Finally, reluctantly, she pulled the comforting blanket from her shaking body and rose from the bed. She crept silently to the door of her bedroom and peeked into the living room.

The parrot was running back and forth along its wooden perch, his talons making the tapping sound she had heard. The white feathers caught a ray of moonlight from a crack in the drapes and glowed eerily, causing the bird to look like a small ghost. Elijah saw her pale face peering from the bedroom door and stopped pacing. He stared back at his audience, his head cocking from side to side. The small black eyes glittered in the moonlight.

"Elijah wants your soouuul!" he shrieked.

Judy ran back to her bed, jumped in, and pulled the cover over her head.

She trembled like a frightened child. Finally, a thought came to her, something like knowing that parrots live long lives, or that they had to have their tongues split to speak, something she had known for a long time but never had cause to remember. *A bird's cage was supposed to be covered at night.*

The staccato tapping came into the bedroom again—Elijah running on his perch. Judy knew she had to get the cage covered before he screamed his awful desire again. She pulled the blanket from her face and dragged her body from the bed. She let her feet pull her into the living room.

Elijah stopped pacing when he saw her. He stood defiantly on his perch and watched. Judy shuffled through the shag carpet to the side of the cage, then reached for the black cloth that was rolled to the top of the wire frame. Just as her hand found the fabric, Elijah opened his beak. Judy yanked the cloth down before he could scream that horrid phrase again. The bird was silent. Judy returned to bed and eventually slept again.

* * *

The next day at work, Judy asked Suzie to take the parrot.

Suzie screwed up her face and said, "I would, I'd love to have a parrot, but I don't think Boo and Tabby would approve of that kind of addition to our family." Boo and Tabby were Suzie's spoiled cats. "They feel about like you do on the issue of birds—the only good ones are the eating kind."

Later that morning, Judy got another idea. She phoned Mr. Curtis. His groggy voice answered on the third ring. "Hello."

"Hello, Mr. Curtis, this is Judy Myers, from next door." She paused for his recognition.

"Yes, Judy," he said after a moment. "What can I do for you?"

"I'm really sorry to wake you up like this," she began.

"That's all right." He yawned into the receiver. "Excuse me."

"Well..." She felt guilty and embarrassed, but there was no stopping now. "I was wondering if you could tell me who delivered that parrot yesterday. Do you remember the company? Was it UPS? Did they say who it was from?"

"No, it wasn't UPS," Mr. Curtis said. "They drove a little blue pickup truck. I don't think it had a company name on it, just plain blue. They didn't say anything about where it came from. Sorry."

Judy tried to hide her disappointment. "Thanks anyway, Mr. Curtis. I'm sorry to have woken you."

"That's okay. Bye." There was a click and the phone went dead in Judy's hand. Frustrated, she hung up and tried to return her attention to the floor plan she had been studying before the call.

She stopped at a pet store on her way home that night and bought birdseed. It was expensive, and she dreaded feeding the parrot, but she still clung to the idea that starvation would be too cruel a way to get rid of the bird.

When Judy arrived home, she was thankful to see that Mr. Curtis had already left for his job at the bank. She hadn't wanted to see him so soon after the embarrassing call that morning. She put her key in the lock, turned it, and pushed the door open. The smell was staggering.

With an effort of will and a wrinkled nose, she stepped into her home and closed the door. The source of the odor was obvious. Large globs of bird droppings were scattered over the entire living room like dirty little snowballs. They were everywhere—all over the furniture, the floor, some even clung to the walls, sliding slowly down the paneling like white slugs.

Fearfully, Judy looked to the birdcage. The cover was up. She clearly remembered leaving it down when she left for work that morning, not wanting to see the bird so early in the day. Elijah sat on the wooden rod behind the gold bars. The door of the cage was securely latched. He continued preening as if he had not noticed her arrival. Judy dropped the sack of birdseed to the floor, letting her purse fall on top of it.

Elijah looked up at her. He clicked his beak twice, then screamed, "Elijah wants your soouuul!"

Judy sank to her knees, sobbing. She felt a wad of the bird's excrement squish beneath her knee. She cried harder. After a time, she regained her composure and stood up. Not looking at the cage, she went to the kitchen. With a small bucket she used for mopping the kitchen floor, several rags, hot water and a lot of disinfectant, she began to clean her home.

Strangely, she found none of the dung in any of the rooms except the living room, though all the doors stood open. It took her over three hours to clean the manure from the room. Her arm ached with the hard scrubbing required to remove the stains from the furniture and carpet. The whole time she worked, Elijah sat in his cage and watched her intently, cocking his head to follow her movements around the room.

When she finished, Judy decided she wasn't hungry enough to cook a meal. The thought of food made her look to the sack beside the door. For the first time, she entertained the idea of letting the parrot starve. She picked up the sack.

Judy found that she could feed the bird in the same manner in which she had watered him the night before; the small, tan seeds rolled smoothly down the funnel and into the food container. She gave him more water, then pulled the black cover over the cage.

After a quick shower, Judy took a battered romance novel to bed. After reading the same page four times and not being able to concentrate long enough to absorb the text, she gave up and put the book aside. Before settling comfortably down for sleep, Judy listened closely for any sounds coming from the living room. She heard nothing, so she pulled the blanket up to her chin and slipped into a troubled sleep.

The dream came immediately.

She saw a large crowd of people—people she knew came from many different nations and races, even from different periods of history. But she sensed, however, that they all had something in common. They were all screaming at her, telling her something, but she could not understand the words. She was sure that if they would speak one at a time she could comprehend their message. The crowd roared on, unobliging, but their message became clear.

A huge white shape loomed up behind them, and a voice Judy had come to recognize shrieked, "Elijah wants your soouuul!" The people screamed in terror as their eyes bulged and popped from their heads, dangling on spring-like nerves from the black and bleeding sockets.

Judy woke up suddenly, her pulse thundering through her head. Elijah was standing on her chest, his body rising and falling in time with her labored breathing. He stared at her, his evil black eyes pinning her to the pillow, his snowy feathers seeming to glow in the darkness of the bedroom. He opened his curved beak and Judy saw the split tongue flicking like a snake's. The parrot clicked his beak closed, then opened it again.

"Elijah wants your soouuul!" he screeched. His head bobbed up and then plunged down, the scimitar-like beak aimed at Judy's left eye.

Judy screamed and jerked her head aside. The beak tore the flesh of her cheek. She screamed again and pulled the blanket over her head. The sharp movement of the blanket caused Elijah to lose his balance. Judy heard him flapping his way back to the living room. Too scared to get up and check her wound, Judy remained in bed with her head covered.

She awoke the next morning unaware she had slept and still gripping the blanket over her head. Her cheek throbbed. Judy slowly pushed the blanket away. It was stained with blood, as was her pillowcase and pajama shirt. She got carefully out of bed, expecting Elijah to come flying back into her room at any moment.

Judy tiptoed to her bedroom door and looked into the living room. The birdcage was still wrapped in its black cover. She didn't see the parrot anywhere. She slowly crossed the living room to the cage and nervously reached up to take hold of the shroud. She threw it to the top of the cage.

Elijah looked out at her from inside his prison. Judy saw dried blood on his wicked beak. The door was latched. Judy pulled the cover down, a low-pitched whimper escaping her chest. A loud squawk came from under the cloth. Judy hurried to the bathroom to check her wound.

After gently washing away the dried blood, Judy discovered that the cut made by Elijah's beak was not as bad as she had feared—only a ragged-edged gash about an inch long. She cleaned it with alcohol, whining and dancing with the pain. When she was done, Judy looked closely at the unfamiliar details of the face in the mirror. Her flesh was pale, with dark circles under the eyes. Her black hair was matted into thick knots from the blood. She decided to take another shower. Afterwards, she pressed a large adhesive bandage over her wound and took a couple of aspirin to the kitchen.

Judy took her aspirin with orange juice. Then she poured two puddles of pancake batter into a frying pan. Watching the batter spread and bubble reminded her of the dung she had cleaned off her walls. She removed the skillet and washed the half-cooked flapjacks down the sink.

She arrived at work a little before Suzie and was in her own office when her partner came in carrying a large, flat box.

Suzie's usual greeting smile died on her face. Judy waited for the inevitable question. "What happened to you?" Suzie asked, nodding at the bandage on Judy's cheek. She listened quietly as Judy recounted to her the dream and the attack, finishing with the fact that Elijah's cage door had still been shut and latched that morning.

"That is weird," Suzie said. "I don't mean to sound skeptical, but do you think the attack could have been a part of the dream? Maybe you threw your arm up to protect yourself and cut your face with your fingernails?"

"No, it was real. If it had been a part of the dream, the pain of scratching myself would have woke me up. I was wide awake when I saw Elijah standing on my chest," Judy said.

"I guess you're right," Suzie replied.

"I thought about running an ad in the paper to give him away. Do you think someone would take him for free?"

"Oh yeah, some people pay hundreds of dollars for parrots."

"I hope so." Judy looked at the parcel Suzie was still holding. "What's in the box?"

Suzie's smile returned as she said, "Well, my brother has always believed in this philosophy, and last night at the art gallery in the mall I found this picture. I thought it would go well in his office. What do you think?" She opened the box to reveal her find.

Judy gasped as the image from her dream returned, making her cheek throb once again. In the upper left corner of the picture were the words, "The eyes are…" and in the lower right corner the thought was finished "…the windows of the soul." The picture itself was a white background filled with dozens of staring eyes of all colors and sizes. Judy looked up at Suzie, whose own large blue eyes were looking down at her, puzzled. Judy's eyes moved back to the picture, read again the terrifying words, then she slumped back in her chair.

"Judy, what's wrong?"

"That picture. It's just like my dream."

Suzie looked at the picture and then back at Judy, her face troubled. "Are you okay, Judy? Do you want to go home?"

Judy only shook her head, trying to force herself to stop shuddering.

"All right," Suzie said, closing the box on her picture. "I'll be in my office. If you need anything, let me know. Okay?"

Judy nodded, then watched the door close behind Suzie. When she was sure she could not be seen, she dropped her head into her hands and cried quietly for a while.

Judy didn't finish much of the work she had planned for that morning. She kept thinking of her nightmare and the picture Suzie had so innocently shown her. Her head throbbed with thoughts of Elijah.

What will I do if no one will take him? And who would have sent him to me in the first place? His only words echoed in her mind. *Who would have taught him to say that?* Judy left early for lunch that day, hoping she could ease her mind with food.

She sat in a nearby McDonald's, absently chewing cold French fries, her Big Mac only half-eaten. Judy was thinking of the card that had been delivered with the parrot. In her mind's eye she saw again the words, "My name is Elijah. I am 367 years old." Three hundred sixty-seven years old, she mused. *How many people has he killed? How many eyes has he torn from their owners' heads? Everyone in my dream? More?*

Judy looked down at her hamburger; watery ketchup dripped from under the soggy bun like blood from an eye socket. She threw the remainder of her meal into a wastebasket on her way out of the restaurant.

She got into her car and drove back toward the office, but the parrot would not leave her thoughts. *How many souls? One a year? More? Has he lived three hundred sixty-seven years by feeding on the souls of innocent victims like me?* She touched the bandage on her cheek. *How many times has the bird killed and gone unpunished? If I give him away, will I just be substituting myself for another victim? Or worse, what if I have been chosen and the bird returns? What if I can't get rid of him?*

By the time she parked her car in the Franklin Tower parking lot, Judy had begun to think about punishing the demon-bird. *An eye for an eye.* She cringed at the accuracy of that thought.

Judy went into the building and rode the elevator up to the seventh floor. She saw that Suzie had not yet left for lunch; she waved and went into her own office. Elijah was sitting on the ledge outside her window.

As usual, he was busy preening his snowy feathers. Judy's movement caught his eye and he looked up at her. He stared for a moment, then clicked his beak once. It was barely audible through the thick glass.

"Elijah wants your soouuul!" he shrieked.

Judy clamped her hands over her face and began screaming. She didn't stop until she felt other hands pulling on her own and heard Suzie's voice asking over and over what was wrong. Judy pointed to the window. "He's there. He's on the ledge. Elijah."

Judy followed Suzie's gaze to the window. A large white pigeon looked back at them for a moment before taking flight.

Judy stared after the pigeon, her eyes wide in disbelief, tears glimmering in her lashes.

"Judy, I really think you should go home and get some rest. Do you want me to take you?"

"No," Judy answered. "It was him. Really. It was." Suzie only looked worriedly at her. Judy sighed. "I guess I will go home, if you're sure you don't mind."

"No, you just go home and go to bed." Suzie smiled comfortingly.

"Okay, thanks." Judy tried to think of more to say, but couldn't. She picked up her purse and, against Suzie's arguments, the plans she had been studying. She left the office and walked down the corridor to the elevators.

Inside, Judy pushed the button that would send the elevator down and simultaneously made up her mind that Elijah must die. She must kill him.

But how?

As the elevator descended, she got her answer. A large brown cockroach was trundling up the wall of the car and Judy quickly moved to the other side of the small cube. Cockroaches disgusted her. They had been in her duplex once, but she had bought some aerosol bug bombs to kill them. She bought two boxes with two bombs in each box. When she returned home and read the directions on the boxes she found that two bombs were enough for her size home. The extra box was still with the cleaning supplies under her kitchen sink. Judy distinctly remembered the directions saying to remove all pets before using the bombs.

Elijah is no pet.

On the drive home, she had the final argument with the part of herself that said it would be wrong to kill the parrot. He was only a bird, a bird somebody had taught to say something evil. He could be changed.

No, he is a demon. A killer.

Only a bird.

The dream. The attack.

It would be inhumane to kill him, especially with the bug bombs. It would be like Hitler's gas chambers.

No crueler than tearing out someone's eyes and stealing her soul. She got out of the car and went to the door of her home.

She should have expected the smell, but it was still a shock. Like yesterday, the living room was covered in bird dung. Elijah sat on his wooden perch, the cage's cover thrown back. He glanced up at Judy's arrival, then turned his head away, but Judy caught the look of malice in his tiny black eyes.

Forcing herself to be calm, Judy hung her purse on the doorknob and closed the door. She went straight to the kitchen, the globs of manure squirting beneath her feet. The bird dung didn't matter; she could clean it up when she disposed of the demon's corpse. She took the small orange box from its place under the sink and started back into the living room. Once past the threshold dividing the two rooms, she froze, afraid to advance farther.

Elijah had moved on his perch. He stood with his beak between the gold bars of the door to the cage, poised directly over the latch. He casually arched his wings while his head bobbed down and up, his beak popping the latch free. The door swung open. He sat in his cage and watched Judy.

Judy stared back at the bird, her mouth open, her body trembling. *I have to close that door.* She had to close it fast, before he flew out. Judy dragged her feet through the carpet, whining as she went. Elijah sat on his perch near the open door and watched. He clicked his beak and bobbed his head as if he were urging her closer. Judy cringed at every movement the bird made, and nearly sank in terror when he spread his wings as far as the cage would permit. Elijah was only bluffing. He sat in his cage and watched. It took Judy over five minutes to traverse the eleven feet from the kitchen to the corner of the living room where the cage stood.

Once there, she reached out to close the door, her hand trembling like a leaf, the palm sticky with sweat. Her fingers touched the frame of the door and pushed it closed. The door settled into place and she clicked the latch down. Elijah's curved beak darted between the bars and tore into the flesh of her finger.

Judy screamed in pain, clutching the bloody finger to her chest. The taste of blood seemed to madden the bird; he jumped from side to side in the cage, flapping his wings furiously. Judy reached up with her bleeding hand and pulled the cloth over the cage. Elijah became quiet.

Quickly, Judy put the box of bug bombs on an end table and ran to the bathroom to bandage the second wound the bird had given her. When she was finished, she came back and removed the two metal canisters from the box, tossing the carton aside. She put both bombs under the cage, gauging the distance and angles to be sure both would spray into the bottom of the bird's prison. She depressed the buttons on the top of both canisters and the aerosol began to rise.

Elijah made no sound as the gas filled his cage. Judy hurried to the front door, removed her purse from the knob and was pulling the door closed behind her when she heard the parrot again.

"Elijah wants your soouuul!"

Judy slammed the door and hurried to her car.

She drove with no particular destination in mind, but soon found herself at the nearest mall. Judy parked and went inside, where she shopped aimlessly for a couple of hours. When she felt sure the bombs should have done their work, she decided to go home and clean up the mess, then treat herself to a meal at her favorite cafeteria.

Judy pulled into her driveway just a few minutes before she would usually have returned from work. She got out of the car and went inside.

The fist thing she saw was the birdcage. It was laying on its side, still covered. Her inner voice whispered to her about how the poor bird must have struggled. No sound came from the cage. *The bombs must have worked.* Judy closed and locked her front door.

The next thing she noticed was the amount of bird dung in her living room had increased. Swallowing a lump in her throat, Judy walked slowly to the toppled cage. She knelt beside it, her nose filled with the smell of the bird and the aerosol. Grasping the black cloth, she pulled it away from the cage.

Judy began to cry as the shroud slipped from her fingers. The cage was empty.

"Elijah wants your soouuul!" The scream tore through the room. Judy looked up in time to see the parrot leave his perch atop the faucet on the kitchen sink and come soaring into the living room. She screamed and threw an arm up to protect her face. The bird struck her arm, his talons digging into her flesh. The impact knocked her out of her squatting position and onto her back. Her head struck the coffee table and she screamed again.

Elijah flew straight up, turned, and came swooping down at her. His outstretched talons tore the bandage from her cheek. Judy felt fresh blood pouring down her face. She wept in despair, her arms flailing the air in vain hope of warding off her attacker. Elijah dropped between her arms and lighted gently on her chest. Judy's arms fell to the carpet, useless and weak.

The two stared at each other for what seemed an eternity. Elijah's body trembled as sobs shook Judy's chest. What she saw in his small black eyes made her cry even harder. She saw the people from her dream—the people Elijah had already killed. But now there was a new face in the crowd, one in the front row, whom she recognized. One whose face was still torn and bleeding. As she looked at her face in Elijah's eye, she heard a banging noise that she knew must have been going on for some time.

Someone was pounding on her front door. Judy couldn't turn her head away, couldn't call out to them; Elijah held her spellbound. Dimly she heard Mr. Curtis' voice. "Judy," he called, "Miss Myers, are you all right in there?" She only sobbed in reply.

"Elijah wants your soouuul!" the bird called one last time.

Suddenly, the door of the apartment banged open and Mr. Curtis fell into the room.

Elijah was enraged by the intrusion. His gaze left Judy's face and he turned his sin-filled black eyes toward Mr. Curtis. Shrieking, the bird took wing and attacked the neighbor.

Slowly, Judy climbed to her feet, her head pounding from the blow she had taken. She saw that the parrot had already pinned her neighbor into the corner beside her front door. Mr. Curtis was crouched down and holding his head between his knees, his arms wrapped around his legs. Elijah perched on the man's arms, his beak tearing pieces of age-spotted flesh from Mr. Curtis's scalp.

I have to stop this. I have to kill Elijah with my own two hands. Suddenly, Judy wanted very much to feel the bird's life end in her grasp.

Carefully, steadying herself with outstretched arms, Judy advanced toward the battle. Elijah was so engrossed with his present task that he didn't notice her. Judy reached out and took the bird's neck in her trembling hands. Elijah's flesh was warm and vibrant under the soft feathers. Judy had heard this was how chickens were killed. She desperately hoped she could do it right.

She squeezed and twisted with all the force she could summon. Elijah screeched in surprised pain and rage. He tried to fly. His wings beat mercilessly at Judy's arms, but she held tight. Judy felt the parrot's neck snap in her hold. Suddenly the bird was limp and heavy in her hands. Repulsed, she dropped the corpse to the floor.

Elijah lay without moving. Judy didn't realize she was crying again until she felt her body heaving with the sobs. Mr. Curtis, his own face streaked with tears and blood, slowly got to his feet. The two of them stood looking at the body of the parrot for a long while, slowly drawing together to comfort one another.

Warren Pepper's Victory Choir

"You're not afraid of me, are you, Derrick?"

"No sir, Mr. Baker, I'm not." The tall orderly had skin so black it looked as though somebody had poured used-up motor oil over his heavily muscled body. His smile, like the whites of his eyes and the bleached clothes he wore, seemed to glow with a holy fire against the ebony of his flesh. "Why should I be afraid of you?"

"You know what I am," Tim Baker answered.

"I know what you was," Derrick corrected. He lifted a spoonful of oatmeal to the mouth of his patient.

"But you're not afraid of me. You've heard the doctors talk about me. You're thinking about it right now. I can see it in your eyes."

"Well now, Mr. Baker, I ain't one to deny I've heard such talk." Derrick flashed a gleaming smile. "What's past is past, though."

"But you're still not afraid. Most people, when they come in here and see me like this…" Tim glanced down at his body, which was confined in the bed of the mental ward with several canvas straps. "They're afraid."

"What do I have to be afraid of?" Derrick asked as he scooped more oatmeal into Tim's mouth. "You're trussed up like a Christmas turkey."

"You know what I did."

"Yes, I know. But you ain't like that no more. That's why you're here. You're learning that you can't be like that no more."

Tim Baker laughed. Flecks of mushy oatmeal sprayed from his mouth. Derrick's smile never faltered as he wiped the gray flecks from his own arms and shirt and then from the patient's laughing mouth.

"What makes you think I want to change, Derrick? Maybe I like what I am. Maybe I need to…need to do it. Maybe that's why they keep me like this…trussed up, as you put it."

"No sir, you don't like it," Derrick said. "You don't. It ain't natural. You know that. Besides, you ain't done nothing bad in a long, long time. I heard the doctors saying the other day that you're doing real good, 'cept for some occasional crazy talk that still worries them."

"You're right about one thing. It ain't natural. It's supernatural."

Derrick chuckled deep in his thick chest. He spooned more oatmeal toward Tim's mouth. The cereal had been warm when they began breakfast but it had ceased to steam some time ago. Now it looked like so much congealed brain pudding.

"Do you believe in Hell, Derrick?"

"Yes sir, I do. Not that I'm worried about it." He winked. "My momma saw to it all her children were saved in the church. Someday, hopefully not too soon, you understand, but someday, I'll be going to Heaven."

Tim roared with laughter until he finally chocked on the glob of cereal in his mouth. "You're crazy, Derrick. Plumb fucking crazy. There's no Heaven. There's only Hell. I know. I can hear the people in there screaming."

"Now, Mr. Baker, we don't want to hear that. You know I'll have to give you a pill if you keep talking about that. I always do. Doctor's orders. You'll get yourself all worked up and try to hurt yourself again. Don't you want to get to where you can do without these straps?"

"The pill," Tim said, smiling sadly. "Do you think your fucking pill helps? It just makes the screaming louder. The only difference is that I can't tell you about it because I can't move my mouth. It just hangs open with slobber dripping out. That makes the pretty little nurses want to gag, doesn't it?"

"Well now, I don't know nothing about that," Derrick said, but Tim knew it was a lie.

"How long you been working here at the loony bin, Derrick?"

"I've been here a month and three days now."

"Who's your favorite patient?"

"You are, of course, Mr. Baker." Derrick smiled and Tim laughed a sane, friendly laugh. Suddenly the laugh broke into a sob and his face became lined and tense, making him look twenty years older than he really was.

"Please Derrick, tell me you're really my friend. A real friend," he begged in a hoarse whisper. "I haven't had a real friend in so long. These doctors and nurses don't like me. I'm like an animal in a cage to them…something they examine and nod over while they write their little notes. I didn't want to do what I did. Won't anybody ever look at me and not think about that?"

"Of course I'm your friend, Mr. Baker," Derrick answered. "You don't need to fuss over that. I'll always be your friend. As for what you did, that was before I met you, so I don't think much about it. You're just a man I'm trying to help, same as Mr. Hopkins in the room next door."

"Sam Hopkins is just a drooling retard."

"Now, Mr. Baker, we don't need to talk that way."

"I'm tired of being here, Derrick. So tired. I want to go outside. I want to feel the sun and smell the starlight and roll in the grass. And I want a woman. Did you know I've never had one?"

"If you want to take a nap, Mr. Baker, I can probably get you something to help you sleep," Derrick offered. "You look like you could use a good nap."

"No, Derrick, no. That's not what I need. I'm tired in my soul, not in my body. Do you have time? Time to listen to me? I want to talk. I want to tell you what happened. I like you, Derrick. You're not like those doctors who won't believe anything or the nurses who act like they'll get leprosy from coming in the room with me. Please listen to me."

Derrick glanced toward the door of the sterile little room. Through a small, square glass window with wire-mesh reinforcement he could see the round face of a clock mounted on the wall of the corridor outside the room. It was ten minutes before 8 a.m.

"My shift's about over, Mr. Baker," Derrick began, then stopped. He had never seen a man's face look as earnest as Tim Baker's did at that moment. "I reckon I can stay a little while, though."

"Thank you, Derrick. Thank you." Tim's head fell back onto his pillow. He smiled wanly. "I'd shake your hand if I could get mine out of these straps."

"It's the thought that counts, Mr. Baker."

Tim laughed softly. "You should have been a damn politician, Derrick. You always know just what to say without saying anything."

Derrick chuckled again. "What is it you want to tell me, Mr. Baker?"

"I want to tell you about the ears. And about Warren Pepper and his root cellar. That's where it all started, you know. Well, sort of. I guess it really started in Vietnam. Not for me, though. For me it started in Warren Pepper's root cellar. That was about five years after he died.

"Warren Pepper got sent to the war in Vietnam. I remember the day he left. Everybody in the neighborhood turned out to see him off. His dad was crying and cussing. His dad said Vietnam wasn't a war, it was a goddamn excuse for Jack Kennedy to kill young American boys so he could have more American women. I didn't know what the hell he meant...or even who Jack Kennedy was back then. I was only six and JFK had been dead for a couple of years already. I just remember it because it was said by a grown man who was crying like a little kid.

"I guess nobody expected Warren Pepper to come home from the war. A lot of boys didn't. But Warren did. He came home. His mom had a big party that day. I remember seeing Warren at the party for a while—he was about twelve years older than me. He'd been gone for just over a year. I didn't know that one year was too short a time to be in the army. I heard my mom and dad talking about Warren Pepper being "Section Eight" but I didn't know what it meant. Anyway, Warren didn't stay at the party long. He left. Went out the back door and wasn't seen again that day.

"His mom and dad weren't seen too much after that, either. His dad went to work at the refinery in the mornings and came home in the evenings. His mom went to the grocery story every Saturday. Nobody ever saw Warren Pepper, though. I remember his mom and dad got to looking real old real fast.

"And then one day Warren Pepper's dad came running out of the house with a red cloth over his ear. But the cloth wasn't really red. It was soaked in blood. Me and David, my best friend, were riding our bikes when old man Pepper came running out with that rag to his head. It was dripping blood and he was screaming 'He's killing us! He's killing us!' Then Mrs. Pepper came out, too, and she wasn't holding a rag. Her right ear was gone. Just gone.

"Warren came to the door then. He looked sick. He was real skinny, like those concentration camp pictures, and his eyes glowed like little flashlights. He had a big butcher knife in one hand.

"'You sent me there,' Warren screamed. 'You helped them do this to me. Now I'll be able to hear you screaming in Hell.' Then he closed the door. Some other neighbors had come out and were trying to help his mom and dad. We could hear sirens coming.

"Then there was a blast from inside the house. Warren Pepper blew his brains out with his dad's double-barreled shotgun. Both barrels in his mouth. He was a mess. He—"

"You saw him?" Derrick interrupted.

"Oh yeah, I saw him. But not that day. Like I said, he'd been dead for about five years when I saw him."

"Now, Mr. Baker, are you—"

"Let me finish, Derrick. You'll see. Then you can go home and see your wife and tell her the truth about the crazy man at work who's strapped in his bed. You've told her about me and what the doctors have said, haven't you?"

"I...I guess I've mentioned you," Derrick admitted.

"It's okay. People have to talk. It's what keeps us sane, huh?" He grinned.

"Go on with your story, Mr. Baker. What happened after Warren Pepper shot himself?"

"His parents moved away. He'd cut an ear off both of them. I never saw them again after that time they came running out of the house with blood all over them.

"Years went by. The Pepper house stood empty. It wasn't a big house; just a one-story, three-bedroom house in a neighborhood where all the homes looked pretty much alike. Turns out Warren Pepper's grandfather actually owned the house and had been letting Mrs. Pepper and her husband buy it from him a little at a time. He tried to sell it once after that stuff happened. There was a sign in the yard for a while, but nobody would buy it. That was about the same time the refinery closed, so nobody was buying houses then.

"Like I said, years went by. I was thirteen when me and David decided to break into the root cellar of the old Pepper house. It was a mound of earth with a warped wooden door that had been painted red. Most of the paint was coming off and the whole top of the cellar was covered in vines from a vegetable garden that grew wild in the backyard every year. We had to cut some of the vines away just to get to the door.

"You know what a cellar smells like, don't you Derrick?"

"Yes sir, I do."

"Yeah. It's all musty and wet smelling. The Peppers' cellar was like that. It was deep, too. Deeper than the storm cellar my parents have in their backyard. The wooden stairs creaked at first when we started down them. Then they just collapsed. The whole rickety staircase just fell. David was hurt pretty bad. One leg was broken and twisted around behind him. He had a broken arm, too. He was unconscious for a while.

"I had some bruises and a few cuts, but I was mostly okay. Scared shitless, but okay otherwise. I didn't know how the fuck we were going to get out of there. I could tell David was hurt pretty bad because of the way he was laying there with his leg behind him and the broken stairs all around him. But he was breathing and I couldn't do anything for him, so I started looking around.

"There were a whole bunch of jars down there. Mrs. Pepper canned stuff from their old garden, I guess. There were a lot of pickles and tomatoes. A lot. But there were some other jars, too."

Tim stopped talking. He stared at the ceiling in silence. Derrick saw that the patient's eyes were moist. A single tear spilled from one eye and ran down the side of his face and into his mussed brown hair.

"What was in them other jars, Mr. Baker?" he asked.

"Ears, Derrick. Ears. What did you think was in there?"

"I didn't know."

"See, so much of the truth has been forgotten," Tim said. "How long have I been in here?"

"Twenty-two years. Almost twenty-three is what I hear," Derrick said.

"Umm-hmm. Details are forgotten over time.

"Those jars were filled with ears. Big ears, little ears; adult ears and baby ears. Human fucking ears, Derrick. You hear what I'm saying?"

"I understand."

"It creeped me out to see those ears. They were canned like the pickles. They were packed in the glass jars but were able to float around a little bit in the…the juice or canning fluid or whatever it was. I don't know. I stared at those jars for a long time. Until David woke up and started screaming.

"I still couldn't do anything for him, no matter how much he screamed. I know he had to be hurting. I screamed, too. I screamed for help. But nobody could hear us. The neighbors weren't home. It was mid-afternoon and everybody who lived around there was at work. David asked me to move his leg. He didn't want his back laying on it. I did that. It must have hurt real bad because he passed out again.

"Then the sun started going down. It got real dark real fast in that cellar. When it was mostly dark, that's when I saw Warren Pepper sitting in the corner farthest from the door. God, I remember how the hair stood up on the back of my neck when I saw him sitting down there with his knees pulled up under his chin and half his head missing. He was wearing his army uniform. But half his fucking head was gone…his jaw was like a bowl holding this mush—mush that looked like that oatmeal you were feeding me except that it had red streaks in it.

"He moved. It was like he had been sitting there for a long, long time and had to get up real slow. But he got up. He stood up and took a step toward me. I remember pissing. I'd had to go for a while anyway. I just did it. Pissed all over myself. I was so scared. Do you know what I mean?"

"I understand," Derrick said. "But don't you think you was just imagining it? I mean, you was just a boy and you was scared anyway…"

"You're sounding like one of those prick doctors, Derrick. Don't do that. Just don't. He was real enough. Warren Pepper was there with me in his root cellar. You can bet your ass on that.

"He leaned over me and then he had his head back. It wasn't right. It was

206

like somebody had tried to put the pieces of it back together. But they didn't fit together anymore.

"'Hello, Timmy,' he said. Oh, he remembered me even though I'd just been a little kid when he was alive. 'I'm glad you dropped in,' he said. He laughed at that. 'I saw you looking at my ears. Do you know why I have those?' I guess I shook my head.

"'In 'Nam, we cut off the ears of those commie fucks,' Warren said. 'Some guys cut them off as trophies. Not me. I found a better use for them. I ate them, Timmy. You see, if you eat their ears you can hear the little gooks when they're sneaking up on you to shoot you in the back. I killed a lot of gooks while I was in 'Nam, Timmy. Lots of gooks. Old men, women, babies— it didn't matter. They were all commie gooks that wanted to kill Americans. The more I killed, the more ears I collected. I couldn't possibly eat them all. I had to do it in secret. The other guys, they didn't believe in the power I got from eating the ears and they didn't want to know I was doing it.

"'My mom had taught me how to can vegetables when I was a boy. So I started canning me some ears, Timmy. For later. There were dry spells when there just weren't any gooks to kill. That made me real nervous. It made me think I was losing my special power. So I kept a jar of gook ears in my pack all the time so I could eat them when there weren't any fresh ones…just so I'd know I wasn't losing the power to hear them coming up behind me or climbing a tree ahead of me. The snipers were the worst, Timmy. I lost a lot of buddies to snipers.'"

Tim Baker's eyes drifted from Derrick's patient face to the ceiling of the little room. His face took on a pinched, painful look—his eyebrows knitted over his nose and his lips pressed tight.

"It's funny how I remember every word, isn't it?" Tim asked, turning his head to face Derrick again. "It's like Warren Pepper has become one of the voices I hear. But of course that isn't true. I can't hear him. At least, not over all the other screaming.

"'Do you want that power, Timmy?' He asked me that. 'Do you want to be able to hear them sneaking up on you so you can kill them before they kill you?' I told him nobody was sneaking up on me. 'That's where you're wrong, Timmy. See those ears?' He pointed to the jars. There were five jars of ears; I remember that now. He pointed to them and said, 'I killed the gooks attached to those ears, Timmy. They're in Hell now, where their pinko commie souls belong. But they're still coming after you, Timmy. At night they come out of Hell looking for Americans. That's what they were bred for, what they lived their fucking lives for.'

"Then he took a jar off the shelf and opened it. He fished around in it and pulled out a little ear. It must have been a baby's ear. He held it out to me. I remember the smell, kind of like vinegar but with something rotten in it, like a dead mouse or something. I backed away but bumped into the wall. He came at me. Not fast, just slow, with that ear held out in front of him, level with my face.

"I screamed. Oh man, I screamed and screamed…until he shoved that ear into my mouth. I gagged and tried to spit it out, but he covered my mouth with his hand. He covered my nose and mouth with his hand and said he'd smother me if I didn't eat the damn ear. Do you hear me, Derrick? Do you hear how it happened?"

"I hear you, Mr. Baker. God help you."

"God? Leave him out of this shit. I ate the fucking ear. I ate it. It was like chewing the most gristly piece of steak I'd ever had, except that it tasted like vinegar, too.

"But he was right. I could hear things I'd never heard before. But it was all a trick, you see. A nasty trick. I could just hear a little bit. Just enough to know there was more—more that I couldn't hear yet. He gave me the jar and told me to keep eating and I'd be able to hear more. I'd be able to hear everything I wanted.

"I was scared. I was even more scared now that I could hear them a little. And I'd already eaten one. I ate another. And another. But the sounds I heard got worse. It was all screaming. I told him that all I could hear was people screaming like they were in pain. He laughed at me.

"'That's right, Timmy. You're hearing those commie gook mother fuckers burning in Hell. I did that. I put them there. You like it? I killed them all and sent them to Hell where they belong. Eat up and you'll hear more. Their screams are my victory song, Timmy. You need to hear the full choir.'

"I tried to run. I went to where the stairs had been, but of course I couldn't get out. I screamed for help again. David woke up. Warren Pepper was standing behind me, but I guess David couldn't see him. David just moaned and asked me to please help him. He said he thought he was going to die from the pain. That's when Warren Pepper whispered in my ear.

"'He's not in Hell,' he said, pointing to David. 'Eat his ear while he's still alive and it'll drown out the symphony of the damned. I know it gets to you after a while. It did me. That's why I ate my mom and dad's ears.'

"I looked at him then and saw that the top of his head was gone again. His hand reached out to me and there was a knife in it. A long butcher knife. Probably the same knife I'd seen him holding the day he killed himself. The knife he'd used to take his parents' ears. He put it in my hand and pointed to David again.

"Oh dear God. They were screaming in my head and I wanted them to stop. No matter how much I screamed I couldn't block them out. I just wanted them to stop. David was already hurt. I could say he cut his ear off in the fall…" Tim paused. He sighed, but the sigh ended as a deep sob that caused his chest to strain against the canvas strap crossing his upper torso.

"I did it, Derrick. I cut off my best friend's ear and I ate it. It was warm and…different than the canned ears…not so rubbery. It tasted salty from the blood. David tried to fight me off, but he couldn't do much with just one good arm and leg. He passed out again before I'd finished sawing off the ear. The knife was dull.

"The screaming didn't stop. Not even when I cut off David's other ear and ate that, too. Warren Pepper just laughed at me when I did that.

"I could see stars in the sky when somebody finally found us. It was old man Miller, who lived next door to the Pepper house. Then my mom and dad were there looking down at us with David's mom. They said the fire department was coming to get us out. My mom was crying. So was David's mom. I don't think she could see anything but his legs from up there. She couldn't see his bloody head.

"A fireman came down to get us. I clung to him while he carried me up a ladder. The fresh night outside the cellar smelled so good. But still, I heard those dead Vietnamese people screaming in my head. I could hear David too. He had died down there. The fireman was trying to put me down. My dad was trying to help peel me off the fireman. I saw the man's ear and just reacted. I wasn't myself any more. I ripped his ear off with my teeth and swallowed it whole.

"It didn't help. Nothing helps. They—the police—claim I ate all the ears in all five of those jars. That's a lie, Derrick. Warren Pepper ate most of those. He went after them like most people eat potato chips. Of course, nobody else ever saw Warren Pepper in the cellar that day. They tried to tell me that when they were determining whether or not I could stand trial for killing David and attacking the fireman. The police…or lawyers…or somebody was saying I'd planned the thing the whole time just to attack David. They said I knew about the ears and had been eating them for a long time. That's a load of shit. He was my best friend. I wouldn't have hurt him if it hadn't been for

Warren Pepper. You believe me, don't you?"

Derrick didn't answer for a moment. Then he smiled slowly and nodded. "Yes sir, Mr. Baker. I believe you. I think you're a decent man."

"I never wanted—" Tim stopped when the door of his room opened and one of the pretty young nurses came in.

"Derrick, what are you doing here so late?" she asked.

"I was just having a talk with Mr. Baker here," the big orderly answered. He looked back to the patient strapped in the bed. "It looks like it's time for some medicine for you and time for me to get home."

Tim cast a look over Derrick's shoulder toward the waiting nurse. Then he motioned with his head for the orderly to lean close.

"I never wanted to hurt anyone, Derrick. But the voices...the screams..."

The nurse ran from the room shrieking. It took two other nurses and another burly orderly to pull Tim Baker's mouth off Derrick's head. When they got the two men separated, Derrick's ear was gone. Where it had been there was only a dark hole leaking thick red blood.

Tim swallowed and turned his head away.

"I still hear them," he moaned. "They're still screaming."